CARTEL PUBLICATIONS
PRESENTS

GOON

T. STYLES

NATIONAL BEST SELLING AUTHOR OF *RAUNCHY*

By   T. Styles   2

ARE YOU ON OUR EMAIL LIST?
SIGN UP ON OUR WEBSITE
www.thecartelpublications.com
OR TEXT THE WORD:
CARTELBOOKS TO 22828
FOR PRIZES, CONTESTS, ETC.

By T. Styles   4

GOON

BY

T. STYLES

Library of Congress Control Number: 2014947670

ISBN 10: 0996099204

ISBN 13: 978-0996099202

Cover Design: Davida Baldwin www.oddballdsgn.com
Editor(s): T. Styles, C. Wash, S. Ward
www.thecartelpublications.com
First Edition
Printed in the United States of America

By T. Styles   6

What's Up Fam,

It seems like we have been crazy busy finishing up projects in an effort to make sure we bring you the best stories possible. We just recently finished filming our latest movie, "Mother Monster". And let me tell you, being on that set and watching the characters I love and hate from the "Raunchy" series appear before my eyes was an experience that was life altering. Our cast embodied their roles and I cannot wait until you are able to view the final production. We will release both "Mother Monster" and "Pitbulls in A Skirt" in our launch next year so get ready.

Now, onto the novel in hand, "Goon". I'm so fucking pumped about this book! In only a way that the great and powerful, T. Styles does, "Goon" is none short of another classic "Twisted" tale. I couldn't put it down and furthermore I didn't see a lot of the twists T. threw at me coming! I loved it!

Prepare to be up all night with this one!!

Keeping in line with tradition, we want to give respect to a vet or trailblazer paving the way. With that said we would like to recognize:

Edgar Allan Poe

Edgar Allen Poe is an American author and poet. He is considered one of the first American authors who penned short stories and is best known for his, "Tales of Mystery". Some of his classics include, "The Black Cat"; "The Fall of The House of Usher"; "The Masque of Red Death"; "The Murders in the Rue Morgue" and one of our favorite works of poetry from him, "The Raven". Edgar Allen Poe is a master of his craft and The Cartel Publications appreciates his contribution to literary history.

Aight, without continuing to take up your time, I'ma let you go and jump in headfirst!

Enjoy. I'll get at you in the next novel.

Be Easy!

Charisse "C. Wash" Washington
Vice President
The Cartel Publications
www.thecartelpublications.com
www.facebook.com/publishercwash
Instagram: publishercwash
www.twitter.com/cartelbooks
www.facebook.com/cartelpublications
Follow us on Instagram: Cartelpublications

Acknowledgements

To my Twisted Babies.
I love you dearly.

Dedication

*I dedicate this to one of my best friends, Dr. Tonja Martin.
I am blessed by your friendship.
Thank you.*

It was widely whispered that many years ago, in a quaint town in ghetto Mississippi, a human child was born and raised by wolves.

Of course it's ridiculous!

People love keeping up shit.

But, and this is actually true, a similar event did occur. And this child, who would later grow up to be homicidal, had one name that it answered to above all.

Goon.

"From childhood's hour I have not been as others were. I have not seen as others saw."
- Edgar Allan Poe

PROLOGUE

"Somebody's shooting!" screeched a paunchy woman as she gripped her lower belly while charging through the mall. Turning around momentarily to see if the killer was upon her, her eyes widened when she witnessed a tidal wave of terror-stricken people zooming in her direction. Her heart thrashed against the wall of her chest just as her high heel shoe failed, causing her to plummet against the grungy floor, slamming on her knees a bit too roughly. When a pain she hadn't expected sequenced through her ankle she looked down only to see the bloody bone projecting through the flesh of her lower leg. "Help me! Please, somebody!" She begged with an outstretched hand.

The thing was this. The horde was unmerciful and it was each man for himself. Some leaped over her, while others stepped on her limbs in an attempt to survive.

More gunfire blazed through the gallery as another woman screamed. "God, help us all! What's happening?" Each time shots echoed throughout the air, it would give the weary dynamism to push harder. To run faster.

When the herd of souls reached a fork in the mall some advanced right while others moved left, including a spry drug dealer and an old man who needed assistance from a cherry wood cane, else he would be trampled like the woman some feet back.

Proceeding in the same direction, they both continued their search for freedom when the elderly man happened upon a beige door with a white and black sign marked, *Employees Only*. Seeking sanctuary, his wrinkled hand covered the doorknob when suddenly the inconsiderate drug dealer shoved him to the side as if he were going into his own home.

Although youthful, his skin was bumpy and his broad forehead was contracted in rage so that his eyebrows formed an inky line. "Get out my way, old man! Before I burn your ass down." He raised his shirt showing his .45.

With warnings in the air, he slipped inside thinking of his own protection.

Fortunately for the elder, he was able to make it into the darkness with his younger counterpart just before he slammed the door and the sounds of gunfire grew nearer.

More shots fired.

More screaming voices.

The reign of terror seemed endless.

When the senior stepped on the drug dealer's toe as he struggled to get situated he pushed him back roughly. "Move the fuck out of my way," he whispered harshly. The senior was knocked into brooms on the back wall, causing a shooting pain down his spine. Neither could see the other's eyes but they could feel the tension in the tight space. "Step on my J's again and I'ma crack your fucking jaw," he whispered, stabbing a stiff finger in the middle of his chest.

"S-sorry," the old man responded, his voice quavering.

With the matter out of the way, they focused on the closed door again and the screaming from the people outside. The young dealer was hopeful that he might make it out alive until he heard the senior's rough breathing that whistled slightly as he inhaled and exhaled. The dealer was certain if the gunman was near he would hear the elder and this made him uncomfortable. He would've thrown him out but what if the gunman saw him? Both of them may be killed.

In panic mode, he turned around again. He was certainly tiring of the old geezer. So he gripped the collar of the senior's shirt. Removing his weapon, he touched the cool steel to his nose and growled. "Either you stop breathing or I'll stop it for you." He cocked his bird. "What you wanna do?"

"I'll…I'll try to be quiet," he stuttered. "Please don't kill me."

"Good choice," the dealer responded before shoving him back into the wall and aiming at the door, ready to fire at whoever came inside. He deduced that the shooter was some crazed white boy, mad at the world and the parents who brought him into it.

The older man continued to breathe heavily until his respiration ceased abruptly, along with the noise outside. There was no wind down or fade out. As if the mayhem in and out of the closet never existed, it was eerily silent. The type of silence that birthed insecurity and fear.

Suddenly the skills the young dealer adapted on the streets—the ones that kept him alive even though he was a most hated man, due to the nights he and his crew, The Reapers, robbed competitors of their stashes—kicked in.

"You know now, don't you?" The senior whispered closely into his ear. His voice was different but vaguely the same. "That I'm here for you."

When the dealer tried to fire at the old man the warm palm of the senior's hand pressed against his windpipe while his other hand now secured a knife at the dealer's neck. "Don't turn around," he demanded. "I'm very swift."

Suddenly the recollection became apparent.

He was a *she.*

"What did I do?" He was certain she was some bitter bitch he fucked who went through amazing odds to get even by causing a diversion in the mall. "At least tell me who you are!"

Without responding, in the blink of an eye, the elder-turned-Impaler, pressed the blade deeper into his throat, past the skin, past the arteries and through the cartilage until it could go no further. Warm blood oozed over her fingers and splashed to the floor.

Although he was helpless and no longer a threat, the Impaler held onto the dealer's body until she felt his spirit exit this world. When he went limp, she placed her lips against his earlobe again and whispered, "Goon".

PART ONE

CHAPTER ONE
-ROMAN-

"And much of madness and more of sin."
- Edgar Allan Poe

Fayette, Mississippi

Supper was almost ready but all Michelle Clutter could think about was the fresh crack cocaine sitting on the kitchen table that needed tending to. She directed her sons to be home two hours ago to cut the work and they hadn't dawned the door yet. She had something for them niggas though. Just as soon as their boots kissed the floor.

"Fuck them fat mothafuckas at?" she pronounced, weighing 250 pounds easily herself, she felt she had room to talk. Eying the clock on the wall, she shook her head in disappointment. Her graying accidental dreads, which only locked due to being uncombed for five years, brushed her shoulder blades. "Ain't good for nothing 'round here but shaking piss on the toilet seat." She shook her head. "Worthless ass bums."

Michelle was a powerful woman, standing six feet tall with the sturdy bones of a man. She could take a life if she desired with her palms alone. As she considered how her men-children were always late, her full-jawed face frowned before she wiped the sweat off her pitted light skin.

When she realized there wasn't much she could do about it for the moment anyway, she waddled over to the stove, her swollen feet pressing against the sooty floor. She knew one thing. They had better not be fucking with her money. She wouldn't kill them but she had no qualms about placing a few slugs in their limbs for lesson's sake. With a stiff fist nestled into the groove of her hip, she stirred the lima beans brewing in her pot briskly. A lot was on her mind and when she glanced to her right, she wiped the frown away and replaced it with a smile.

Her only girl child, Bay Clutter, was staring at her with admiration. With her mother's loving eyes upon her, Bay grinned slowly, causing the apples of her cheeks to rise like fresh bread in an oven. Her light skin was speckled with freckles in the corners of her brows, highlighting her emerald green eyes. Since Michelle wasn't good with tending to her own hair, let alone her daughter's, she insulted the curls of Bay's mane regularly by keeping it cut low like a boy. She wasn't about fussing with no one's hair on a daily basis. Still, the child was stunning.

If you gave Michelle a jug of moonshine and two packs of Newports, she'd gladly tell you all night that the best thing about being the queen of the dope game in rural Mississippi was taking care of her little girl.

Bay was the light in her eyes.

Although Michelle never cared about the spoils the drug dealer's lifestyle could afford her, she gave five-year-old Bay anything she desired. A cream canopy bed sat in the middle of her bedroom and so many dolls leaned against the baseline of her walls that they made the room feel miniscule.

Although expensive toys and furniture surrounded Bay, the best gift Michelle could've ever given her was a grey pitbull named Ice. The thing was she didn't even buy the beast. The dog came into her possession quite ironically.

Michelle came home one day with him because she had been cooking fried turkeys all day one weekend for paying customers. When she delivered one to a neighbor's house some blocks down, only two months old, Ice followed her home even though she yelled at him and threatened him with her fists. He paid her no mind. The dog was persistent and after awhile he grew on her. Plus, he was a cute little thing so she didn't see the harm in throwing him a few bones here and there to keep him alive, just as long as she didn't have to care for him much more.

The moment Bay and Ice met, it was love at first sight. As if they were always one and had finally reunited.

For the first week Bay took to spending so much time on the floor with Ice that she started crawling around like him. She was so good at recreating his mannerisms and barks that a few times when Michelle wasn't looking, she thought Ice was in the kitchen behind her, only to see her only girl child smiling up at her with wide eyes.

Ice wasn't the only person Bay could imitate. She could recreate the grumping and growling Michelle did as she scolded her brothers so well it was frightening. But with Ice, things were different; Bay roamed the home as if she wanted to give up her own life to be a dog like him.

For months Michelle laughed at she and Ice until one steaming afternoon she smelled a foul odor behind her old beige couch in the living room as she was shelling peas. When she looked behind it to investigate the smell, she saw two piles of shit. One from Ice and the other from Bay.

From that moment on, she had her sons keep Ice outside until he took his morning dump. She also separated Bay from Ice until she promised to stop acting like an animal. "You don't adapt to other species, Bay," Michelle taught. "You make 'em adapt to you. That goes for humans too."

She sure loved Bay and her boys too. She inherited the dope business when her husband died four years earlier, due to a gunshot to the back of the head, so she was forced to step up to care for her family. And before long, she learned the business. She considered life to be good. You wouldn't be able to tell she had paper stashed under the floorboards by looking at her home. The house was shack-like, giving the impression that it could be forced down if threatened. But she didn't care for impressions so they didn't move to a fancy house. She loved her home and they would have to take her out of it on her dying bed.

As Bay sat on a stool, her legs dangling below her body while Ice licked at the bottoms of her dirty feet, Michelle stuffed her fist in her waist and said, "What you smiling at?"

Bay's grin spread across her face. "Nothing."

"What you talking 'bout, girl? If I don't know nothing else, I know for a fact something's always brewing in that mind of yours. So speak it, child. You know there ain't nothing you can't ask me for."

Bay beamed wider and pointed at the oven.

"Oh, that's what you want," she chuckled. "Meat from the bird I got warming." She threw her head back and laughed heartedly at something no one else would find that much humor in. "You was never one for waiting for chow time now was you?"

Bay scratched her head. "No, ma'am."

"Well, since you and Ice being good and all I 'spose it won't be a problem tearing off a slice for ya."

She opened the oven and put the large turkey, which sat in a steep silver pan, on the table. The odor of the bird was intoxicating and caused Bay's insides to stir. Her mother was a great cook.

Cleanliness was another matter altogether.

Using her fingers, which recently cooked crack, she snatched a piece of meat and stuffed it in Bay's mouth. Then she pulled another for Ice and sat it in her palm. He slurped up his treat before running his tongue to clean any meat juice left behind off her fingertips.

When she was done with the turkey, she used the same hand Ice licked clean to give Bay a hefty piece of cornbread. Bay licked the butter off her mother's index finger and then licked her lips. When she was done, Michelle leaned closer and said, "Now don't tell your older brother nothing about the favor I showed you. He's in his feelings since I hit him on the head for snooping 'round my pot earlier." She looked at the clock again and grew agitated. "I'm gonna hit him on the head with something else if they don't hurry up and get 'round here."

"What you feeding her now?" Sam Clutter asked as he tossed his black book bag on the wobbly wooden chair in the kitchen. He yawned and stretched his arms before dropping them by his sides.

There was her oldest son.

Always greedy, he could spot someone chewing even if their mouth wasn't moving. "You stuff her so much she can't fit most of her clothes."

"Fuck you worried about what I feed her?" Michelle asked pointing a long finger at him. "Huh?"

"Mama…"

"Mama shit! Don't make no never mind what I do for her." She turned the oven off, removed the silver grates from inside and grabbed the knife to carve the turkey. "Now where the fuck were you?" she asked pointing the blade in his direction. "Let's talk about that shit."

"We went to meet Billy Bob like you said. But he wasn't at the spot." He pointed at the bag. "The work right there though. You can check it if you want to."

Michelle tottered toward the table and opened the bag. After eyeballing her product and determining it was intact, she closed it and said, "I thought I was gonna have to come looking for you with a bullet in the chamber. Good thing you back," she said with a lowered brow. "And stop talking about Bay so much. You a man. What a man doing banging on a little girl? His own sister at that?"

Sam was suddenly reminded why Michelle was one of the most dangerous drug dealers in Mississippi in that moment. He knew nobody but Bay was immune from her violence if she got worked up enough. "I'm not trying to make you mad, mama. Just saying she's growing, that's all. And with you keeping her hair low, people saying she looks like a boy. Ask anybody and you'll hear the same thing."

"Then tell them same people to come see 'bout me. And since you wondering so hard, I feeds her like I do 'cause I want her to know her mama." She looked at Bay and squeezed the child's chin. "I want her to know I loves her. Want her to know that I'm always here even if the world tries to break her down for being a black girl in this racist ass state." She sighed and turned the eye off under the beans. "And everybody knows the way to the heart is through the gut." She slapped hers and it sounded off like a drum. "If you had a woman instead of fussing around me you'd know that." She turned around and focused on the table. "Now tend to that work over yonder. It needs cutting." She wiped her hand on a grungy towel on the stove handle. "Where your brother anyway?"

"Right here, mama," Jim Clutter said as he waddled into the kitchen. His were calves so swollen they looked as if they would pop. He rubbed his eyes that were as green as Bay's and their deceased father's. "What time dinner gonna be ready?"

"Dinner ready now. The mac and cheese over there," she pointed at the kitchen counter, "and I just took the bird out. But neither one of ya'll gonna get shit until that work is cut and bagged. You know the rules. In this house it's all about the fucking money."

****

After Jim and Sam packaged the work they, wiped the coke residue off the table and sat down to prepare for dinner. It was dusk and since the stove was cooled, Michelle placed her sawed off shotgun back in the oven were she hid it on the regular. The Clutter family sat around the table, with heads bowed, ready for dinner by way of prayer.

"God, we come to You to thank You for this meal. I pray the love I poured into the meal will come through on my chillen. Lord. I know we may not always do the best in Your eyes but I pray that You show us the way. Protect my chillen. Protect my family and protect my business. Amen."

The lights went out.

"Get on the mothafucking floor!" a man announced as the front door in the living room was kicked in. The crackling sound of wood caused the heart of every Clutter present to pump harder than the AK 47 sitting in the palm of the intruder's hand. "Anything moving getting slayed."

The robbers couldn't see them because they were in the kitchen but the matter at hand was evident. Two men had done something Michelle never thought possible. Broke into her home.

Since it was time for combat, Jim grabbed his shotgun that was securely latched under the kitchen table and Sam snatched the .45 that sat on his lap no matter where he was in the house, even on the toilet. Michelle, always on point, pulled the oven door open and gripped her sawed off.

When she was loaded and ready she moved toward Bay. She gripped her shoulders and looked down at her. "You listen here, child. I don't want you to come out of this here oven no matter what you see!" Michelle's dreads, which always smelled sour, brushed against Bay's face. "Am I getting through to you? Don't leave this oven until you see my face, else I'll give you something for disobeying me."

"Yes, ma'am." Bay looked as if she was on the verge of erupting.

When she saw how horrified Bay was, Michelle thought about telling her how much she loved her in case she didn't win the war but she thought against it. There was no need for goodbyes because she would be returning. Just as soon as she finished blazing. So she hoisted Bay up, placed her in the oven and walked over to the table to greet her sons.

She hugged them roughly, wiped her tears and said, "Now let's go get them niggas out our house." She looked at the back door. "Jim, open the latch and let in Ice. We need all the help we can get."

Jim quickly did as he was told and Ice came rushing in from the outside, baring teeth dripping with foaming spit. From the glass on the oven door, Bay could see her mother and brothers rush toward the living room with guns in the air.

****

Bay awoke in a panic. She had the worst nightmare of her life. At least she hoped it was all a dream. When she sat up straight, her head knocked against the gas panel above her. It confirmed what she hoped was unreal. That she was still inside of the oven and her mother had not returned.

Bay leaned forward and looked out of the window on the oven. Her heavy breaths caused small fog circles to appear on the glass, making it difficult to see. Using the palm of her hand she wiped them off and squinted to look out into the kitchen.

"Mama," she whispered as she placed both of her tiny hands on the window. "Mama, please." She looked around as far as she could see, wondering what happened to her family. With each passing minute, she began to weep so hard her chest tightened and her tummy knotted. Assuming the worst, she closed her eyes and leaned her head against the window. "Mama, please! Where are you?"

She was startled when suddenly she heard Ice scurrying over the kitchen floor quickly in her direction. When she raised her head she could see that he left red tracks leading toward the oven. In order to bark, he opened his mouth and dropped what was in his jaws.

The finger of one of the intruders.

Seeing his friend inside, Ice whimpered before jumping up and nailing both paws on the oven window. When he jumped down two bloody paw prints remained. Who did the blood belong to?

Bay immediately went hysterical. "Mama," she cried louder, not caring who heard her. "Mama, please!"

Ice didn't want to hear his loyal buddy in such distress so the animal did all he could to get her to come out. From leaping up and down to pacing and whining in place, nothing worked because Bay knew that although Michelle loved her she could also be stern and violent if disobeyed. With her head lowered, she cried softly into her palms hoping that in the end the strong woman who could kill a man with her bare hands would prevail.

****

The next morning Bay awakened to Ice's rough tongue licking her eyelids. At some point, she was brave enough to leave the oven hoping that Michelle would strap her for disobeying her because at least it would mean that Michelle was alive.

Bay's boldness had limits. She left the oven but didn't leave the confines of the kitchen so she had no idea what was going on in the rest of the house. Before she knew it, the exhaustion she felt from being afraid forced her into sleep. Now it was morning and she stood up and stretched the kinks out of her body. Ice, who lay by her leg, arose also and placed his massive head in her lap.

Suddenly hunger pangs attacked Bay, causing a growling sensation to roll throughout her belly. Ice heard it too. It was mealtime. He hopped up on the chair and brought his large jaws down on the turkey's leg before he dragged it down.

With the bird on the floor he licked her face again, letting her know that it was time to eat. Bay crawled over to the turkey, lowered her neck and bit into it like a dog. Ice took the other end and they both ravished the meat until it vanished. Her mother would have a fit if she'd saw her child carrying on like Ice but Bay was starved. There was no time for manners. Once the food was gone, Bay began crying. Loneliness set in and although she couldn't articulate exactly what she was feeling she had a sense that her life would forever be different.

Where was her mother?

Her brothers?

Why had they left her alone?

It was time to investigate. Slowly she stood on her feet and walked toward the living room. Her heart rocked in her chest and she almost turned back. But the curiosity of being a child was stronger than the cravings of an addict for his drug of choice. She had to explore. She had to know. Luckily, she wouldn't be alone on her journey. Ice, forever loyal, followed closely behind.

The moment Bay bent the corner, the rough smell of rotting flesh permeated throughout the air and caused her stomach to churn. What was the horrible smell? Had Ice pooped in the house again? Her mother would surely lash him for it if he had.

When Bay walked further she noticed the front door was wide open and the living room was wrecked. And when she looked down she stopped in place when she saw what looked to be her mother lying on the floor with a bullet hole in the center of her forehead.

"Mama!" Bay screamed as she ran toward her, skidding down like a baseball player sliding into home base. Once on her knees, she scanned the living room and saw her brother Sam across the way. He was on his knees, slumped over as if he were praying. But he wasn't. A gaping bullet hole in the back of his head snuffed out his life and mashed his brains. Jim suffered a worse fate. The entire right side of his face was jerked off by the intruder's AK 47, exposing the pearly bone matter beneath.

Huge tears developed and Bay tried to pick her mother up. Instead, her head wobbled around as Bay struggled to bring life back into her body. "Mama, wake up! Mama, I'm scared!"

Bay tried with all of her might and although Michelle's head swayed, her eyes would never open. She'd seen the last of life on earth and it was time for the next level. And to think, it was all because of the cocaine Michelle kept in her house that everyone in the city knew about.

It was just a matter of time before some brave thugs came a calling.

And they did.

After crying on and off for two hours, grief stole the rest of Bay's energy and once again she drifted off to sleep.

Later that night Bay awoke to the loud sound of crickets chirping. The moonlight from the opened doorway lit up the living room. Slowly she peeled her head off of her mother's cold body. Where was Ice? She hoped her friend didn't leave her too. Although she didn't have much to drink in the last two days, her full bladder pressed downward, causing an urge to pee.

Slowly she walked to the bathroom and tried to flip on the light but it would not activate. One of the robbers cut the power to immobilize their victims, in the end giving them the upper hand.

Using outstretched arms, she found her way to the bowl. Her mind was jumbled with confusion. After she finished, she plodded out without flushing and stopped in her tracks in the hallway when she heard Ice growling. In all of the years she had her dog, he never snarled at her. Afraid her friend would attack her since the adults were dead, she was about to run into her mother's room until she heard another animal barking.

With her curiosity in gear again, she moved slowly toward the living room. When Bay bent the corner and saw a large brown hairy dog, which looked angry, her eyes widened. He had come in through the open doorway. All of the lights were out but the moonlight shining from behind the dog gave it the appearance of a wolf.

At first the angry animal was vying for Ice's attention but when it focused on Bay's green eyes, it directed its aggression toward her instead. Protecting his family, Ice lunged for the dog and embedded his teeth into the back of its throat just before it reached Bay. The two animals rolled around on the floor, over the bodies in the living room as each fought to reign supreme.

Stronger and more vicious, the wolf managed to dig its claws into Ice's eye, knocking it from the socket. With Ice weakened, the wolf moved toward Bay again. But Ice was a pitbull and he was loyal and strong. Using the little energy he could muster, Ice charged the animal and lodged his teeth into its back, forcing its attention on him again. The two scuffled for one more minute until the wolf's body lay amongst the rest of the dead.

Victorious, Ice hobbled toward Bay. Bay wrapped her arms around his bloody neck and the two made it to her mother's room, which had been ransacked by the intruders. Although it was in shambles, she felt safer there than in her own room. But her mother's bed was so high that Bay could not pick Ice up to place him on the mattress with her. Plus, he was in so much pain he whined no matter what she did. So she decided to lie on the floor with him. Using her mother's large print bible as a pillow, Bay curled up on the floor to get some rest, with her bloodied hero next to her.

For the next five days Bay and Ice survived in the house on snacks hidden in her mother's room. When they were gone, they raided the warm refrigerator and the cupboards. When all was gone and spoiled, Ice, who could barely see due to his missing eye, would hunt small animals to keep them both alive. At first Bay balked at eating dead animals until the pangs in her stomach got so great she was left with no choice.

Time flew by and strangely enough, things became normal for the child. Bay Clutter now lived in an environment similar to that of Holocaust victims. Her mother was no longer her mother. She was a rotting corpse that kept the company of maggots and flies and Bay was angry at it all. Having nowhere to go, Bay was now immune to horror.

She was immune to fear.

For one month, they remained in a house thick with the odor of rotting flesh. Until one day Bay was in her mother's bedroom eating meat from a squirrel Ice had recently killed when suddenly she heard a voice.

"Michelle Clutter, you in there?" yelled a stranger in the house.

Who was in the house now? And what did he want with her?

Ice immediately growled at the closed door, waiting for whoever was brave enough to set foot inside. "Clutter, are you—"

When Bay heard the stranger stop talking, she opened the door and walked toward the living room. Her toes pressed into the wooden floor until she was standing at the entrance of the hallway.

Billy Bob Adams didn't see her at first. He was busy staring at the four corpses, three humans, and one dog. His red hair and beard made his skin appear extra pale and the spots on his face due to picking his skin because of his meth habit made him gross. Witnessing the carnage, he covered his mouth and nose because the smell was so strong it caused his stomach to whirl. When he realized he was not alone, slowly he raised his head and observed the filthy child. "You been living here?" He wiped his red hair backwards before tugging on his long red beard. "Alone?"

Answering on Bay's behalf, Ice growled.

"You going to answer me, boy?" he said to Bay, ignoring the angry dog. Sweat poured from his neck and dampened the cream BILLY BOB HOUSE OF HORROR t-shirt he wore. "Talk, boy!" Although she was pretty, her short-cropped hair gave him the impression that the child was male.

When Ice growled again Billy focused on it. "You sure are a ugly little bastard, aren't you?" He surveyed the carnage again. "You know, before I came here I had intentions on having firm words with your mother, kid. Seeing as how she promised to deliver a package and all. But now," he looked at her body which had turned blue, "well now it all makes sense." He pulled a white handkerchief from his pocket and put it over his nose. "Well this house ain't fit for nobody, let alone a kid." He paused. "So what's your name, boy?"

Silence.

"So you won't even tell me your name, huh?"

Silence.

"Well since you got that word Romans on your forehead," he said looking at the large words, which imprinted on her skin from the Bible she slept on each night, "I'll call you that."

Bay, who would now be called Roman, stared at him unsure if she could trust him or not.

"Well," he looked around again, "I guess you got to come on with me, kid. I got to burn this place to the ground."

Roman's feet remained planted.

Growing agitated by her silent treatment, he leveled and evil glare her way. "You listen here. Now I'm burning this piece of shit house down. Me and your mama had business and I don't want the cops snooping around thinking I was involved. So either you coming with me or you can stay in here with the rest of these stiffs and burn to death. Don't make me no never mind."

Billy Bob left out of the door before returning with a dirty yellow canister. He walked inside and poured the gasoline over the floor. But when he moved to Michelle's body Ice growled. Fearing the animal would attack, Billy Bob reached under his shirt and pulled out a small .22 caliber. "Boy, you better get a hold of that dog before I give it something to growl about."

Roman rubbed Ice's head and he stopped snarling instantly.

Billy Bob laughed. "Least you got him under control. I'll give you that." He continued to water the bodies with fuel. When he was done he said, "Go on, hop in the back of that red truck out front." She rubbed Ice's head. "You can take the dog with you."

Roman trudged toward the door but before leaving she dropped down next to her mother's body and her knees slammed into the floor. Despite the fact that none of her mother's original features remained, she kissed her forehead anyway. It would be the last she'd ever see of her mother and the memory would remain in her mind forever.

Suddenly, emptiness lay in the base of her gut.

Who would love her now?

When she was done, she stood up and walked out of the door with Ice following closely behind. She tried to rid herself of the hate she was feeling for Michelle. She knew it wasn't her fault she was murdered. Still she felt alone. She didn't know the strange white man or his intentions.

Once outside, she climbed into the hatch of the dusty red Toyota pickup truck and waited. Ice leaped in also. What was happening? She cried hard when she looked at the home she had known all of her short life. What would happen to her now? What kind of man would Billy be? Where would he take her?

Her questions evaporated in her mind when she saw a flash of fire through the open door in the bedroom. In an instant, clouds of smoke crawled out of the doorway and Billy Bob walked out and climbed into the driver's seat as if nothing was happening. Before driving off, he removed a cigarette from its pack and lit it. Then he cranked the handle for his window until it was rolled down and a cool breeze along with the scent of smoke seeped inside.

"Ain't it something, Roman?" He surveyed the house. "How it takes years to create memories and only seconds to burn them down?"

Roman looked at the flames and tears strolled down her face. Her mother was in that house. Her brothers were in that house. Her life was in that house.

"Like I said, your mama owed me product, Roman." He took a puff. "And I lost a lot of money and a good partner when she didn't deliver. When I saw her cold body I thought it was a lost cause. And then I found you." He threw his head back and laughed. "I don't believe in slavery, but I guess in that way, you belong to me now."

"Where we going?" Roman asked under her breath.

"Baltimore."

CHAPTER TWO
-YOKO-

"All that we see or seem is but a dream within a dream."
- Edgar Allan Poe

Baltimore, Maryland

Meanwhile in another ghetto part of the country, moonlight glowed into a tiny apartment. "You know I always knew I was gonna have my son in this place," Andrew said as he sat on the edge of the windowsill, which overlooked the snow-laced streets of Baltimore City. He grew up in Magnolia Gardens apartments, the same place where he was born, and he wanted the same for his child.

The window was open because the room was unbearably hot due to the radiator, which stayed on blast because it was temperature controlled by the landlord. "It's always been a dream of mine." His eyes rolled toward his wife who was breathing heavily in and out due to labor pains. "My father was born here and so was I." He sighed. "And even though people said he left us for another woman, I still feel like his spirit is here, in this building." He smiled. "Thank you for doing this for me. I know you wanted to have our child in a hospital."

When the labor pains subsided she looked over at her husband, her eyes Asian-like courtesy of her father. The gold chain that should've weighed down his neck possessed by its excessive diamonds swung like the pendulum on a clock.

She wiped the brown hair that clung to her face and, despite the pain, forced out a smile. "You always get what you want, don't you?" she grinned. "Even when you plotted to take me away from your brother."

He chuckled, hopped off the windowsill and waddled toward her. Normally she wouldn't be so brash but he figured the pain of bringing a child into this world made her bold and forthcoming. He crawled to the top of the mattress, lifted his leather blazer slightly in the back and took a seat on the edge of the bed. Once settled, Andrew reached for her hand and she embraced him.

"I am a wealthy man, Daisy."

"You're telling me something I don't already know," she smiled.

"It's true. I have more money than a man should be allowed. I have men who would fight for me and give their lives if it would be pleasing in my eyes. But the only thing I wanted in this world was you and Vincent had that. Does that make me wrong because I desired my brother's wife? And made her my own?"

"You know the answer to that," she said breathing in and out of her puckered lips. "We are both foul. And we both should pray to be forgiven for our sins." When she felt more contractions she squeezed his hand harder. And when the pain slacked she loosened her grip. "I'm sorry, Andrew. I didn't realize my strength."

He chortled. "When are you going to realize I can take it? You can't hurt me, even if I'm smaller than you." He winked. "I love you, Daisy. Always have. And I know it's not right that I took you from him but from the moment I laid eyes on you, I knew you belonged to me. Somebody had to get hurt in the process and unfortunately it was my brother."

"We could've had the baby in our own home. Or in a hospital. Are you trying to make him jealous? What if he sees us walk out of this building with our first child? It would hurt him even more." She paused. "He lives downstairs, Andrew. You both own this building so—"

"No!" he yelled, quickly correcting her. "My father owned this building and he left it to me. I let him stay here out of pity."

"But it's a dope house."

Andrew found that hilarious considering all he'd done to welcome his new baby into the world by making it beyond presentable. "It may be but I cleaned it up," he said firmly. "Look around. I brought in brand new furniture, fresh linens. Shit, this bitch look more like a five star hotel than a dope house," he bragged. "Naw, baby. I brought you here because I was born here and my daddy too. This apartment"— he looked up at the ceiling— "this raggedy mothafucking apartment, believe it or not, holds tradition." He paused. "Real men are born here. And money is made here."

"But he will see us."

"My brother living downstairs don't have nothing to do with my motives for wanting to have my first child here and I wish you stop questioning me."

She smiled and then the contractions gripped her again. "I'm going to make you happy, Andrew." She breathed rapidly in and out of her nose and mouth. "I'm going to make you happy you made me your wife. Because despite my past life with Vincent, my heart always lied with you. Never your money." Suddenly pain gripped her again. "Andrew, you got to go get Pam," she said breathing laboriously. "I think this is it."

Andrew hopped down and rushed out of the bedroom and returned with the help. It was time to have a baby. Pam had her two younger cousins, who acted as her assistants, bring hot water and washcloths into the room. Together the three of them coached her on until her child, who was female, was brought into the world. Pam cleaned the infant up and held her in her arms. "Awe, it's a girl." She grinned. "And she gonna be a fine ass little shorty too. Just like her daddy."

When Andrew heard Pam's words, he walked over to her and she lowered her body so that he could view his daughter. When he nodded she walked the infant over to Daisy.

"Leave us alone," Andrew said in a heavy breath.

"Why I got to go?" Pam bucked.

"Yo, get the fuck out of here before I slap the shit out of you!" he yelled scaring her instantly. He may have been small but he was mighty and so were his threats. He loved his cousin but she played too much when he wanted to be serious. When they were alone he looked at his wife. "She's like me. Isn't she?"

"How do you know, Andrew?" Daisy asked with bulging eyes. "Even if she is, what's wrong? I'll love her no matter what."

"Her limbs look like mine in my baby pictures. Why is it that Vincent gets a son of average height? And my child is…she's a…dwarf."

"Baby, I know it doesn't seem that way now but we could raise her to be happy and strong. All we have to do is give her love. If we do our job, she'll be a good person and treat people fairly. And because of it, they will treat her the same. All she needs are parents who love her. Will you help me?"

"You could love her?" he yelled. "Even if she is like me?"

"I would love anything we made together, Andrew." She kissed her on the forehead. "You know that." She paused. "Aren't I your wife? Didn't I put it all on the line to be with you?"

"Yes."

"Then to ask me that when you know how much I love you is outrageous."

He paced the room and shook his head. His future life with his daughter went into speed play in his mind and he didn't like the show. "I don't know…I don't know what we gonna do. I mean…I don't think I can handle it. I don't think I can take my brother laughing at me because of my daughter." He stopped pacing and looked up at her in the bed. "We have the same parents. Both dwarfs. Yet he is regular height and has a regular son. And me." He exhaled. "I'm a laughing stock. All of my life."

"Why is it always a competition? We have our family and he has his. Isn't that enough?"

Andrew stopped pacing and using the small ladder, crawled back on the bed and sat down next to her. He gazed at his wife and his child. "I don't want to resent her," he said softly. "I don't want to pour all of the things I hate about myself onto her."

"Then don't."

"It will be too hard."

She frowned. "What are you asking me? To give her up?"

Silence.

"Can you at least try to love her, Andrew? Try to be a good father?" she pleaded. "She needs you. She needs to see how a strong man with the same symptoms can still rule the world. She needs to see that she can be powerful, despite her condition."

When he saw how much his wife loved their child already he said, "You're right. You're right, Daisy. I'm so sorry for making you feel that you or our child is inadequate. Just give me a few moments alone." He got up and walked out of the room.

When they were alone Daisy gripped her baby tighter. "I love you so much," she said as a cloud of fog escaped her mouth before rising in the air. Now that she was not exerting a lot of energy, she noticed that the cold air was settling in the bedroom, causing a freezing temperature.

Slowly she eased out of the bed with her baby. She underestimated the toll her body took from giving birth as she moved toward the window cradling her baby tightly in her arms. Once there, she slumped down and looked at Baltimore City. The tiny apartment where she was, was only two stories up, not much at all, but her view seemed large.

Andrew was a strong man who never allowed his height to hinder his rise in the world when it came to business. He was a powerful dealer who had a small army and a lucrative drug distribution market in the city. Yet she was in his life long enough to see how people treated him upon first sight. And the things their evil words did to his mind. And to his self-image. The bloody murders that occurred from people making him the butt of their jokes were only an afterthought. Even though he wiped out their lives, the pain was still everlasting, lingering, like an evil spirit that couldn't rest.

Daisy glanced down at her baby girl again. "He will never treat you right even if he promises," she admitted as tears rolled down her face.

****

The hallway was too small to be moving furniture, yet the hateful couple was doing it anyway. "Can you stop pushing me, mothafucka?" Maria yelled as she held firmly onto the far end of the twin mattress as they walked it down the steps in their apartment building. "Don't get mad at me because this bitch is covered with bed bugs. I told you we should've tossed it when Dale first complained of itching."

"But I paid fifty bucks for it," Vincent advised as he gripped his end and pushed in her direction. "Now it's gone in the wind."

"Fifty bucks ain't shit, nigga."

"I don't have money growing off trees like my midget brother." He looked at Andrew's limo sitting on the curb. "Everything I have I earned." He acted as if he did more with his life outside of drinking twenty hours a day.

For reasons that were deeper than the center of the earth, Vincent despised his younger brother. It wasn't just because he took the only woman Vincent ever loved by flashing his drug money in her face and sweeping her off her feet. He also disliked him due to the way his father treated him when they were kids.

Since Andrew was the same height as his parents, and Vincent was not, their father spoiled Andrew rotten. If he wanted something he got it and Vincent would be forced to watch the preferential treatment and pretend it didn't bother him. But it always hurt badly. In the end, it made him bitter and pulled their relationship apart.

Vincent's connection with his father was dark.

Very dark.

When they made it to the bottom step Maria poked her butt out and pushed the glass door open. The frigid air rushed inside the hallway causing pillows of fog to rise from their breath and float over their heads.

"Well next time, don't buy no bed from a crack-head."

Verbally insulting each other the entire way, they walked the bed toward the alley. Years of alcohol abuse caused Vincent to lose breath too soon so he said, "Just leave the bitch here. This good enough."

"But the dumpster ain't nothing but ten or fifteen feet away. Stop being trifling. We live in this neighborhood."

Annoyed at his girlfriend, Vincent unhanded his end, forcing her to release hers too. "Listen, woman, I want to go back inside and drink my beer. If you want to kick this bug infested mattress to the dumpster than so be it. I'm gone." The sound of his boots stepping on the snow disappeared when he entered the building.

Needing five seconds away from him, Maria leaned up against the brick wall and removed a cigarette pack from her pocket. She thought about their conversation and her life with Vincent. She realized every day that she was dumb for giving birth to his son because now they were stuck together forever. Like gum on the bottom of an old boot. She started to abort the baby but the yearning to have a daughter in her image convinced her to bring the child to full term. Her disappointment was great when she realized the baby was male but she tried to love him just the same.

In her defense, in the beginning, it was hard to deny Vincent. When he was inebriated he was funny, sexual and a pleasure to be around. As a matter of fact, that's how they linked up, at a bar in the city. She was having a bad day due to losing her man to her best friend and he recently lost his wife to his shorter brother. But you'd never know troubles plagued him that day because he poured on the charm and she was won over. And then the morning came. He was a mean man who was consumed with everything else but her.

One of these days, she was going to rid herself of him. If only she knew when.

After taking a deep breath, she lit a cigarette and was startled when something fell out of the air to her left. At first she thought it was one of them fat ass city rodents but when she heard an outburst of crying and looked down she saw it was a beautiful baby wrapped in a blanket. "What the fuck?" she picked it up and looked up at the sky. The moment she did, she saw Daisy's startled face. She was sitting in the window and appeared beyond guilty for what she'd done.

Daisy wasn't doing some act of kindness by dropping the child on the mattress. She didn't know anybody was outside and planned to release the child to its death. But now…well now Daisy considered the matter a sign. If she couldn't kill her baby maybe there were bigger plans for her small child.

"Oh my God," Daisy said covering her mouth. "She's safe! You saved her!"

"Daisy, is that you?" Maria asked although startled at what was going on. Did she just witness a crime? A mother trying to kill her own baby girl?

"Yes," she said trembling.

"It's a good thing I was here. She could've died." She paused rocking the baby gently to calm her down. "I'm bringing her up now. Open the door."

"No," Daisy said shaking her head and extending her hands out of the window. "Please don't do that."

"Daisy, I'm confused! You just dropped your baby and now you don't want her?" Maria removed her jacket and wrapped it around the infant so that she could stay warm. "Are you telling me it was on purpose?"

"You don't understand, Maria. If she stays with me I'm afraid for her life." She paused wiping her tears. "Before you say anything, I have money." She disappeared and returned with several stacks of cash. Fully loaded, she released it from her grasp and green bills floated to the bed where her child just landed. With the baby in one arm, Maria used the other to collect every last bill, stuffing them into her pocket before her greedy boyfriend saw her newfound fortune.

"I don't know, Daisy," she whispered. "I might not be able to get this to go past Vincent."

"Then I'll pay you. For as long as you keep her, I will pay you. You know I'm good for it, Maria. All I ask is for your silence and to keep where you got the baby away from Vincent."

"Well what's wrong with her?" Maria examined the beautiful child. "She seems perfect to me."

Silence.

"Nothing," Daisy cried wanting to hold her daughter in her arms again. "Do whatever you can for her and I will give you whatever you desire. Just please...never tell her about this night. She must not know how I treated her. It will ruin her for life."

CHAPTER THREE
-ROMAN-

"And all my days are trances..."
- Edgar Allan Poe

"You an ungrateful nigger," Billy Bob yelled as he sliced into the cherry red tomatoes on the counter. The rest of his apartment was a mess but when it came to his kitchen, things remained spotless.

"I told you he ungrateful," Cindy Lou, Billy's girlfriend said. She scratched her scraggly blonde hair, causing a few strands to fall onto the pizza he was making. "Don't know why you got him here anyway! Seems odd to me."

"What is wrong with you now, boy?" Billy Bob asked ignoring Cindy. "Your mama dead! Deal with it!"

Several months passed and still he assumed that *she* was a *he* and Roman didn't care enough to correct him.

"Nothing," Roman said with an attitude as she stood next to the counter, gazing at the ruby red tomato and imagining how it would taste in her mouth. Her weight decreased drastically since Michelle was not cooking for her. She was almost skin and bones.

High off meth, Billy Bob had been up all night cooking and making calls. On a wobbly wooden table across from him sat a collection of stolen goods that he was trying to move for cash.

Billy Bob Adams was many things. He lived in Mississippi ever since his mother, Terri Adams, pushed him out of her pussy in the backyard of their broken down home. But after doing one too many niggas wrong, he relocated to Baltimore where he and his meth-addicted, married girlfriend, could hide within the city.

He worked as a mule for Andrew Hammond, a local dealer who moved crack throughout his building. Andrew didn't like Billy Bob because he was racist but when it came to bringing back a package untouched from Mississippi, he proved loyal. But when Michelle was murdered he had no more use for Billy Bob, so he cut him off, especially when he learned that he was on meth. There was no way he could trust an addict so their relationship was severed.

"Don't tell me nothing wrong," Billy said as he placed the tomatoes over the fresh pizza before throwing it in the oven. "And don't expect me to change my mind about letting you eat either. Boys who cry don't get a thing in my house and that includes a meal."

"He's right," Cindy said as she plucked some ice cubes from the tray in the freezer before tossing them in her cup. Nobody wanted her opinion but she lent it anyway. "You gonna grow up to be a faggot with an attitude like that. Better straighten up."

Hungry for the second day in a row, Roman about faced and sat on the floor. She enviously watched Ice, who lay in a ball some feet over, chew on a bone. Billy Bob may have treated Roman poorly but he tended to the animal well after discovering that although he had one eye he was a good attack dog.

When the yellow phone rang on the wall Billy Bob wiped his hands on the soiled white towel on his shoulder and answered. "Hello."

Cindy Lou walked to the back of the apartment to go to the bathroom.

"Who do you think you talking to, Charlie?" He checked the temperature on the oven. "An amateur? If you place an order, I'll get your product. I don't care what it is."

While Billy Bob busied himself with the call, Roman tiptoed over to the counter. With his back faced in her direction, she was hoping she could slide a few tomato cubes off the counter and toss them down her throat. The moment she placed three dices on her tongue Billy Bob turned around and hit her so hard in the face the back of her head bumped against the oven and the stolen tomato cubes shot out of her mouth. "I'll call you back, Charlie," he said. When he hung up he focused on Roman. "You know why I hit you?"

Roman was too afraid to answer.

She was in so much pain.

Michelle never abused her and she found herself hating everything around her now even more. She wiped her clammy hands on the black BILLY BOB HOUSE OF HORROR t-shirt she wore that was too large and swallowed her frame. Billy Bob ran a small Haunted House in Essex, Maryland, in October and couldn't give the t-shirts away.

"I don't know why you hit me," she responded rubbing the back of her head.

"I hit you because you got caught stealing. If you gonna take something you had better not let the person you stealing from see you do it." He wiped the stray tomatoes into his hand and tossed them into the sink just so she couldn't have them. "From here on out if you want to eat you better get it when I'm not looking. If you're gonna thieve, be great at it."

Roman stomped out of the apartment, down the steps of the hallway and out the front door. The ground was cool against the bottom of her feet and she cracked her knuckles.

What the fuck was a Billy Bob anyway?

She hated him.

She hated her life without her mother and she hated Baltimore City. How she wished she were bigger so that she could show him she could take care of herself and run away.

She was outside for five minutes when a yellow cat walked up to her wanting to be rubbed. She stroked his fluffy fur for one minute before she gripped him by the neck and snapped it, leaving the animal limp. Now she felt better. She was changing into a monster and yet Billy didn't know or care.

The next day Billy Bob, in one of his meth rants, placed locks on all of the cabinets and the refrigerator.

He was evil supreme.

The only thing he allowed Roman to drink was water.

The poor child did all she could to eat. When Billy Bob left the house she tried to steal a slice of bread and he came home right as she placed a corner in her mouth. He stole her in the face so hard her tooth lodged into the flesh of her upper lip and he had to yank it out in the kitchen.

There was one thing that he couldn't keep her from and that was toothpaste. Since she and Cindy were the only ones using it, she would squeeze out globs at a time on tissue paper and eat it throughout the day. After awhile it wasn't just a means to survive, it became a favorite.

When Billy Bob was low on meth and finally took a nap in his room she tiptoed toward the counter to steal three saltine crackers from the pack. When she turned around he was standing before her. It was as if he knew when she would make a move. He backhanded her so hard she knocked her head into the edge of the counter and cut her face.

In the end it was obvious that no matter what her plan, Billy Bob was sneakier.

****

The sun was beaming in the pickup truck and burning Roman's legs. Four days passed and Roman still hadn't eaten a bite outside of her minty toothpaste. She was famished. Even in that moment, she could feel her stomach rolling. But what could she do? She did all she could to win Billy Bob over.

It dawned on her that if she wanted to survive that she needed to make peace with him. With Michelle gone, he was all she had in life. Although little, she tried to straighten up his house but he would grow angry and claim he couldn't find anything. She even tried to stay out of his way, hoping he'd take pity on her and let her eat. But he'd grow frustrated, believing she was stealing from him and forced her to stay where he could see her. Nothing she did worked and the baby fat Michelle grew on her limbs with love continued to dwindle, making her appear scrawny and unkempt.

Billy Bob was in the driver's seat and a bottle of cheap liquor rested between his lips as he fed his fleeting thoughts.

The humid air from the rolled-down windows caused her eyes to dry but she remained silent. She was a child but she figured the less he knew she was there, the more he'd like her. Not to mention, the smell of bananas in the grocery bag caused Roman's stomach to churn. Every so often, she would pull a piece of tissue from the box and cover her nose to stop the smell from tempting her because she knew he'd never give her one. He'd rather see her die first.

Besides, Billy Bob was in a bad mood. Due to recent security upgrades at the electronic stores he frequented, he wasn't able to get any big-ticket items and without money he couldn't get high.

His foot was pressed down on the gas and he was speeding and swerving up the road like he was on the highway alone. How could he support his meth habit without money? Halloween wasn't for another six months so he wouldn't have the revenue from that small business, through which he sold homemade costumes to supply his needs.

Having nowhere else to direct his vexation, Billy Bob looked over at Roman with disdain. "You're old enough to help me out, you know," he said taking a large swig. Tiny balls of tissue paper covered her lap as he glanced down at her. "And I'm going to figure out how." Although he was talking shit, there was one way he could've made money that he didn't take.

One day his good friend, Herbert, asked to have his way with the little boy and he'd pay him five hundred dollars. Billy agreed and told Herbert to meet him later that evening at his shop in Essex. With the plans in order, Billy told Roman to get nice and clean and they drove to the location. When they arrived, the man's mouth watered as he looked at Roman with lustful eyes as they stood out back of the building.

"Thank you, Billy Bob," he said rubbing his hands together. "I won't harm a hair on his head. Trust me," he licked his lips, "I'll be gentle."

The moment he moved to touch Roman, Billy Bob stabbed him in the arm and then the legs. "Fuck you do that for?" he screamed.

"Because I was hoping what you wanted wasn't real. Hoping a man I've known all of my life wasn't no pedophile and that my ears deceived me. So I got the boy all nice and clean so that I could look in your eyes. To see if you were the no account fool you seemed to be."

"So I can't have him?"

"You not only can't have him, if I ever see you around my shop or any kid for that matter, I'll tell the world who you are and together we will kill you."

Horrified, he hobbled to his car with haste and drove away. Billy may have been a hot mess but when it came to men raping kids or any variation thereof, he didn't play that shit.

When he almost hit a parked car, a cop flicked his lights and trailed Billy Bob until he slowed down. "What is this shit about?" he said to himself as he pulled over and parked. He hid the bottle under the seat and gripped the steering wheel tightly until his knuckles turned white. Looking over at Roman, he said, "Don't get a case of happy lips all of a sudden, boy. Stay quiet."

A tall white police officer with a red forehead walked up to the driver's side window with his thumbs hanging over the edge of his belt with authority. His head was small and flat and his large ears stuck out from under his police officer's cap. "License and registration please," he said sternly as if Billy was already wasting his time.

"Uh…hey, officer…what's wrong?"

"License and registration please."

"Can you tell me what I did?"

"License and registration!" he yelled, causing Billy's eyes to flutter.

Billy Bob trembled as he popped open the glove compartment for what he requested. When he located the documents he fumbled around in his wallet for his driver's license. "I don't mean to cause a problem, officer. I just want to know what I did is all."

The officer snatched the documents without hesitation or an explanation. Billy Bob scratched at his face and his right knee bounced as he waited for the verdict. The suspense was killing him. From the rearview mirror, he observed the officer easing into his patrol car and running his paperwork. While waiting, he flipped over the latest heists in his mind and tried to remember if he had any open warrants. He didn't believe so but he'd done so much dirt he couldn't be sure.

When the officer returned with his identification he also delivered a ticket. "Here you go."

Billy Bob's eyes rolled over the fine the cop gave him but he couldn't understand. "What's this for?"

"It's for littering," he said. "And it carries a one hundred and fifty dollar fine."

Billy Bob wanted him gone but he couldn't believe the charge. It seemed so petty. He needed more answers. "But I didn't throw anything out my window."

"Well someone on your passenger side must have," he responded. "It looked like tissue paper." The cop looked at the bald headed little girl in the passenger seat. "Maybe it was her. Whoever it was, it ain't my problem." He tilted his cap. "Good day." He walked off.

When Billy Bob focused on Roman she was smiling and eating a banana. The peeling sat on her lap and an empty Coca Cola soda bottle was thrown on the floor at her feet.

Billy Bob shook his head and laughed heartedly. Now he understood what occurred. Roman caused the diversion to grab a bite to eat and it worked. Not only was it bold but also it was extremely smart for a child.

"First off, are you a girl?"

"Yes."

"Why didn't you tell me?"

"I dunno."

He chuckled again. "Okay, kid. You got one over on me with the tissue." He nodded. "But since you're so good, it's time to help me bring in the big bucks. Welcome to the crime world. I'm sure you'll be a star."

CHAPTER FOUR
-YOKO-

"There are some secrets which do not permit themselves to be told."
- Edgar Allan Poe

Ten-year-old Yoko could barely see over the edge of the tub as she sat inside of it for her bath. Completely naked, the frigid water caused her lips to tremble.

Had she been forgotten?

Would her mother return to finish bathing her? Unable to clean her own body, especially her private parts without assistance due to her short limbs, she was worried that if Maria didn't return soon they wouldn't have time to go to Chuck E. Cheese's and celebrate her birthday like she promised.

She was hopeful her mother would return soon when she heard the voices of her parents escalate in the hallway. "Maria, I'm tired of this shit! How the fuck you gonna tell me you ain't got no money but then you taking that midget to Chuck E. Cheese's?"

"Vincent!"

"I'm serious! You care about that little mothafucka more than you do your own kids!" he roared. "You know we need all the money we can get 'round here."

"Why? So you can buy liquor, drunk?" She paused. "I'll fucking kill you if you call her that again," Maria warned. "Do you hear me? I'll fucking kill you dead! That's my little girl whether you want to be a part of her life or not!"

Yoko, who was given the name by Maria because she said her eyes were Asian, tried to hum her favorite tune to take her mind off the awful things her father was saying about her.

What was a midget?

And why did he despise her so much?

Yoko did all she could to be the nicest and prettiest little girl ever but whenever she was around, Vincent would kick her and tell her to get out of his face. Nothing she did ever worked but it didn't mean she would stop trying.

Yoko was still shivering in the tub when her nine-year-old brother Joshua burst through the bathroom door, whipped out his penis and pissed around the toilet, missing the bowl completely. It was the main reason the bathroom smelled like urine all the time. When he was done he pulled up his jeans and climbed in the tub with his clothes on.

He was mentally detached but when it came to his sister, he loved her completely and where you saw her, he would follow. "Yoko," he said cheerily splashing the water around. "Yoko, Yoko!"

With flailing large arms that looked like boulders to a dwarf child, she grew scared hoping he wouldn't hurt her by mistake. Yoko adored him as much as he loved her and when able, she took care of him as best she could. But as the years rolled by, although they were about the same age, Joshua grew taller and stronger and Yoko had a harder time controlling him.

It wasn't his fault. Joshua, Vincent and Maria's second child, was mentally challenged. His birth certificate said he was nine years old but his mind was closer to that of a four-year-old than anything else. Maria was intoxicated when she gave birth to him and it was one of the reasons she and Vincent argued so much.

"Yoko, Yoko!" Joshua chanted excitedly as he slapped at his light skin until it reddened with each blow. His curly hair dampened and fell in loose loops around his face. "Look, Yoko! Water!"

Naked and completely terrified, Yoko slid backwards and leaned against the back of the chilly tub. "Joshua," she said in her soft voice. "Remember you can't hurt Yoko."

"Can't hurt Yoko," he said as he continued to flail his arms in play but softer. "Won't hurt Yoko."

"That's a good brother," Yoko smiled. "Yoko loves Joshua."

"And Josh loves Yoko," he grinned before slapping himself in the face again.

With Joshua calming down somewhat, Yoko looked at the edge of the tub and contemplated trying to make an escape. But when she raised her arm she wasn't even close to the edge. The only way to make a better go at it was to roll over on her belly. That way she could use her hands to push herself up. But turning her back on her brother could make things worse. What if he playfully charged her and she drowned?

As Joshua grew more excited, Maria stomped in the bathroom after ending her argument with Vincent, only to see her youngest son in the tub with Yoko. "Joshua, no!" Maria screamed, heart pounding, as she rushed toward him, picked him up and shook him so hard Yoko was afraid his head would pop off.

"Mama, please don't," Yoko begged as her eyes protruded. "He was just playing with me! Don't hurt him!"

"But he's not supposed to be in here with you," she scolded him. Maria pulled the door open and yelled, "Dale, come get your fucking brother! You were supposed to be watching him!"

Hearing his mother's frantic voice, nineteen-year-old Dale rushed into the bathroom and gripped Joshua by the hand, forcing his fingertips to turn brick red. One half of Dale's head was braided and the other half sprouted curls. The only reason Joshua was in there to begin with was because he wasn't monitoring his brother. On some freak shit, his girlfriend Courtney turned a hair braiding session into a dick suck in his closet and he took eyes off of him for one moment. That was all Joshua needed to slip away.

"Sorry, ma," Dale said scratching the extra curly part of his head. "I got him now."

"Sorry shit! What if he would've hurt Yoko? Huh? You know she can't do anything by herself. She not like ya'll. She needs us to look after her! You know this, Dale!"

Yoko knew what Maria was saying was true but it still hurt her feelings. She wanted to be independent but

Maria never gave her a chance to prove herself. She did the same thing to her brothers. Maria did everything for Yoko, which handicapped her even more in the process. Yoko craved independence.

"You're right, ma," he said as he rolled his eyes at Yoko and then walked out, closing the door behind him.

Maria was on some obsession shit when it came to Yoko. Although she was not her birth child, Yoko wasn't aware. It didn't matter to Maria that she was a dwarf or that she didn't share her blood. It also didn't matter that Yoko wasn't as strong or tall as her other children. She was the only other girl in a house of men and because of it, they had an unbreakable bond. In Maria's mind, Yoko's dwarfism was the best gift she could've asked for because it meant she would be small forever. She'd always be her doll.

Although Maria doted on Yoko, Vincent didn't feel the same. It wasn't easy for her to convince Vincent to allow the child to stay in the beginning. For starters she wasn't forthcoming about where Yoko came from. First she claimed the child was born to a friend he never met and was abandoned. When he asked for more information on this mysterious friend, she gave him different names and did an awful job of keeping her lies straight. After awhile she decided to write down the information she told him and he stopped asking questions when she presented the same answers.

Besides, why argue with Maria? Originally, money flowed in from Daisy and Maria gave him a cut although she kept the source a secret. As long as the cheddar rolled in, he didn't see a problem with the baby.

That was, until the child grew up. As the years went buy Vincent started to realize she didn't have the same growth spurt like Joshua who was close to her age. "She's a dwarf," he said one day as he saw her playing. "I couldn't figure it out at first but now I know. It's just like my brother! Tell me the truth!"

"She's not a dwarf! She's your niece," Maria sobbed. "And she needs us or else she'll be alone."

"She has to go! I'm not taking care of his responsibilities!"

"I'm sorry for lying but please don't put her out. And please don't tell Yoko. It will kill her!"

This new information almost sent Vincent over the edge. He couldn't believe he was raising the child of the man who stole the only woman he ever loved. A man he despised. Unfortunately, that was last year, around the same time the money Daisy was giving stopped. Maria did all she could to find Daisy to ask about payment but she couldn't find her and Andrew seemed to have fallen off of the face of the earth.

In the long run, Maria didn't care. She already fell in love with the child and would care for her with or without Daisy's payday. The money was never important but Vincent felt differently. If she wanted the dwarf to stay, it would cost her. Every little dollar Maria earned washing hair at a salon down the street, she would give it to him. Not only so he would allow Yoko to remain, but also so that he would keep the secret that they weren't her parents away from the child.

"Sorry, Yoko," Maria said as she turned the hot water knob on to take the chill out of the tub. "Are you okay, honey?" Maria wiped her long fine hair out of her face. "I was so scared just now." She turned the knob off.

"Yes," she smiled with wide eyes. Yoko may have been a dwarf but she was beautiful. Not one blemish or flaw was present on her face or skin. She was kindhearted and filled with love and Maria wanted her to remain that way forever.

"Are you sure you're okay? That boy can be wild, Yoko. He's not right in the head and you must be careful." She washed her feet as she went into her mind and dealt with her own guilt. "Sure it's my fault," she said talking to the wall over Yoko's head. "I know I'm the cause of why he is the way he is. With my drinking and all." She focused on Yoko. "But you got to be careful around him. Understand?"

Yoko didn't see it the same. Outside of Maria, Joshua was her only friend.

"Yes, mama. I understand."

"You know something," she said wiping her under arms rougher than Yoko thought was necessary. "You're the only one in this house who cares about me. And I love you so much. I'll never let anything happen to you, Princess. Ever," she said as she poked the tip of her nose.

****

When Maria, Yoko and Joshua made it to Chuck E. Cheese's it was jam-packed with screaming children. Balls of napkins littered the floor along with edges of wrapping paper and other trash. It was a madhouse but Yoko was super excited.

Unlike Dale and even Joshua, she didn't get to go many places. She wasn't even allowed to go to school or outside because Maria feared the children would be mean and hurtful and she never expressed her fears to Yoko. She made like everything was fine in the world. Homeschooling was Yoko's way of life. The only time Yoko got to be around children was on the one day a year where Maria would splurge and take her to Chuck E. Cheese's for her birthday.

Yoko was just about to zip way from Maria when she gripped her hand and looked down. "Be safe, Yoko." She wiped her soft hair behind her ear. Tears welled up in her eyes and Yoko didn't understand why she was so sorrowful.

"What's wrong, mama?"

Maria ran her hand down Yoko's face and smiled again. She knew she was older now and although she was the same age as a lot of the kids present, she was different. Maria could no longer protect her from the upcoming pain. "I'm sorry in advance, Yoko. So sorry."

Yoko didn't understand what her mother meant but at the moment she was too excited to care. Instead, she and Joshua zipped toward the house of balls as they fought the pecking order of children waiting in line. Once they found their place on the stairs, they waited eagerly to submerge themselves into the colorful pool of balls.

"Yoko, Yoko!" Joshua cheered as he moved anxiously in place. "Balls, Yoko!" he pointed at the house. "Balls! Can we play?"

"Aren't they nice, Joshua?" Yoko grinned trying to maintain her excitement. After all, she was the big sister and she had to show him how it was done. "We just got to wait in line that's all," she said joyfully while trying to be patient.

When Joshua grew overly excited, Yoko tried to calm him down. Plus, there was a pretty little girl behind her who, although taller, appeared to be around her age. Yoko didn't have any friends and figured if she was nice to her that the little girl could come over her house and they could play together.

Trying to find a talking point, something they had in common, Yoko examined the little girl's hair, which was as long as hers. Then she focused on her bright smile. "I like your red dress," Yoko said to her. "It's pretty."

Instead of being flattered, the child rudely rolled her eyes, turned around to her friend and whispered in her ear. When she was done they both looked at Yoko and laughed hysterically. Yoko was confused on what was so funny but it was their turn to get into the colorful balls so she walked up the stairs with her brother in tow.

As she jumped around in the pool of balls, she was careful not to go into the center with the rest of the children, because unlike them, the only thing you could see on Yoko at any given time was her head. But it didn't stop Joshua from flailing around like a madman excitedly.

When Yoko saw the little girl with her friend, she replayed their interaction in her mind. What was funny? Why didn't she smile back when she was trying to be nice? If Yoko had one of her dolls she would've gladly given it to her so that she would know she wanted to be friends. Yoko desired to be around a girl her age. Someone who liked the same things she did but it never happened.

Yoko's mind was too busy on the little girl when suddenly she saw Joshua move to close to her. "Get off of me, retard!" the little girl yelled. "Before I tell my mother!"

"Joshua, come," Yoko hollered and tried to raise her arm so that he could see her. But Joshua was too busy with the little girl to bother with his sister.

"Yuck! I said get away!" The little girl pushed him back. "I'm telling! You tried to touch my butt!"

"Don't do that," Yoko said to the little girl as she finally made her way toward them. Yoko was unable to move around as quickly or as much as other kids because she got winded easily. "He…he didn't mean anything," she said trying to catch her breath. "He's not that smart."

"Yoko, Yoko, Yoko!" Joshua chanted as he circled his sister, unaware of the drama brewing on his part.

When Joshua got in the little girl's face again, the child slapped him so hard he sobbed. Now Yoko was mad. Nobody fucked with her brother! Nobody!

She pushed toward the little girl and through the balls Yoko kicked her in her lower shin, the only place she could reach. It wasn't hard enough to cause any real damage but it didn't stop the child from blowing things out of proportion.

"Mama, mama," she screamed as she climbed out of the balls. "The midget hit me! It hit me!"

That was the second time she heard the word midget in reference to her that day. The first time was with her father and now with the little girl she wanted to be her friend. She didn't know what the word meant but she could feel the tension when the word was used against her.

It was filled with hate.

Yoko turned around and faced her brother. "Joshua, we have to get out of here. Something bad is getting ready to happen."

"Yoko, Yoko!" he continued jumping around, out of reach of his sister. "Balls! I like balls!"

"Joshua, we have to leave," Yoko pleaded, on the verge of crying. Suddenly she didn't want to be independent anymore. She wanted her mother.

But Joshua was having too much fun to listen to his sister. He was face deep in the funky balls and the only thing she could see at the moment was the bottom of his soiled white socks. "Joshua, please," Yoko persisted. "We have to leave now!"

Yoko was still focusing on her brother when suddenly she was hoisted up. Before she knew what was happening, she was tossed in the air and moving rapidly toward the edge of the ball pit. When she landed, her forehead banged against an exposed bar across the way and she was knocked out cold.

****

The next day Yoko was in a hospital bed scared and confused about what happened to her. And why did people look at her differently than they did her mother or brothers? Just like the little girl and her father, Yoko heard various orderlies refer to her as a midget during her stay. It was as if Yoko had done something wrong simply by being born.

It wasn't until an elderly black nurse walked into her room to check her vitals that she experienced a moment of kindness. "Hey there, pretty lady," the nurse said in a warm voice. "How are you today?" she placed the stethoscope against Yoko's chest to check her breathing before moving it to her back.

"What am I?" Yoko asked the woman as tears rolled down her cheeks. Her eyes narrowed.

"You're a pretty little girl," she smiled. "That's what you are."

"Then why do people hate me?"

"Nobody hates you, honey," she responded as she scanned over Yoko's health chart. She was doing all she could to avoid the topic but the little girl was persistent.

"Then why did that girl's mother hate me? Why did she throw me in the air? Why does my daddy hate me? Why does..."

"Relax, honey," the nurse said realizing the child was on the verge of a mental breakdown. She already suffered a concussion and had a gaping wound across the top of her head. She didn't need her making things worse by panicking. "Your mother will be back in a minute. She's downstairs buying you some treats."

"Please tell me what's wrong with me." Her eyes glazed over. "Nobody will talk to me."

Realizing she needed to hear the truth, the nurse sat on the edge of the bed and touched the top of her tiny hand. "Sweetheart, you are going to have a difficult life," she sighed. "And I can tell in your eyes that you are kind and unfortunately that will make you a victim. You need to be strong and you need to prepare yourself because you will be exposed to the worst of humanity." And just like Maria, the nurse said, "I'm so sorry, honey. I'm sorry in advance."

Now Yoko understood what Maria meant.

CHAPTER FIVE
-YOKO-
MANY YEARS LATER

"The boundaries which divide Life from Death are at best shadowy and vague."
- Edgar Allan Poe

Eighteen-year-old Yoko leaned against the sooty brick building. A burned out jack was stuffed between her cracked lips and she smashed it under her timberland boot after releasing it. Her still moist hair, due to wetting it earlier, was pulled back into a tight ponytail, forcing the corners of her eyes to reach higher. Like always, she clutched a metal pipe in her right hand and she clanked it against the ground every ten seconds as if it were a heartbeat.

"Either give me the money you owe or you're wasting my time." She exhaled a puff of smoke into the crackhead's face who was standing over top of her.

"Yoko, come on!" he waved the smoke out of his face. "You know I gave you more money than that." He rubbed his arms and rocked slowly before scratching his chin. "I don't feel good. Don't do me like this. At least give me my money back."

"Nigga, you think I'm stupid?" she barked. "You gave me ten dollars and I handed you back what was due." She paused. "Now get the fuck up out my face before I go off on you."

When her brother Joshua tried to walk off, lost in his own mind, she tugged the leash that was secured to his belt buckle. Joshua moved by the beat of his dangerous mind, which was why he stayed in trouble. It was important to keep eyes on him at all times. It was Yoko who kept him safe and made sure he never went too far. "Josh, no," she said to him "Stay."

"Yoko, Yoko," he chimed.

"I'm here, baby bro," she said winking at him. "Be easy. You can't go too far."

When she focused back on the fiend, she wiped her long hair behind her ear and rubbed her scarred face. The man before her was running game and she didn't trust him. Outside of her own family, who she would die for, Yoko hated average height people, including the nigga before her who was begging for handouts. In her opinion, average heighters were always trying to get over and he was no different.

"Listen, you little bitch," the crackhead said as he leaned down. "If you don't give me my money back I'ma—"

"You gonna what?" she pushed off of the wall and moved closer to him. Her face contorted into a glare and she secretly begged him to say some smart shit out of his face so that she could lay him flat.

"I'ma fuck you—"

The moment he spoke ill she whacked him in the ankle with the metal pipe bringing him crashing to his knees before he could finish his statement. Believing he was still too tall because he was able to look her in the eyes she smacked him again on the neck causing him to slam face first into the concrete. Now she was staring down at him. She liked it better that way. "Talk that shit now, nigga," she said glaring at him. "Now you beneath me. Where you belong!"

"When I get up I'm gonna kill you, you fucking midget!"

"That's how you feel?" she said hitting him again across the face. "You wanna hurt Yoko?" Turning her attention to Joshua she said, "Yoko hurt! Get him!"

Before Yoko yelled the code words, Joshua was in his own mind. The lights and sounds of the city always excited him and he would often lose focus. But the moment he discerned her frantic voice, he gave her his undivided attention. With wild eyes on the crackhead, Joshua dropped down and pounded him so badly he fell unconscious. When he was done his nose was bloodied and two teeth rested next to his body.

Not wanting Joshua to murder the man, she knew she had to call off her brother before it was too late. "Yoko fine," she said rubbing his back. "Yoko fine now."

Slowly Joshua rose and looked down at his older but smaller sister. His knuckles were crimson red. Breathing heavily, he patted the top of her head and said, "Josh loves Yoko."

"And Yoko loves Joshua back," she winked. When she saw a crowd closing in on the scene she yelled, "We got to bounce, baby bro!" She walked over to her red bike with the white streamers floating from the handlebar. It was built for a toddler, training wheels and all, but she rocked it as if it were a souped up Benz with wicked rims.

Yoko climbed on the seat and slid her feet on the top of the big blocks of wood that were secured to the pedals. Once on top, she made sure the tips of her feet were under the rubber band.

"Let's rock out, Joshua," she said when she heard the sirens. "Trouble's near."

Although Joshua was walking normally, he was still much faster than her if she was on her feet. Yoko needed the bike to keep up with him and other average height people. At first the difference in her attitude caused problems in the house with her and her brothers. They could move around better than she could. But now she learned to adapt to the big world.

As Yoko rolled down the street, she thought about the day the woman tossed her across the ball pit. As if she wasn't a person with feelings. The nurse was right. Yoko's life was hard and the older she got, she realized things didn't get any better. It was as if she were all alone.

People treated her like a freak.

Children were mean to her for no reason, adults made jokes about her for their amusement, and when she met a man and gave him her heart, she learned quickly that he was only interested because of some strange fetish he had for dwarfs. Before long, she stopped caring and decided to use her handicap as an advantage.

If a nigga wanted to fuck her, she'd charge him and make a few bucks in the process. If she had larceny in her heart, she'd borrow her brother Dale's gun and commit robbery. She didn't care what she had to do because these days it was all about the paper. She suffered a lot for diving in the streets though. Through the years she was shot, robbed, raped and beaten more times than the average person and yet she was still alive. Yoko wasn't naïve anymore and if it wasn't about her family, in her opinion it wasn't about shit.

****

The sun fell behind the building across from where Yoko sat on the porch as she glanced up at the sky. She was alone, and darkness was enveloping the city. The best part of her life was coming.

Nighttime.

And she was hoping her front row seat was adequate enough to see the madness that took over her neighborhood when the worst of the city came out of their holes.

Instead of action and some good drama, Roman, the neighbor who lived upstairs, walked outside. Before plopping down on the step next to Yoko, she asked, "Anybody sitting here?"

Yoko looked back at the tall girl with the green eyes and two thick French braids running down her back. Although her stunning looks were the first thing one thought of when observing Roman, it would be unwise to stereotype her because she was anything but a beauty queen.

Irritated with her presence, Yoko shrugged and said, "Last time I checked this was a free world." She clanked her pole against the step and continued to watch the city. "Don't ask questions. Just do you."

Thinking Yoko was trying to play her as soft, Roman snapped on her ass. "Ain't nobody ask you about a free world! You can keep all that other shit you popping to yourself. I was just being polite." She sat down but scooted away from Yoko or else she feared she'd steal her in the jaw. "I can't stand these rude ass Baltimore bitches."

Upon breathing in the insult, originally Yoko's plan was to rise up and stand behind Roman. So that the moment she caught her off guard she could bring the pole across the back of her head. Instead, she fell back for a second. Because despite the rudeness, she could feel she was different. Although Roman tried to get out on her with her sharp word-play, when Roman looked at her Yoko could tell Roman saw her as a person.

Not a dwarf or midget.

"Ain't nobody trying to hear that shit," Yoko snapped although she liked the girl immediately. "You the one who came out here with all that mushy shit. Don't have one seat. Have several. Whatever you do just leave me the fuck alone."

Roman waved her off and pulled out a small tube of mint toothpaste. When Yoko saw she was eating it she started to say something negative but Roman asked, "Want some?"

Yoko looked at her green eyes with the freckles in the corners and then the tube. "What the fuck," she said sticking out her finger.

Roman placed a dab on top of it and Yoko licked it down. Yoko shrugged and said, "Hey, who am I to talk?"

With nothing else left to be said, they observed the darkening city. For an hour, both of them sat in silence as they viewed Baltimore as if it were a stage. As if they had been friends forever, they sat on that step and made separate observations. Yet they laughed at the same things, feared the same things, and before long something was evident. They both shared the same personalities.

They became best friends.

Each day they would come outside, hoping to see the other. They found security in their budding friendship even though the world viewed them as awkward.

One short.

One extremely tall for a girl.

But both the same.

As the months went by their bond grew stronger and unspoken rules developed between the two of them. If one had something, they both had it. If one was wronged, they both were wronged and somebody had to pay. And if one was sad, so was the other.

One cool day they were sitting on the porch trying to get away from it all. When suddenly a black Escalade pulled up to the corner store across the street. Once parked, a lanky character sporting a red Bulls basketball cap eased out of the driver's seat, slammed the door and talked to a few of his friends inside of his ride. He was loud and clearly desired to be seen.

He was the epitome of a true clown nigga.

But when one of the men inside of the truck pointed across the street at Yoko who was sitting on the step, the skinny character cracked up laughing. They called her sexy red midget, dwarf, and the like and Yoko hated it all. As she watched the group make fun of her, her skin grew hot to the touch.

With a lowered brow she said, "I'm so sick of that shit." She sighed and looked over at them, wishing she had her brother's gun to blast extra holes in their faces. "People love treating me like a joke." She shook her head and watched them laugh. "Like I ain't got feelings." She choked back tears because she hated softness especially in front of her homie.

"Fuck them, Yoko." Roman spit on the ground in front of her. "They clown ass niggas." She wiped her mouth off with the back of her hand.

"That's easy for you to say. I'm 4'4 and you the total opposite." She shook her head again. "The funny thing is shit like this always happens when I start to believe that maybe shit is changed."

"When you think that?"

"When nobody makes fun of me for awhile. And when I became friends with you." She exhaled. "That's why I hate average height mothafuckas."

"Hold up," Roman said putting her palms out. "I ain't like the rest. Don't lump me in with them clown ass niggas. You just a regular bitch and I've treated you like one from the jump."

"First off, you not average height. You tall as shit for a bitch. Got the nerve to be pretty too. I been told you that. And second of all, I'm not talking about you so get out your feelings. Don't play the martyr. You know I fuck with you. Always have and always will." She looked over at the guys. "But them...they different. Just mean."

Roman looked at the driver bop inside of the store as she considered what her friend was truly saying. She could tell in Yoko's body mechanics that her feelings were hurt and that plagued Roman. It had her wanting to do something about it.

About five minutes later, the clown came back out with a paper bag filled with snacks and soda. He handed it to the dude in the passenger seat.

"Don't be too long," the passenger yelled. "We got somewhere to be."

"Nigga, shut the fuck up," the clown said gripping his thickness. "I told your bitch ass to drive because I wanted to get my dick wet first. But you ain't have no gas. Remember? Now you gonna have to wait." He laughed all the way to the building behind his truck before he disappeared inside.

Although she couldn't see him anymore, Roman kept her eyes on the building. "You want to do something 'bout it?" she said slyly.

"'Bout what?" Yoko asked clanking her pipe on the step, already moved on to the next thought.

Roman nodded at the building the jokester crawled into. "You know what I mean. Do something 'bout that bitch ass nigga who thought he was on stage a minute ago. I'm curious to see how he performs with a gun to his face."

Yoko grinned. "I'm with that shit if you are."

Roman stood up and spit again. "Meet me in the basement of our building. I got to go to my apartment and do something right quick."

****

Curtis Ryan hung in Brickhouse Lucy's apartment doorway. The pizza she cooked earlier warmed on the top of the stove and gave him more inspiration to get inside of her place.

He was starved.

For pussy and food.

Brickhouse Lucy's titties spilled over the ruby red top she wore and the curve of her ass cheeks hung out of the mini dress. Although he wanted to fuck, she was leaning against the doorframe reminding him about all of the reasons she wasn't going to give him no good-good.

"I'm not trying to hear that shit, Curt. I'm sick of you telling me you feeling me and then running back to your weak ass baby mother." She inched her tiny mini up a tad, basically showing her entire snatch. "I know ain't nobody fucking you like me. Come real with it. I'm just trying to fig-ure out when you gonna realize you lost the best thing you ever had."

When he saw her glistening clit his dick rose like fresh bread in a hot oven.

"Look at this pussy. Ain't it pretty?" she continued, taunting him. When he tried to touch it she smacked his knuckles.

"You worrying about dumb shit, Lucy. Let me come inside right quick." Curtis gripped his dick, trying to calm it down. The pulsing was maddening and it ached. "So I can fill you up."

"So you can rip and run the street with your niggas later?" She put her hands on her hips. "I know they outside in your truck, ain't they? This ain't no gas station. Don't come here for a fill up."

"Man, ain't nobody even outside." He was growing frustrated. He raised his right hand in the air and put the other on his chest. "I swear on my life! On Allah!" Curtis continued as if he were Muslim. When he made the trip to her building he hoped it would be easy enough to fuck her right quick. Based on his calculations, he deduced that he would be back in his truck right now.

But he underestimated how much energy it took to get up with a bitch who was fed up with his bullshit. "Come on. Let me in right fast." He paused. "So we can do what grown folks do." He ran his dry index finger along the side of her face. "Later on, I'll come back, scoop you up and we'll get something to eat. You with it?"

For a second, Lucy considered his whack ass proposal. She was even smiling up in his face when all of a sudden she slammed the door against his nose, causing it to bleed a little. "Fuck wrong with you, bitch?" he yelled as he banged his fist on the door, causing it to ring out in the hallway. "That's why all I do is fuck you, slut! You ain't good for nothing else!"

He could talk shit all day long if he desired. Lucy was done with his creep ass. And when he'd turn around he'd find out why. Because the moment Curtis' eyes adjusted, he was staring into the face of what he thought was a nigga in a black hoodie. White paint covered the cheek and forehead areas while black paint concealed the eyes. Curtis noticed that the nose looked large and a little fake but it didn't decrease the fear in his heart. It was obvious the dude wanted something from him.

When he glanced down he saw what looked to be the silhouette of a gun sticking out of the white face crook's pocket. "Give it up," she said in a deep voice.

"Man, don't do this shit," he stomped like a bitch. "I just got hit last week!"

"I'll say it once more." She paused. "But there won't be a third time. Give it up."

Afraid for his life, Curtis turned his pockets inside out, giving the crook all he had on him in the moment. When Roman stuffed her pockets with her newfound wealth she said, "Your toll is paid. You're free to roam."

Slowly Curtis walked toward the steps. "You not gonna kill me if I walk down are you? Shoot me in the back of the head or nothing?"

Roman shook her head no.

Curtis took one step, and then three. But right before his Jordan made the fourth, Yoko hit him with a swift blow to the ankles. She was so short that he didn't see it coming. Curtis rolled down the steps like a pinball, seconds before his chin crashed against the guardrail, breaking his neck in twenty places.

He was paralyzed for the rest of his life.

CHAPTER SIX
-ROMAN-

"But why will you say that I am mad?"
- Edgar Allan Poe

The sun beamed upon the black church crown of a 6-foot tall grey haired black lady as she promenaded up the tree-lined street. She was humming *Jesus Loves Me* and moving unhurriedly toward a white woman who was watering her plush green lawn in a suburban Maryland neighborhood. A golden basket full of fresh green tomatoes hung from the crease of her arm as she made her way up the block.

As she looked down at the address in her hand, she tried desperately to read it. But as it had been all of her life, it was too difficult because the words appeared unsteady. She would have to wing it.

The elderly woman was Roman.

With some good facial prosthetics from The House of Horror Shop that Billy owned, she was able to conceal her real identity. Even down to the wrinkly hand gloves she wore.

Once at the white woman's walkway, Roman sang, "Beautiful day, ain't it?" She looked up at the sky and squinted. "Glory be to God."

The woman turned the hose off, wiped the sweat from her brow and said, "Pardon?"

"I said, beautiful day, ain't it?"

She smiled and looked up at the blazing sky. "I guess it is. Way better than yesterday for sure." She scanned the woman over. She looked harmless enough so she asked, "Now what can I do for you?"

Roman raised the basket. "A Maryland farmer I am. All my life." Roman cleared her throat. "Interested in—"

"I'm sorry," she said cutting her off. "I've done my grocery shopping for the week already." She turned the hose back on and watered her plants. "Good luck though. Try Margo three houses up."

"Ma'am, I...I'm not a sales person." She cleared her throat. "But farm good I do." She smiled and raised the basket again. "What do you say 'bout this deal. You can have this whole basket for five bucks." When the woman didn't seem interested Roman grabbed a tomato, walked up to the running hose and placed it under the water. "This one is free. Try it."

The woman accepted the tomato and took a large bite. Her eyes widened with delight. "Wow, this is...delicious." She took another chomp and before long finished the entire fruit. "You know what, I'll buy the entire basket." She wiped the sweat off her forehead. "Come inside. Let me get my purse."

Roman, glanced up the street, winked at Billy Bob and plodded into the woman's home.

As she stood in the foyer, the white woman said, "Stay right here. I'll be right back."

While she was gone Roman lodged a wad of gum into the lock of her front door so that it would remain open when she left. When she came back she handed Roman twenty dollars instead of five. "Listen, I know we agreed on five but my husband owns a farm too. I know how hard you work. Why don't you take this instead?"

When Roman saw the money she dipped her chin toward her chest in shame. This was the first time, in all of the jobs she and Billy Bob did together that she felt guilty about her motives.

"Are you okay, ma'am?" the woman asked Roman.

"Uh...yes," she smiled. "Just feeling a little under the weather that's all. Thank you." She handed her the basket. "Thank you for everything."

"No problem," she smiled kindly. "Let me put these in the kitchen. I'll walk you out."

When she left Roman removed the gum from the lock and rolled out before she could return. In quickened steps, she hurried up the sidewalk, until she reached Billy

Bob's silver Dodge Durango. The moment she eased inside, he drilled into her.

"Did you do it?" the sores on his face due to years of meth smoking were wetter and wider. And the teeth that were brave enough to remain in his mouth had decayed, while the others split along time ago.

Roman nodded. "Yes. I did it."

"Good," he grinned rubbing his hands together as he glanced at her house. "I saw when you were coming back. You were too lax. You better watch your surroundings when you pulling a job. You leave too much to chance and someone could've followed you."

She nodded in understanding.

"Now all we have to do is wait," he said to himself.

"But…I got to tell you something," Roman swallowed. "You gonna be mad."

As the years rolled by, twenty-three-year-old Roman grew fiercely loyal to Billy Bob despite being afraid of him. Although she never loved him as much as she loved her mother and her brothers, it felt just as close. Due to his drug habit, he couldn't think the same and it was Roman who made sure he was cared for and safe.

In turn, he taught her how to break and enter. Steal. Rob. Lie. And even be conniving. She learned quickly, mainly because it was important to her to please him. In her mind it was them against the world and if she had to break into someone's home to feed them then so be it.

For the most part, before Yoko entered the picture, Roman was a loner who talked to herself. One day when he came to the apartment, he heard Roman imitating a conversation he had with Cindy Lou and he was blown away. He noticed how she was able to impersonate his voice and Cindy's interchangeably. Billy Bob realized the greatest thieves were wonderful illusionists so he used her natural talent to his advantage.

At first Roman didn't understand why she had to dress like different people to pull heists until he explained it to her using good old fashion racist Mississippi ethics, even though Baltimore was now their home.

"The only thing more suspicious than a black woman is a black man. You must learn to be a chameleon. You must remain unseen. Like the devil."

From that moment on, she became whatever character she had to, to complete her heist and she was good at it. So good they never, ever got caught. When it came to the money he made off of her, it was clear that Roman paid her mother's so-called debt long ago. But Billy Bob kept his claws into her heart, never letting go. Using guilt and fear as a weapon.

"What do you have to tell me?"

"I took the gum off," she said softly, afraid to disappoint him. "I mean I put it on but took it back off." She dug into the pocket of her long skirt. "Because she gave me twenty dollars instead of five like I asked."

He snatched the bill out of her hand and slapped her in the face. It didn't hurt as much as it usually did because she was wearing the mask. "What the fuck is wrong with you, nigger? Huh? Do you realize how much jewelry is in that house?"

"But she gave us more," Roman said with her quivering lip.

"What do we give a fuck? It's about the big bucks! Not about who's nice and who's not. That heart of yours is gonna get us in trouble. Get rid of it!" Then he looked her over. "Wait, where's the basket?"

The moment he asked for it her eyes bulged and she trembled. He repeated over and over that the basket had to come back with her. On the surface it looked average but examined closer, it was unique to Billy Bob because it was used to sit pumpkins in during Halloween every year at his shop.

"I left it, Billy," she spoke in a drawling voice.

"Why would you leave the basket?" he yelled, his spit sprinkling on her nose. "You know it's from my shop. Too original. You have to go get it." He paused. "It's sad, kid. Because you know what you have to do now." He paused and looked over at her. "Don't you?"

She shook her head no.

"You have to kill her."

Upon hearing his statement, her long brown hair moistened under the grey wig and she could feel sweat trickling down the back of her neck. "No, Billy. Please."

"You knew this would happen sooner or later." He reached in the glove compartment and handed her a knife. "Murder is always the next step in what we do. Now go do it."

She shook her head no.

"What the fuck is wrong with you?" he yelled. "Huh? You not killing me, or your mother or your brothers. You're killing somebody who doesn't even know you!" He scratched his face again. "Somebody who before you gave her those tomatoes didn't know you were alive."

"But I don't want to," she said as tears and sweat crawled down her face. "She's innocent."

He was asking her to do the impossible. Something she never thought she would be responsible for…murder. After all, she remembered how she felt when someone broke into her home and snuffed out her mother's life. Maybe the old woman was someone's mother too. The raw feeling stayed with her always and not a day went by where she didn't recall seeing their faces in her mind.

Billy Bob sat back in his seat in frustration. It was evident that he was losing control. He would kill the woman himself if he could get within a stone's throw of her. But he realized the moment she saw his pus filled face she would jump on the phone and call the cops. Roman had to do it. There was no other way.

Billy picked at his face again. "You know who that woman is in there?"

She shook her head no.

"She's a racist, Roman. She hates niggers," he continued as if he was Dr. King himself. "I once saw her give the word to string up a kid on the east side for smiling. She thought he was flirting with her." He leaned up and got closer to her face. "They hung that boy by the neck on a tree out front of his house for everyone to see. Even his mama was present. And that's the kind of woman you want to stay alive?"

Roman's heart rate quickened and she was feeling something she hadn't felt since her mother was murdered. Rage. If Billy wanted to ruffle her feathers, he was doing a good damn job. But he knew he had to go deeper.

"I didn't want to tell you this but I 'spect I can go ahead and do it now. You're old enough to know. There was a group of people responsible for your family's death. More people than you are aware of. It was a conspiracy." He sat back in his seat and looked in the direction of the woman's house. "And that bitch up the street was one of them."

Roman was so angry now her veins pulsated. "My mom…she killed my mom?" Her bottom lip flopped loosely and a string of drool eased off of it and fell on her jacket.

"Yes, Roman." He placed a firm hand on her shoulder. "And she's also the one who gutted Ice and tossed him in the alley in the back of our building all them years ago."

For years Roman wondered what happened to her loyal companion. Ice didn't bother anybody so she didn't understand who would be so cruel that they'd kill an animal. She had no idea that Billy grew tired of the dog growling at him whenever he would see him strike Roman. So he placed sleeping pills into his ground beef meal and when Roman was asleep, Billy sliced into his underbelly releasing him from his misery.

"But if you don't care about your family or your dog I'll just go home." he placed the car in drive but she stopped him.

"No," she said softly.

"No what?" he said in a sly tone.

"I'll do it."

It worked!

Because she was still naïve, she allowed him to infiltrate her mind.

"When you kill her don't look in her eyes. They'll haunt you, Roman." He paused. "Stick her in this area and then her heart." He placed his hand on his chest. "And don't pull it out until you can't push any further."

Roman's body seemed to vibrate as she pushed the door open and plopped out into the street. With visions of her mother lying in her own blood fresh in her mind, although still in an elderly costume, she was now walking swiftly with murderous ambitions.

When Roman reached the yellow door, she knocked forcefully and the moment the woman opened it she prodded the blade into her stomach and pushed her to the floor, slamming the door behind her.

Once inside, Roman straddled her and covered the woman's mouth while she stabbed her in the heart. "That was for my family and Ice." A single tear fell from Roman's eye but she wiped it away before it dropped on the lady's face, leaving with it her DNA.

When she heard the woman mouthing something, she lowered her ear so that she could hear a dying racist's last words.

"What are you saying?" Roman asked angrily.

"G…goon," she stuttered.

****

Roman sat on the top step popping sunflower seeds when the apartment building door opened and Yoko strutted outside. "What up?" Yoko asked. "Why you ain't tell me you were out here? I would've came out with you. I was bored as shit in the house."

"No reason. I was just chilling."

Roman attempted to hide her face when Yoko stood behind her. She wasn't in the mood for convo. But even Roman underestimated how close their bond had grown. Even if they were silent, never saying a word to each other, they would still know if the other was hurt.

"What's wrong with you?" Yoko asked using the pole to sit on the step next to her. She snatched the bag of seeds and popped a few in her mouth.

"Don't come out here with that bullshit. I ain't feeling it right now."

"Bitch, don't tell me not to come outside with shit. I'll bust you in the back of your head with this pole first." She raised it for effect. "And just so you know, that's something I been wanting to do since I laid eyes on you. Now what's going on? Stop wasting time."

Roman shook her head and wiped the tears away that were streaming down her face. "Nothing, man. Just leave me the fuck alone! That's why I hate your little ass sometimes. Always want a bitch to talk when she prefers silence."

Yoko laughed. "Roman, I love you. But you should know this. I'd rather kill you dead than to see you this sad without knowing what's going on. Now what's up?"

Silence.

She realized she wouldn't leave it alone. "Billy made me do the ultimate today."

"What's that?" she squealed. "He raped you?"

"Fuck no!" Roman stared at her with red eyes. "Murder."

Yoko shook her head. "And you mad because?"

Roman frowned at her friend's insensitivity. "I'm mad because that ain't me, Yoko. The woman I killed today was nice. She didn't deserve that shit! Robbing hood niggas is not a thing for me. You know I don't have a problem with it. But killing innocents? It ain't in me, Yoko." She wiped her tears away with the back of her hand. "It just ain't."

"You taking shit out of proportion. Murder is the next step up from the robbery game. You ain't know?"

Roman observed her as if she had dicks for nostrils. "To me there is never a need for murder. Unless a hood nigga pressing you and you got to make a move."

"A hood nigga?" she giggled. "Bitch, have you looked into the mirror lately? You a hood nigga too." She paused. "You know what your problem is?"

"Do tell," Roman said sarcastically.

"Your problem is that you think you're the only one in the world who laid a nigga to rest. Wake up, bitch! Niggas get robbed and murdered every day. The only thing you did this beautiful morning was contribute to the American way. If anything, you should be commended."

"But that's not what I'm about, Yoko. I believe in having a code. Everything in life should have a code."

"And what's yours?"

"Any nigga getting money on the streets better hold tight to their pack and their life. But innocents are out of rotation and shouldn't be killed."

"Let me tell you like this. Leave the code shit to computer programmers. Keep your mind on the dollar. If anybody walks outside of their house they subject to get the business. Kids and innocents included." She paused. "And if Billy Bob's racist ass put you up on game he a better man than I thought." She shrugged. "I'm just saying."

Roman loved Yoko but at the moment she viewed her in a different way. She was starting to feel like she couldn't trust her. A person without a code in her opinion was dangerous.

"Your outlook on life is all the way fucked up." Roman grabbed her toothpaste from her pocket and squeezed a sliver on her finger before licking it off. "What you think a goon is?" she asked changing the subject.

"A thorough nigga," Yoko responded cheerfully. "Like me." She grinned. "Somebody not to be fucked with."

Roman nodded but wasn't sure if she was interested in the moniker the old woman gave her. And she doubted the woman was using it in that manner when she killed her.

"Why you ask?"

"No reason," she lied, refusing to tell her about what the old woman called her.

"Answer me this shit, Ro," Yoko said bringing back up the conversation. "If we both went to court for murder, you with your code and me without, who do you think the jury would convict?"

"Both of us," she answered without hesitation. "But tell me this. Who would be able to sleep at night? Someone who wouldn't kill a pregnant woman for her paycheck or the other who for fifty dollars took her and her unborn baby out?"

Silence.

"I don't sleep at night as is," Yoko said secretly knowing Roman made a good point. "So putting a few mothafuckas out they misery for the dollar ain't nothing but a thing to me. It's just how I feel."

"One day you'll want someone to have a code. I wonder if you'll feel the same then."

"I guess we'll have to see."

CHAPTER SEVEN
-YOKO-

"Who shall say where the one ends, and where the other begins?"
- Edgar Allan Poe

Holding a can of beer, Yoko sat on the porch in front of her building doing the regular. Wasn't shit popping off as usual and at the moment all she was thinking about was her life. Was this the only thing she would amount to? Quaffing and sitting on the porch day in and day out? Would she ever find love? Would she ever get out of the hood?

No, she said to herself. *You don't deserve to be anywhere else. Remember? You're a nobody.*

When her beer was finished, she was just about to go buy another when Roman stepped outside. "Fuck," she said rubbing her flat stomach before plopping down next to Yoko. "It's hot as shit out this bitch." She looked at the beer can, picked it up and shook it. "Damn! I got you on the last one...you could've left me some. You knew I was coming outside." She sat the empty can down.

"We can walk to the store in a minute. I got a few bucks on me."

Roman yawned. "This city feels dead as shit today."

"What you think it should feel like?" she asked clanking her pole on the steps. "It's Murdermore, baby."

Roman shook her head and laughed at her feisty buddy. Over the months of knowing her best friend, she was certain of one thing. That she was a braggart, often telling people of the heists they pulled off together just for points no one was giving out. The only good thing about it was that in her stories she never mentioned Roman. She made out as if she did everything on her own. To most Baltimoreans, she played herself like a clown. Nobody believed that she robbed this dude or killed that nigga for a pack. How could she? She was a dwarf.

No doubt the city was scared of a new dark figure that plagued Baltimore but it wasn't 4'4" tall Yoko. It was the 6-foot tall nigga that was sneaking up on dealers who moved work in the dark cracks of the city, waving two brand new guns in the air.

Although she was hiding out in plain sight, the city never considered Roman. She was the perfect height but her light green eyes and mellow voice were different from the dark eyes of the perpetrator. How were they to know she wore contacts and a fake nose to distort the feminine features of her face? The nigga they feared went by the name *Goon*.

She would whisper the word in their ear after she took their work or before she murdered them.

No one had any idea that he was a she. That she was Roman.

There hadn't been a figure since Wayne Perry who pumped as much fear in the hearts of young hustlers on the East Coast. When she waved the weapons in the air you either anti-up on the work and money or make your peace with the concrete beneath your feet. Roman may have had a problem with killing innocents but she held no qualms about murdering hood niggas who disobeyed her orders. To date, she killed 12 with the number increasing with every uncooperative hustler who crossed her path.

"You ever think you'll get out of Baltimore?" Yoko asked.

"No," Roman scratched in between two of her cornrows. "Not unless somebody saves me."

"What that mean?"

"What would a real man want with a woman like me?" she asked seriously. "I'm nobody's type." She exhaled. "Too tall. Too weird and I kill for a living. I used to have this dream about having a family. A husband. A son and stuff like that. But even if someone did save me, I've done too much dirt to ever feel comfortable. I would always worry that someone would take my son or my husband from me. Like Karma would be waiting around the corner saying, 'Naw, bitch. You don't get to be happy.' Get it?"

"Yeah, I get it," Yoko said under her breath. "I want what you want too. But a little different."

"What you mean?"

"I want to be looked at for me. Without people judging me for my height."

"Shit that's easy. Give niggas a reason to respect you and they will."

Yoko nodded. "I'll work on that," she said smart-alecky. "And if you don't have a son by the time you're thirty I'll steal one for you."

Roman laughed. "What's up with you and this kidnapping fetish of yours?"

"I don't know," she shrugged. "It's amazing how different people act when you snatch 'em up. Some of the hardest niggas, once in the back of a trunk, go soft as ice cream."

Roman laughed her off. "Fuck all that. What's up with the beer?"

They were about to walk when Roman saw an event go down across the street next to the corner store. Vale was leaning up against the brick wall where he served Baltimore's zombies. A barrel was pressed against his throat by a snatcher and Vale looked horrified. When his hands flew up in the air, the robber grabbed his money and work that was stashed behind the dumpster before taking off in the wind.

"Did you just see that shit?" Roman asked with her jaw hung. "In broad daylight!"

Yoko laughed and clinked her pole against the step again. "Hell yeah I saw that shit. I keep telling that nigga his hustle game is unsatisfactory at best but he don't listen." She shrugged.

"Exactly. Who the fuck turns their back to the city when they moving product?" Roman giggled. "Well, better him than me."

"Who you think it was?"

"You ain't see the watch on the hot boy's arm when he held that gun to his face?" Roman dug in her pocket for a stick of gum before offering Yoko a piece. "It was a gold Tag Heuer watch."

"I'm good," she said, not wanting gum. "But what that mean? How you know who it is based on his arm wear?"

Roman stuffed the pack back in her jean pocket. "It's the same one Damien bragged about robbing from that D.C. nigga who was fucking Trina upstairs. He was out here showing everybody!"

"You saw that shit from way over here?" Yoko questioned with a tilt to her head.

"Bitch, if I don't have nothing else sweet about me, my vision is on point. Believe that."

After getting his shit stolen, Vale rushed across the street and stomped up the steps leading to Roman and Yoko. Tired and out of breath, he asked, "Did y'all just see that shit?"

"These eyes ain't just green for show. Nigga, the entire city of Baltimore saw that shit," Roman chuckled. "It was a movie. My man, thanks for the show."

"I don't know why you insist on hustling on that corner," Yoko added. "Any nigga with a vendetta can look out of any one of these buildings and peep your entire hustle game. Including where you keep your shit."

Vale was more embarrassed now that two bitches were schooling him. "Fuck!" He ran his hands down his face and looked up the block. As if Damien was gonna come back in any minute and say, "I'm just playing."

"You know who did it?" he asked looking at Roman.

Roman chuckled. "Nigga, don't come at me on no snitch shit. Just do yourself a favor in the future and protect the package. *Always*. You know the rules."

"I might know who did it," Yoko interrupted. "If the price is right, that is."

The moment she parted her lips, Roman wanted to crack her jaw. Her chatter game was nonstop and was one of the reasons they stayed in trouble. Yoko enjoyed bragging and showing how thorough she was in the hopes that people would take her seriously. That wasn't Roman's thing though. She felt it best to be judged by the way she cocked her weapon and pressed the trigger if need be.

Her friend was the leader of team Too Much.

"Tell me who it is, Yoko," he begged. "That's the second time this month this happened to me. The nigga Motion not trying to hear no shit about me getting pushed on again."

"I'ma do you one better 'cause I fuck with you. I'll get the pack back for you."

If there was one thing Yoko knew about Damien it was this—he had been trying to fuck her for years. She reasoned if she laid her game down just right she'd be in the nigga's crib before the sunset holding Vale's work and anything else she could find in his apartment.

"What's it gonna cost me?" he questioned with an accusatory glare. He thought the midget was being greedy and he wanted to slap the shit out of her.

But Roman peeped the daggers he was throwing her friend's way and decided to check him. "I don't know why you looking all hard," Roman said as she scratched her head and looked upon the streets. "You know you have to pay the fine. Ain't no use in getting mad with Yoko." She spit on the side of the step.

"Yeah, but is it gonna cost me everything?"

"I wouldn't say that," Yoko responded. "Five hundred dollars will get me right."

"Fuck," he yelled again. "You robbing a nigga too?" He paused. "Is that what this is? Where the fuck is your gun? You might as well point it at me!" he pouted. "I mean you really gonna hit me like that?"

"It's your call. I'm fine sitting right here and watching the day pass me by. You in a bind, not me."

"Yeah, she ain't the one who got raped for an entire pack," Roman added.

Vale considered his dilemma. The stolen pack was valued way over five hundred dollars. If she could return it he could replace what was lost with his own stash and not miss a beat. But if she didn't he would be out of fifteen hundred minimum and be forced to deal with Motion again, which he wasn't trying to do. Besides, the only language Motion knew these days was murder.

"What if I snatch you up when you ain't expecting and get the information about who did it out of you for free?" He acted as if he was joking but the duo didn't find him hilarious.

"My man, you ever make another threat like that and I'll make you a memory."

"What you gonna do, baby boy," Yoko said clapping her hands together. "Time is money."

"Okay," he responded, still panicky about how Roman delivered her threat. It was as if she really meant it. Unlike some who believed Goon was a dude, he always thought she was the right height to pull of the heist but no one ever believed him. "You get that pack and I'll give you five."

"Make it six," Roman added. "Thanks to that shit you were just popping, I feel the need to go with her."

Yoko winked at him.

****

Damian sat on his living room sofa in his apartment, butt naked from the waist down. The dwarf he had been trying to fuck for years was finally bending over between his legs and blessing him with her superb suck game. With his stiff chocolate dick nestled between her pink lips, she went to work as if she owned him. Damien was finding out what a few niggas with the proper money already knew, that when it came to oral sex, Yoko was the baddest.

Both of Damien's hands rested on the sides of her head and he pumped in and out of her mouth as if he were playing pool.

Eight ball.

Corner pocket.

He didn't know what changed in her heart to get her to come see about a nigga, but he was grateful all the same.

"Keep it right there, mama," he coached with his tongue hanging out the side of his lips like he was dying of thirst. "I swear to God that mouth feel right."

"You got it, daddy," she said as she ran her tongue around the tip. "I told you I would be the best. Now you believe me, don't you?"

"Yeah you told me that shit," he said as he thrust harder, hoping to gag her for all the times she said no. "Damn, bitch." He continued as he looked down at her short legs and fat yellow ass. Since he was geeking, she popped both cheeks because she knew he was watching. "You got a nigga going crazy." He stabbed into her throat harder and she took each push like it was nothing.

The thing was that Yoko's throat was strong and flexible. She could take the best and since she sucked niggas off with larger dicks, Damien's situation was lightweight.

"I'm glad you like it, baby," she said as she jerked him for a second before swallowing him whole again. As she gave him her best, she looked up at him and smiled with his stick in her mouth. He was so turned on that if he could've taken a picture he would've. Framed it and everything. "I'm just trying to taste the sweetness. Damn you're so sweet."

As he enjoyed the moment and the shit she talked, suddenly a quick thought flashed across his mind. If he were drunk he would've missed it and he was appreciative that he was lucid. The thought was as clear as his own reflection in the mirror.

Danger was near.

As he enjoyed Yoko a few seconds longer, he considered who she was and what she represented. She didn't fuck with him. Never had. So what changed suddenly? Why was she really there? No longer taken by the fat ass and the pretty, scarred face, he thought about her motive.

Something was up.

Before sounding the alarms, he pumped one more time in her throat. "Keep it right there, Yoko," he begged as he glared down at her. "I'm almost there." With one more push, he released his juice down her narrow throat.

When he was done he snatched his dick off of her tongue and pressed the .45 that he kept tucked under the cushion on the sofa against her forehead. "Thank you, bitch," he paused. "You did a good job. Now tell me what the fuck you *really* want?" He stuffed his dick back into his tighty whities with one hand and waited for an answer.

"I know you better get that gun up out of my face," Yoko warned as she wiped her mouth with the back of her hand. The watch he wore while he ganked Vale was still on his wrist.

"Fuck you, midget! Don't tell me what to do with my gun!" he pressed it harder against her face. "Tell me why all of a sudden you changed your mind about a nigga? When you been acting like you can't stand me." He cocked the gun. "I'm not dumb, Yoko. I know something's up."

"On the contrary," Roman said rising from behind the sofa. "You're worse than dumb." With a gun in each hand, she placed one on each temple. "You know what time it is. So where's it at?" She cocked both .9 milli's and tapped his head.

"You should've checked the front door again when you was in your room," Yoko grinned. "You been wanting a bitch so bad, you can't even see straight." She took the watch off his arm and put it on hers.

"I knew it," he said as he lowered the weapon. "I shouldn't have trusted your ass."

Yoko snatched his piece from his hand and pointed it at his chin. "Fuck that shit," she said. "Where the work you took from Vale?"

"Is that what this is about?" he chuckled trying to make light of the matter. "Because the nigga is soft. Sending two bitches to do his job. Please don't do this. I mean what the fuck ya'll care about me taking that nigga's work for?"

"We don't," Roman said. "It's about the paper he's gonna give us." She pressed the barrels harder against his temples. "Now where's it at?"

"The nigga been robbing other mothafuckas for ages," he snitched as if they were police. "Let him come see about me if he want his package back."

"I'm not gonna ask you again, Damien," Roman warned as she felt her blood boiling over.

Breathing heavily, he said, "You know I'm not gonna let this slide, right?" He beat his chest and shook his head softly from left to right. "I can't let it go, man. The hood gonna be talking about how two bitches got me."

Roman looked at Yoko and nodded. "Thanks for making my job easier." With that, she squeezed both triggers and exploded his head like a dropped watermelon. Still holding the guns, she wiped his brain matter off of her upper lip with her wrist. "I had to push on him. The nigga threatened me."

With splattered blood on Yoko's face, she said, "So what part of the code is that?"

"I guess you can call it the murder code." She winked.

Yoko laughed. "My bitch."

****

Bottles of vodka lined the wooden floor and knocked against each other as the bass boomed from the Lighthouse sound system. Sending the entire apartment in an earthquake like tremble. Vincent and his three friends, who had way too much to drink, talked loudly about their lives that were as meaningless as a month-old newspaper.

"Let me tell you what your problem is, nigga," Vincent said as he pointed his finger with his bottle clutched in his palm, "You *asked* if you could fuck her. That was your first and only mistake."

"What you talking 'bout now?" Novo responded.

"Sometimes you got to pay these bitches no never mind and take the pussy. That's what they want." He took a huge swig. "They just don't want you to know it."

Novo shook his head. "See, I know what you doing. You trying to get a nigga ten long behind a rape charge." He leaned back into the worn leather sofa and it moaned. "Ain't nobody 'bout to go to jail for no stank pussy. 'Sides, it comes too easily to a nigga these days."

"You only saying that 'cause you ain't had no pussy worth taking. Trust me, ain't nothing like snatching box from a slut. It's an aphrodisiac. Pussy be so wet and tight it clenches the dick like a fist." He formed a mitt with his hand. "Trust me."

Novo, Ryan and Zoo looked at each other and shook their heads. Not only was Vincent talking recklessly but he carried on as if Maria wasn't in the bedroom. But after a swig or two, they realized what everyone who visited the Lighthouse home realized. The way he treated Maria was normal. He could care less if she heard him. It was as if he wanted her to so that she would leave him but she never did.

"Yoko," Vincent yelled, "Bring me another beer."

Hearing her father's call, Yoko, who was lying sideways on the bed, popped up. Dale, Joshua, Farmer and Mills were sitting at a table in the room they all shared. Earlier in the day, Yoko snuck a bottle of their father's best vodka and tilted it with her brothers although they never drank as much as she did. Drinking nonstop, she was twisted and Yoko loved it that way. She enjoyed the liquor he bought because it always seemed to make her drowsy. And make her feel tall.

"Yoko, did you hear me call you?" yelled Vincent again. "Bring me a beer!"

"What you waiting on?" Dale asked. Although he was pushing thirty, he hadn't left the nest and it looked like he never would. "Go give him what he wants before he walks back here."

Yoko sat up on the bed, rolled on her belly and slid down on the large hardback cookbook on the floor, which acted as a step. When she was on the floor she grabbed the silver salad tongs that leaned against the wall to open the door. Yoko used the tongs for everything she needed to grab.

She used them to do stuff that was within a normal teen-ager's reach and that included pulling her underwear up and down and cutting on the lamp by the bed. As the years went by, Yoko grew creative in her approach to getting around the world. Hardback books were in almost every place of the house and when her brothers were mad they often kicked them out of the way or put them on the shelves, knowing she couldn't get to them. It never worked for long. Because Joshua, her saving grace, was always available if she needed him and because of it they were extremely close. She trained him on what she needed and he was always ready to assist her.

Although things changed, the best thing about the time that went by was the new bond Yoko built with her father. She was a thug on the street but when it came to her daddy, she became childlike and longed for his affection. He went from not taking any interest in her at all to asking her to go places and do things with him almost every day. For some reason, it seemed to Yoko that she had become the apple of his eye and it made her feel tingly inside. All she ever wanted was to be daddy's little girl and now she was.

The moment Yoko bent the corner, Vincent yelled, "There's my princess." His eyes were red and glassy, revealing no emotion. But Yoko didn't see things that way. She associated any attention he gave her with love. "Go get me a beer, sweetheart. And then come over here and show these niggas your new routine."

"Aight, daddy," she grinned. "But I don't want them stealing my moves later on when they leave," she joked.

"If they do I'll kill 'em, baby girl," he responded.

Yoko opened the fridge using her tongs, pushed a stool in front of it and grabbed an ice-cold beer. When she was done she closed it and rushed to Vincent and his friends who were sitting in the living room as if they were about to watch a movie. "Here you go, daddy," she said handing him the beer.

"Thanks, baby girl. Now do that dance for me." Vincent turned to Novo. "Hey, nigga! You the closest to the radio! Put that new Jay Z shit on! That's her favorite shit."

Novo fulfilled his request and the moment Yoko heard the first verse she sat the tongs down, stood in the middle of the floor and placed her hands on her hips. When the music got good, she gyrated back and forth like she was killing the game. His friends pulled out their camera phone and recorded every last move. She was doing her best to mimic what she'd seen so many young Baltimore women do in the hood and she hoped she was doing it right. She wanted Vincent to be proud when he looked upon her and it appeared to be working.

Vincent and his friends bopped their heads and appeared to be enjoying the show as Yoko danced for dear life. She jiggled around the room and when the song got real good she tried to raise her arms to each beat but could only lift them halfway. The harder Vincent laughed, the harder she danced.

When she was done Vincent clapped wildly and said, "Come here, princess."

She scooted toward him. "Yes, daddy."

He dipped in his pocket and handed her ten dollars. "That's for always doing what you got to do to make your pops laugh."

****

Later that night, the Lighthouse clan walked up the street to get cigarettes with the money Yoko got from Vincent. Although she was childlike around her pops, the moment she hit the streets she was primitive.

Yoko was on her bike so she was able to keep up with her brothers. The pipe she went everywhere with was nestled in the white basket in the front. She may have looked innocent but she wasn't.

Although Dale sold drugs, he did a bad job and often it was Yoko who would have to go outside and move the work, or else people would come looking for her brother.

"Ya'll hear about the nigga Goon?" Dale asked. "They say he murdering niggas left to right."

"You mean did *you* hear about the nigga?" Farmer responded. "You the one call yourself fake ass hustling. You the type the Goon goes after."

"I do what I do," Dale said somewhat embarrassed.

"You mean Yoko do," Mills winked at her. "You should be blessing her with more money than you do for real."

Dale waved them off. "Yoko know I look out. Don't you?"

Yoko nodded but was still stuck on Goon. "I know who Goon is," she said trying to gain points.

They looked at her and laughed. "Who?" Farmer asked.

"I can't tell you."

They laughed again. "Lil sis, chill out and stop telling people shit like that. Somebody might believe you one day and put you out of your misery."

Yoko didn't appreciate how he didn't believe her. But no one did.

When they went back home they noticed that Novo's children were at her house. Although they weren't really young, they were teenagers and still irritating. None of the Lighthouse clan liked other children but Yoko despised them even more. They were always mean to her and if they weren't nasty, they would mistake her as another child and invite her into awkward play situations.

"Fuck," Dale said when he heard their voices in the back. "They probably going through our shit and everything. Why pops keep inviting them mothafuckas over?"

"Don't worry, I'll get 'em out," Yoko said under her breath, always trying to impress her family. She wanted them to know that her height had advantages, hoping they would love her more. Especially since they didn't believe her tall tales about Goon.

Always the hero, while the brothers remained in the living room, Yoko snuck quietly toward their bedroom. The door was cracked and from the hallway Yoko could see Sarah and Amanda, who were sisters, playing with the cards on the table her brothers were just using.

Since they were occupied, Yoko slipped in unnoticed, slid under the bed and waited for a few minutes. After enough time passed, she crawled from up under the bed growling and moving in their direction as if she were a monster.

Horrified, fourteen-year-old Sarah went screaming out of the room, calling for her father while seventeen-year-old Amanda, who was eye to eye with Yoko, placed one hand on her hip and slapped her in the face with the other.

"That shit's not cool," she yelled. Although it was evident that she was afraid, she was doing a good job of saving face. "And I would appreciate if you don't do that shit again. Else you gonna get fucked up 'round here."

Yoko was stunned and something about the feisty girl made her interesting. At this point in her life, most people knew how dangerous Yoko could be. Although she was young, she was a fighter and wouldn't hesitate to unleash on anyone who got her wrong. And if she couldn't do a good enough job she would get Joshua. So why wasn't Amanda scared?

Yoko was still holding the place on her face that Amanda struck when Maria stumbled into the room. Since she was recently diagnosed with cancer, she wasn't moving the same and often stayed in the bed with throbbing headaches. Her condition broke Yoko's heart and she would sometimes avoid her so she wouldn't see her in pain.

Slowly she pulled the yellow cotton belt on her robe and staggered up to Yoko. "Why are you changing? You used to be such a sweet little girl. What has happened to you?" She bent down to look her in the eyes.

Yoko waddled over to the bed and climbed on top of it. "Why you say that?"

"Do you want people to look at you like that?"

"Like what?"

"Like an animal." She walked closer to her and got on her knees.

When she was about to fall, Yoko touched her arm. "Mama, you have to be careful. You aren't well. Sit up here with me."

Maria balanced herself. "I'm fine, Yoko. I just want to look you in the eyes so that you can feel me." She paused. "You already have a mark against you for something you can't control your height. Why give people more ammunition by acting like a goon?" she continued in a compassionate tone. "You're beautiful, Yoko. Always remember that, despite how the world treats you. Despite how I treat you." Maria stood up using the wall for support, opened the door and steadily walked slowly out.

Two days passed and Yoko was still thinking about what her mother said. Her words were hard but resonated in her soul even if she didn't want them to. And what did she mean by how she treated her? Yoko didn't want to be a joke but she would rather people were scared of her than fuck with her on the regular. Being the victim was over and although she loved her mother, she didn't plan on changing anytime soon.

A few days later Vincent asked Yoko to dance for him and his friends again. This time he instructed her to wear the tight pink bikini she wore when Maria took the children to the community pool. The bikini showcased her rising breasts and large behind. She was a woman now and things spread differently on her body. Yoko tried to tell him that it was too tight and didn't fit well but Vincent wouldn't hear it.

"Dance for me and my friends anyway, Yoko. It would make me so happy."

So Yoko did what he wanted but felt awkward in the process. Although her limbs hadn't grown, her breasts and private areas matured. So she decided to do lighter moves and hoped her father would appreciate the routine so that she could maintain some self-respect.

But Vincent didn't seem as excited about the dance as he had in the past. His friends didn't either. They turned off the cell phone cameras and sighed. "Why so stiff, Yoko" he asked, only halfway amused. "You usually do a better job of dancing for me than that."

"I don't feel comfortable, daddy," she said as her head hung low. "I feel like my bathing suit is too small. Can I do it when I buy a different one?"

Vincent said, "Sure, princess." He looked at his friends. "I understand. If you say so." He exhaled and reached in his pocket and gave her five dollars, half of what he'd given her before.

That entire night, Yoko could feel the space between her and her father as she moved to get closer. And later when his friends left Yoko walked up to him and said, "Daddy, I'm making dinner. Do you want anything?"

He looked down at her and said, "You embarrassed me tonight. You made me look like a fool. I told everyone how good you were and you were terrible. No I don't want to eat! I don't want to see you right now."

Since the bathroom was the only place she could get some privacy, she pushed the cookbooks that were up against the wall in front of the door, turned the knob and trudged inside. She unbuttoned her pants and using the tongs she pushed them to her ankles, scooted the stool next to the bowl and climbed on the toilet seat.

Yoko was confused and her heart was heavy. She didn't understand what people wanted from her. It was as if she had to perform just to be loved by Vincent. But she needed him. Truly she did. And as she replayed how her father treated her, she determined she could do better. She made a decision to do whatever he wanted if he would give her another chance. No matter what it was.

She was about to get off the toilet when Joshua rushed inside without knocking. "Yoko, Yoko!" he chanted in between slapping his face rapidly like he always did when he saw her, which presented red handprints over his cheeks.

Although Yoko still adored Joshua, she preferred not to be near him when she didn't have her pole. It wasn't because she thought he would hurt her intentionally, but because he was always so excitable he often injured her all the same. She couldn't count the number of bruises on her face and upper body Joshua caused simply by being too thrilled.

"Joshua, you have to get out," Yoko said softly. "Remember you aren't allowed to be in the bathroom when I'm here."

"Yoko naked! Yoko naked!"

"Yes, Yoko is naked so you can't—"

Yoko's statement was halted when Joshua knocked her off the toilet with a blow to the face. When she was on the floor Joshua scooted up to her head, released his pants and stuffed his penis inside of her mouth on a mission to her throat. She could taste the salty juices oozing out of him and the taste made her nauseous. His long pubic hairs clogged her nasal passage.

Yoko's eyes started welling with tears because she could not breathe. She slapped at his thighs and when she looked up at her brother she didn't recognize him. It was like he blanked out and became someone else. "Suck it, bitch," he said sternly. He pulled it out allowing her to take one breath before stuffing it back into her throat. "Suck it good! Suck it better!"

Yoko couldn't believe what was happening.

Why was he doing this?

When he knew how much he loved her?

None of her questions were answered. Because at the end of the day she came to one realization.

That she was being raped.

By someone she loved.

CHAPTER EIGHT
-ROMAN-

"There is something in the unselfish and self-sacrificing love of a brute..."
- Edgar Allan Poe

R oman sat on the floor of her room looking down at the dictionary, scanning it with her finger. Although she knew small words she hadn't learned enough vocabulary since living with Billy Bob to consider herself intelligent in the least. But she was sure how to spell the word Goon. The last word her first murder victim mouthed before dying and a word she could not erase from her mind.

Moving down the G's, she squinted to read the letters. For some reason the words appeared to hop around on the page and when she blinked she couldn't stop them from shifting. Was this normal? Did everyone see words the same?

The definition read:

n. slang 1. A thug hired to intimidate or harm opponents. 2. A stupid or oafish person.

But because the letters seemed to whirl around the only thing Roman could decipher were the words *thug* and *hire*. She may not have been brilliant, but she was smart enough to perceive the word hire meant for pay. She couldn't help but wonder after all of the work she put in for Billy why he hadn't given her so much as a pile of lint.

"Roman!" Billy Bob yelled. "Come here. I need help."

Roman pulled down her blue BILLY BOB HOUSE OF HORROR t-shirt and rushed to his aid. When she saw him he was sitting on the recliner with his face etched in agony as usual due to his addiction. "Come rub my feet. I'm not feeling good. You need to care for me! When I die, who else gonna take care of you?"

She was on her way to him when there was a knock at the front door. As she was trained to do, she rushed toward it, grabbed the large silver baseball bat lying next to the wall and threw it open. "What you want with us?" she asked a man who was standing on the other side.

"To speak to Billy," he said with a glare as he stared at him through the door. "He owes me some paper and he ain't paid me yet. So I'm collecting."

Roman's head spun toward Billy who didn't bat a lash. When he nodded, she whacked the man in his head and knees before he had a chance to elaborate. Since he was shorter, like most, he couldn't handle her swift blows or bottled rage. She was like a rabid dog without a leash and before he knew it, he was sprawled out at the bottom of the steps in the hallway.

Roman was so focused that she didn't see Yoko standing there.

"I guess you got the answer to your question," Billy Bob said as he walked behind Roman. He was delighted at how flagitious Roman had grown. Many debtors were afraid to come to his house because of her. One never knew how she'd act. "Don't come around here no more. Unless you want to get hurt."

He looked up at the woman standing above him. Her brows were squeezed together and her nostrils flared. It was as if he harmed her personally. "How did such a slimy creep get you to be so loyal?"

Upon hearing the insult, Roman was about to spin the man's head around, which would have killed him but Billy yelled, "Don't! You've done enough!" She put the bat down and he looked at the man. "Get out of here. Before you won't be able to."

Receiving his exit papers, the man pulled himself together and rushed out of the building's door. But when he made it outside Yoko hit him in the knees with her pole, sending him falling again. She looked back at Roman and winked and she smiled back.

"Come outside later," Yoko said. "I go to talk to you."

"Bet," Roman responded.

When the man left, Billy hobbled back up the stairs before plopping on the recliner. Trying to put him at ease, Roman dropped to her knees to make him comfortable. She smiled at him and massaged his feet. "Who was he?"

"Somebody who wants what I don't have."

She tugged his toes, and an odor resembling boiled eggs permeated from his feet and was hard to ignore. "Why don't you have it?"

"Because we have to pull a bigger job, Roman. We need enough money to pay him and the other bills around here. And with Halloween coming if we don't move now I don't know what will happen. I need supplies to make the costumes."

Roman focused on his feet again. Most of his toes didn't have nails but she wasn't concerned. She loved everything about him.

"I'm worried about you."

"I'm fine." He got up and walked around her.

Roman scanned his body and noticed he was frailer than he was when she first met him. "You don't look well these days, Billy."

"If you're worried I guess you better not leave me then. Because you're all I got."

Her eyebrows rose. First, because he was exhibiting emotion for the first time and secondly because she didn't have any place else she wanted to be. "Where will I go, Billy? No one wants me but you."

He took a moment to examine her closely. He could think of a few places a woman like her could go. Hollywood, Rome, Africa…with her beauty, she could go anywhere and the sky would be the limit. He saw the men snooping around in their building trying to figure out who the tall, attractive girl was living with him. Although she was not glamorous, he couldn't help but realize how beautiful she was. Standing 6 feet tall with her green eyes and her wild curly hair, she resembled a Calvin Klein model more than a specialized killer.

"I hear you talking," he said as he diverted to his usual mean antics. "But only time will tell." He shoved her to the side, stood up and hobbled to the mirror next to the door. "I forgot to tell you. With Halloween coming I have someone bringing by supplies for the costumes. Paints and stuff like that. Normally I deal with a UPS driver, but the owner told me his son is bringing my order instead. Make sure you let him in. Tell him to put them on the kitchen counter and I'll pay him later."

"I will."

"I'm serious." He pointed a long finger in her face. "I know how much time you be keeping with that midget downstairs. I don't want you to miss my delivery."

"I won't, Billy. You can trust me." She moved to hug him and he pushed her away.

Her adoration made him feel unworthy and he despised her stirring up his emotions. He never showed her one ounce of love so why did she love him so? "I don't need all that affection." He slapped her hand away. "Just make sure you listen out for him." He grabbed his wallet and car keys. "You are smart enough to handle that, aren't you? 'Cause God knows you're dumb when it comes to everything else." After the rampant insults, he walked out of the house leaving her alone.

So that she wouldn't disappoint him, Roman opened the front door, jogged down the steps and sat on the front porch to wait for the driver. The deliveryman didn't come right away but Yoko came outside to keep her company.

"Billy racist ass home?" she asked as she squinted and looked out into the city.

"Naw," Roman said. "Not sure where he at. Why?"

She sat down. "I'm not looking for him if that's what you thinking." She seemed sad but Roman wanted her to take her time with whatever she had to say. "Has anybody ever...you know...raped you?" She paused. "That you loved?"

"Somebody raped you?" Roman asked with her head jerking in her direction.

"No," she said quietly. She'd been raped before but never by her brother. "And keep your voice down. This is a private conversation." She looked at the door behind her before focusing back on Roman. "I just want to know if something like that happened to you that's all."

Roman shook her head but was leery about her response. She took a few quick breaths and attempted to slow down. "No but if I knew something like that happened to one of my friends I would tell her to tell somebody she trusted."

"What if she can't?" She paused looking into Roman's eyes. "What if the person who did it was mentally unstable?"

Roman did a double take. She understood what was happening now; Joshua raped her. "Then I would tell her to weigh what is more important. The love of herself or the love of that person. Once she made her decision I would tell her to live with it, keep it inside and never mention it again."

Yoko nodded and wiped a tear away that snuck up on her face. "Okay, I never want to talk about this again. Deal?"

"Done."

Yoko turned around and faced the city. "Oh, before I forget. Dale told me he's trying to get to know you. And wants to know why you faking."

She squeezed her eyes shut and shook her head. "Girl...get to know me? For what?"

"He said you were cute and shit, for a tall bitch." She giggled. "And that he sorry he came at you the wrong way when you were at my house the other day." She clanked her pole against the step. "Told me he wants to take you out tonight. If you let him."

Roman thought about what she said. Although she didn't care about Dale she did appreciate his attention. She was lonely and sometimes that emotion weakened her. She was interested until he asked for a little kiss and she gave him one. Only for him to push his finger into her pussy, scratching her insides in the process. If Billy didn't come home early she believed he would've rape her.

By T. Styles 100

"What do you think? Should I give your brother another chance?"

"I wouldn't fuck with my brother with Billy's dick," she laughed. "He's not trustworthy and he got a lot of secrets." She looked out. "More than us both put together."

Roman rubbed her legs just as a black pickup truck was coming down the block. Yoko was still running her mouth but Roman tuned out a long time ago. She was zoomed in on the truck with grey wooden carts in the hatch that pulled up to the front of the building. When the driver parked and walked around the back of the hatch Roman stood up and observed him. He had taken her breath away.

His tall lanky body seemed to hover over the truck and she could tell before he even stepped into her presence that he was at least 6'4, way taller than she was. Since everybody she knew, including Billy Bob and Yoko were shorter, in her eyes he was a God.

Jackson hoisted the crate over his left shoulder filled with supplies. The moment he caught a glimpse of Roman's doe eyes and pouty pink lips, he was struck. As enamored as she was with him, he was equally drawn to her.

"Who is this fake ass pretty boy type nigga?" Yoko asked trying to throw salt in the game.

"I don't know. But I'm trying to find out."

"Well I don't like him," Yoko warned. "If I were you I'd be careful."

"Well you ain't me so fall back."

When Jackson approached Roman, although she was standing on the top step, she noticed that they were eye to eye. "Mind opening the door for me, sexy?" he asked her. "Or are you gonna make me wait?"

She swallowed. His directness was something she was not used to. It was refreshing almost. Quickly she rushed to open the door for him and noticed she needed to look up at him. She followed him upstairs to her apartment and when he was near, she caught a whiff of his manliness. It smelled as if he'd been in the fields all day but it wasn't offensive. In fact, it was like an aphrodisiac and she felt things awaken in her body she never felt before.

As he walked through the apartment, Roman examined his frame. His light brown hair was cornrowed to the back and his eyes seemed to sparkle. With his eyes being brown and Roman's being green, she wondered if they had a child what color its eyes would be.

The white wifebeater he wore showcased the definition in his muscles but it wasn't like he was trying too hard. Jackson hadn't been in a gym a day in his life but you'd never know it to look at his body. The sun's rays sneaking through the windows as he stood in the living room bounced off his brown skin, causing it to look like golden syrup.

In all of Romans' life, she never met a man more attractive and she doubted she ever would.

"Where can I put it, pretty?" he asked giving her another compliment in less than one minute.

She blushed and quickly put the smile away when she realized she probably looked moronic. She pointed toward the left and said, "On the table."

Jackson placed the order down and walked back toward the door but stopped short of leaving. "The name's Jackson Tate. And you are?"

"Roman."

Upon hearing her name, he tilted his head. "Wow. Roman. A powerful name for such a beautiful girl." He squeezed her chin softly. "I like it." He winked. "Tell Billy he can pay me later. But whether he does or not, I have to be honest. I feel myself coming back for you. I hope that's cool."

✹✹✹✹

Cindy Lou steered the car while Billy Bob sat in the passenger seat rubbing his noxious smelling feet. Normally Roman would be irritated with Cindy's presence but today was different. She wanted Billy to have someone to keep his attention so that she could think about her new friend.

By T. Styles   102

Ever since she met Jackson, she was in a world of her own and nothing anybody could say or do would bring her out of it. Repeatedly she replayed in her mind how he called her pretty and sexy and suddenly she wanted to live up to his standards. But where would she start? She wasn't a beauty queen. A thug maybe. But beautiful? If only she could see him again so he could explain himself, tell her exactly what made her so special, she'd know where to start.

"What you thinking about back there?" Billy asked with a scowl on his face. "I been talking to you for the last five minutes only for you to ignore me."

"Sorry," she whispered.

"Leave the girl alone," Cindy said jealously. "You show her too much attention as is. She's a woman now. With her own thoughts and perspectives. Keep your mind on me. Where it belongs."

"Don't tell me where to keep my mind." He frowned. "I'm talking to the girl anyway." He looked back at her. "Like I was saying, sorry don't pay the bills, Roman." He focused back on the road and now he had her full attention. "I was saying we have to hit another house. Cindy knows about a few that will be good scores." He ran his finger in between his toes and sniffed it before putting his sock on. "It could be our biggest hit."

"Okay, Billy," she responded as she looked at the back of Cindy's head and rolled her eyes. "Whatever you want. You know I got you."

It was no secret that she hated Cindy but her involving herself in Billy's and her affairs by finding homes made her despise her even more. Roman preferred as few people involved in the robberies as possible. She also didn't like Cindy because with Billy, she was slumming. And when she was done getting high she'd rush back to her rich husband.

"These people were involved in your mother's murder too," Billy added.

As always, whenever he wanted to give her a reason to commit crime he would lie about who killed her mother. It was unnecessary. She didn't need a reason to maim anymore. Roman's life was bland and committing crime was the only thing she knew she was great at.

"We're going to move on it tomorrow, Roman," Billy said.

****

When they walked into the grocery store Billy bossed Roman around as she tossed everything he wanted in the basket. She just placed a few cans of corn into the cart when she saw Jackson and a pretty brown-skinned girl with an ass too large to be real chattering. Roman was stuck. She knew it was unlikely that a man like him would be single but she didn't want to see him with another girl either.

Jackson was all smiles until he looked ahead and saw Roman ogling him. He acknowledged her with a wink and swaggered in their direction, leaving the woman back by the frozen goods. "Sir," Jackson said nodding at Billy first. "I trust the product I dropped off was to your liking."

There was that smell again that was unique to Jackson that drove Roman bat shit.

Billy may have been frowning but the young man had Roman and Cindy's undivided attention.

"Yes, but I asked for canary paint and got yellow," he grunted. "I told your family before to make sure my orders are exactly as I specify. Don't know why you can't get it right."

Instead of getting angry, he said, "You're correct, sir. I'm sorry about that. I'll make sure that it doesn't happen again." Jackson's eyes moved slowly off of Billy's ugliness and onto Roman's prettiness. Although the frumpy House of Horror t-shirt threatened to drown out her figure, he could see through the threads as if he had x-ray vision. "I'll bring you over some fresh paint tomorrow." The comment was for Billy but you'd never know it as hard as he eyeballed Roman.

"Good," Billy grumbled. When he saw him goggling Roman seductively he pinched her on the back, out of sight of Cindy and Jackson. Roman immediately adjusted her sight. With Roman under control, Billy Bob looked at Jackson. "I'll look for the package tomorrow."

"Good day," Jackson said before touching the tip of his baseball cap and tilting his head slightly forward. He looked at Roman once more and winked again. "Later, pretty. Remember what I said the last time I saw you."

"Bye, Jackson," Cindy waved as if he was talking to her.

When he walked away Billy Bob said, "I can't stand that motherfucker. Think he's better than everybody else 'cause his people own that factory." He looked over at Roman who was still staring in Jackson's direction. "Well, back in my day my people would own him."

"I don't know, Billy," Cindy said licking her lips. "I think he's nice enough."

"You would."

Billy was used to Cindy being a whore so he wasn't surprised in the least. But he would be damned if he'd let Jackson dig his claws into his prize. "Don't even think about it, Roman." He paused. "Niggers like that never go for niggers like you."

CHAPTER NINE
-YOKO-

"Deep into that darkness peering, long I stood there wondering, fearing."
- Edgar Allan Poe

Yoko sat on the step outside of her building, thinking about her life.

Again.

There was one thought that prevailed above all others. And it was that her brother raped her. When she was with Roman time passed and she didn't think about it much. But when she was alone the pain was almost unbearable.

The part that hurt the most was that after the rape, Joshua moved around the apartment like he hadn't done anything. Didn't he realize what he took from her? How much he hurt her and how she would forever be changed? She questioned herself daily and it had her looking upon men in a different way.

As if she couldn't trust them.

Yoko realized he wasn't equipped. He was born with alcohol for blood. In the end, it was just as Roman said. She would have to forgive him and move on, or else she'd harbor hate where it couldn't be received. But where had he learned something so foul? He was like a vessel, which could be filled with love or hate. So who taught her brother such evil things?

Yoko was still in her head when Amanda walked up to her. She took a few moments to check her out before asking, "Can I sit down?"

Yoko shrugged as if she could care less even though she wanted nothing more. She focused on the busy street and squinted at the rising sun.

Amanda took a seat, rubbed her hands down her jeans and smiled at Yoko. "You do coke?"

Yoko looked at her, frowned and shook her head. "Why would you ask me some shit like that?"

Amanda shrugged and looked out at Baltimore City. "Just wanted to know." She shrugged. "I'm holding, if you're interested." She exhaled. "You still being rude? Because you seem like something on your mind."

Yoko clanked the pole against the concrete step, sending her signature ringing noise out into the city. "Yeah, the fact that you asked me if I did cocaine."

"You still thinking about that?" she asked. "I'm on something else now."

She scooted closer to Yoko, causing her to feel ways she hadn't before. There was something about the scent of cigarettes from Amanda's lips and coconut hair oil from her mane that caused Yoko's heart to quiver. She wanted her there and yet she wanted her far away.

But why?

She'd never been into girls before.

So what changed now?

"The last time I saw you, you were jumping from up under a bed. And scaring me. You still being mean?"

She shrugged. "You still on that shit?" She paused. "I thought it was funny. Plus ya'll were in my room and I wanted you out."

She shook her head. "You could've asked. It's sad 'cause I like you, Yoko. If you wasn't so mean you'd make some nigga a real wife."

Yoko couldn't help but feel as if she were pushing her off on someone else. As if she were a charity case. Fuck she mean make a real wife? "Listen, if you want to kick it with me out here then let's do that. But don't come at me sideways again about some random nigga."

"What I say wrong?"

"Where you wanna start?" Yoko attacked. "I'm gonna be with whoever is in the right place to mentally receive me in the moment. I don't have to change. They change for me." She stood up. "Period." She walked into the building, leaving her alone.

For the next few days, Amanda was relentless. She made all kinds of excuses to be with Yoko before she settled on asking her if she liked cards. They would play two player games as they got to know each other better. Yoko found herself falling for her and wanting to get closer even though Amanda constantly asked for money. If Yoko had it she would give it to her but it didn't stop her from feeling used.

Being with Amanda seemed right. If only she could rid herself of the guilt she felt for wanting to be with another woman. Her mind was wrecked on a consistent basis. To make shit worse, Amanda started kicking it with Dale. Yoko felt stupid that she was feeling Amanda only for her to like her oldest brother. What type of shit was that?

Things really came to a head when Yoko saw Amanda kissing Dale in their living room one evening. Yoko's stomach twirled and anger consumed her as she watched them make out. She never felt rage toward her brother, despite the shit he'd done to her and she wanted the emotion gone. That type of feeling wasn't for them.

They were blood and bitches like Amanda came a dime a dozen. Still, there Yoko was, sitting on the front porch trying to cool off when all of a sudden, who came outside? Amanda. The cigarette and coconut smell that she had grown accustomed to followed. "What do you want?" Yoko asked.

"Why you out here by yourself?" Amanda asked as she opened the building's door and sat next to Yoko. Amanda wiped her lips with the back of her hand and Yoko figured she was ridding herself of Dale's dick juice.

"My pops drinking upstairs with his niggas. So I'm chilling here." She looked at the door. "And my best friend not home. She'd normally be out here chilling with me." Yoko looked over at her briefly. "You seen Joshua upstairs?"

"Yeah, he's in your room looking at TV. Some cartoon I think."

A weird moment of silence filled the air.

"Can I ask you something?"

"What?" Yoko was tiring of the questions.

"How come your dad likes to see you dance? It's creepy."

"Why you say that?" She scratched her throat. "My pops cool."

She frowned and shook her head. A bum was waddling up the street with a cup in his hand. She focused on him, as if what she was about to say was difficult. "I don't think he's cool." She shrugged. "I know he's your father and all but I think it's weird he wants to see his daughter dancing in front of his friends and shit. But that's just me. You should be careful. I think they put your dancing online as a joke."

Yoko didn't know what she was trying to get at but she didn't have time to think about it because as usual, her father called her name from the hallway. She was starting to notice that he mostly required her attention when he was drinking. Yoko sighed and said, "Let me see what he wants. I'll be back."

"Okay, I'll hang out in your room." She got up and followed her into the apartment.

Yoko walked through the kitchen and toward the bathroom before going to see her father. She pushed the hardback books against the toilet bowl, crawled up them and grabbed her pole that was sitting on the sink. She pushed her jeans down and took a seat, with the pole resting in her lap. She loved Joshua, but she doubted there would be another man who would take anything from her she didn't set out to give.

Her mind was on life when she heard chattering outside of the door. When she focused she could hear Vincent talking to someone else. "Where is that fucking midget?" Vincent joked. "I called that little fucker five times already and she still not here."

Yoko's heart dropped in her chest when she heard him talk about her so coldly. She wasn't green anymore. She knew exactly what midget meant and how much it hurt her feelings. Sure she heard him disrespect her in the past but she thought since their relationship tightened that things were different.

"You better be quiet before Maria hears you," Novo said to Vincent. "You know she hates when you call that bitch a midget."

Yoko's heart ached. They carried on as if she were a trick on the street.

"Fuck Maria!" he yelled. "She better hope I don't throw her ass out for that young bitch up the block I been digging in."

Yoko didn't like him cheating on her mother at all and she was suddenly starting to look at him differently.

"I been trying to find a reason to move that young slut in," he continued slyly. "Put that blunt out though. I see Zoo over there eyeing it and I'm not sharing with no nigga not putting in."

The conversation was over but the damage was long-standing. Yoko was devastated. All she tried to do was be there for him. What made her more embarrassed was that Amanda seemed to have known what she didn't. That Vincent could care less about her.

Something had to be done.

But what?

****

Roman and Yoko were sitting on the front porch with Yoko's brothers, kicking it and talking about life and bullshit. It was cooler outside than normal but when you were in the hood the weather didn't matter. You became immune to the elements and they were no exception.

"Did y'all hear that they still don't know who killed Damien?" Dale said as he sipped his vodka from a white cup.

"I heard the dude Vale running around telling everybody he the one," Farmer said as he plucked chips out of the bag. "And that nobody better fuck with him again."

Roman listened to their many stories and she thought the shit was hilarious. She knew very well that it was her birds that chopped off Damien's head. But if Vale wanted to take the credit, so be it, just as long as he did the jail time too if he were caught.

Yoko on the other hand didn't find his antics so humorous. She had big problems with him boasting about a crime they committed. She wanted street credit for everything she was involved in and was too stingy to share. "The nigga may have said he put in work but he's a fucking liar," Yoko said. "And he better slow his roll before the real executioner finds him and delivers to him the same fate."

Roman's eyes widened as she listened at her friend. She carried on as if she was the reason Damien no longer existed. Roman squeezed those triggers, not her. "Settle down, Yoko," Roman said through clenched teeth. "Who cares about that clown anyway? We all know Vale ain't capable of murder. Just let him do him."

"I know nobody cares about him. I'm just saying it's wrong to take credit for something he didn't do."

Thinking his little sister was hilarious, Dale said, "Well if you know so much, who did the shit? Since you keep talking 'bout it."

Roman looked over at Yoko and pleaded with soft shakes of her head for her to remain silent. But she wasn't receptive. "Let's just say it's somebody you all know." Yoko pulled up the sleeve on her jacket and showed the watch she stole from Damien before Roman murdered him.

Dale looked at the timepiece and past his sister. His gaze was fixed on Roman and suddenly he was enlightened. "Come to think of it, shawty, you are 'bout the right height." He laughed. "Maybe you do get down like that."

Upon hearing that statement, Roman jumped up and rushed down the stairs in a hurry. She was livid. She was seeing red. Yoko followed as fast as she could but she needed the help of her bike, which was sitting at the bottom of the steps, to catch up to her. When she rolled up behind Roman she said, "What's wrong with you? I didn't say nothing. My brother did."

"Get the fuck outta here!" Roman yelled. "You hot. And I don't fuck with hot bitches."

"Who you calling a bitch?" Yoko yelled pedaling harder.

"You heard me. You talk too fucking much." She stopped and turned around. Looking down at her, she said, "From the moment we became friends, I've had your back. I've done shit with you in the dark I wouldn't tell a soul and we made a little money in the process. But that's not good enough for you, is it? It'll never be enough."

"I think you blowing shit out of proportion," Yoko pleaded.

"And I think you talk too much. I don't get up with niggas like that. They make me uncomfortable and with the shit I do, I need to be comfortable." She paused. "You need to know this shit too. If we ever stop kicking it this is gonna be the reason why."

"So you threatening our friendship?" Yoko asked trying desperately not to cry.

"No, friend, you did that." She pointed at her. "Talking too much is the game of the weak. And I'm worried about you, Yoko."

Roman wiped a tear that rolled down her face and Yoko was emotionally destroyed. She knew the woman before her was hard bodied and if she was crying, it meant that she was really concerned. Outside of Maria, she didn't think it was possible for another soul to care so much about her fate.

"But he lied, man," Yoko said. "I was just trying to set shit straight."

"Who cares? I'm trying to stay out of jail not go in it!"

"I was just telling my brothers! They won't say nothing. Promise"

"First off, them niggas back there don't act like your brothers. They use you. And just so you know, your so called father gets you drunk from the liquor bottles he gives you and then lets his friends rape you." She paused. "Be careful who you call family. 'Cause I was the only family you had." Roman stomped away.

CHAPTER TEN
-ROMAN-

"And the fever called 'living' is conquered at last."
- Edgar Allan Poe

Roman pulled t-shirt after t-shirt out of her closet in search of the perfect outfit. After seeing the pretty girl Jackson was with in the grocery store, she was seeking something special to wear for when he showed up with the delivery. When she realized the obvious that everything she owned was the same, blue jeans and tons of Billy Bob's House of Horror's t-shirts, she grew disappointed.

It was obvious that when it came to clothing selections, she failed miserably. She ended up choosing the best of the worst. A red Billy Bob House of Horror t-shirt and a regular pair of blue jeans that were tighter on her frame.

After getting dressed, she unleashed the braids from her hair, which allowed her naturally curly mane to sprout like wild flowers. She didn't like much about herself but over the years she appreciated how crazy her hair could get. It was similar to her personality. Beautiful and untamed.

Once her hair was in order, she rushed to the kitchen and grabbed a cherry Kool-Aid packet. With it in her hands she dipped to the bathroom placed water in her palm and sprinkled a little powder inside of it. When it was blood red she spread it lightly over her lips and cheeks.

She looked in the mirror at her reflection. "I feel so stupid," she said hoping she was judging herself to harshly again.

She was about to scrub everything off when she overheard activity in the living room. As far as she knew, Billy Bob was gone but when she bent the corner he was closing the front door and walking inside. When he saw her face he tossed a brown paper bag on the floor before taking a moment to examine her from head to toe. "What you trying to do? Play a whore for Halloween?"

With eyes bulging, she said, "No."

"Then what's with the red shit on your face?"

Silence.

He shook his head and sat in the recliner. "Get over here and do my feet."

Roman rushed toward him, dropped to her knees and removed his boots. As usual, his toes stunk unbearably but she massaged them as if they were not offensive. As she stretched the kinks out of his toes he looked down at her with disdain. Her beauty was irritating and he tossed a few ideas around in his mind on how to lessen her beauty. Perhaps a few slashes across the face would do the trick.

"I know you been looking at that Jackson boy. But if I find out you talking to him I'm gonna throw you out on the street. The only man you need is ugly old me."

****

Later that day, Billy Bob went out of town with Cindy Lou to purchase some things in Atlanta for the House of Horror. Although he was out of town, his voice played over and over in her head.

Stay away from Jackson.

He doesn't want you.

He was right. She was an idiot and there was no reason to believe that Jackson would ever be interested in someone like her. Plus she didn't want to be homeless if she was caught. Billy was a man about his word and proved it to her when he starved her as a child.

Roman was on her knees on the living room couch looking out of the window. At a time like this, she would be with her best friend. She missed Yoko but decided that she was done with her.

Forever.

The moment she heard the song "Believe" by Raheem Devaughn, her heart throbbed. When he parked across the street and looked up at the building, only to see her nodding her head to the beat, he hopped out but left the car running so that she could enjoy the music a bit longer.

As usual, he walked around to the back of his truck, grabbed a large crate and then activated his alarm that cut the music off. Roman rushed to open the front door and the moment he was standing before her, he said, "That was my cousin."

Her eyes widened with confusion.

"The girl you saw me with at the grocery store the other day. Just wanted you to know." He paused. "Can I come inside?"

She shook her head no. She was afraid of what she would do with him if they were alone.

Jackson placed the crate down, stood up and looked into her green eyes. "So are you two...I mean...together?"

When she understood what he meant she shook her head no. The idea of being with Billy Bob was beyond gross and caused pangs to her stomach. As it stood, she could still smell the odor from his toes on her fingertips. Being romantic with him was the last thing on her mind.

"Can I come in now?"

Before she could say no, he opened the door wider, yanked her into the hallway and pulled her against his body. "Why are you trembling?" he asked so confidently.

She swallowed. Any other time she'd be in control, but around him she was fumbling. "I'm...trembling because of Billy. He doesn't want me with you."

He shook his head. "When you're with me you don't have to be scared of anything." He looked into the apartment. "Not even him."

When his point was made he released her, picked up the crate and walked it inside. "Tell him he can pay me later." Without another word, he bopped out and left her to her thoughts.

When he was gone she leaned up against the door and slid down to the floor. She felt she appeared stupid based on how she acted and knew he was done with her. But she didn't know Jackson Tate. He was unwavering and the next

Goon   **115**

day, he showed up without an order for Billy. Despite not knowing if he was home or not, he got out of his truck and leaned against it. And when he saw her looking, he demanded with his finger for her to come to him.

A few Baltimore thugs wondered what the strange rich kid was doing around their way but he wasn't moved in the least. He leaned against that truck as if he belonged anywhere he went. Including one of the most violent cities in America.

The moment he beckoned her, she threw open the apartment door and rushed down the hallway and across the street. It wasn't until he looked down at her feet that she realized she wasn't wearing any shoes. He said come so she made it quick. "You get what I like, don't you?" he grinned. "Total submission to me."

Roman didn't know what he meant but she could tell that he was a man who knew what he desired. If he wanted her to submit and it meant getting to know him, she would do it. Besides, around him she felt safe. Around Jackson, she wasn't some goon with a fetish for money or gunpowder. She was a woman who was falling in love with a man.

"I like you, Roman. But I want a woman who can obey me. One who would listen to what I say and follow. Is that you?"

She nodded. "It can be."

"Good...then go change your clothes. I want to take you somewhere."

"But Billy Bob will be back in—"

"I'm not asking Billy Bob, Roman. I'm asking you. Now go."

Great with taking orders, Roman rushed inside without another word. Jackson sat in his truck for five minutes and when she returned she was wearing a pair of blue jeans and one of Billy Bob's new red plaid shirts. Her hair was wild and curly and she was smiling brightly. "This the only thing I could find."

He got out and opened the door for her before re-turning to the driver's seat. "I've never met a woman who could make an outfit like that beautiful." Shaking his head, he said, "You never cease to amaze me." He threw the car in drive. "So I guess you're coming with me."

She thought about what she was doing, leaving with Jackson, a man Billy forbade her to see. She knew if Billy found out there could be trouble but there was one problem. There was no saying *no* to Jackson Tate. "Yes, I guess I am." She paused. "Can you tell me where?"

"It's a party for me. I'm going to college in two weeks. And I wanted to show you off before I bounced."

****

As they pulled off, Yoko walked outside of the apartment building to get a better look at the truck. Her lip curled up and she clanked her pole against the guardrail lightly. She felt it was mighty funny how Roman could ig-nore her calls and knocks on the door but could hang out with Rich Boy Floyd. In her mind, Roman was playing her for a man.

"This bitch always talking about code but then put a nigga before her friend." Her eyebrows lowered and then pinched together.

In her mind, the reason Roman cut her off had nothing to do with her inability to hold a secret. It was Jack-son's fault. And as she watched them pull off, she had noth-ing but detestation in her heart for their budding relation-ship.

****

When Jackson opened the double doors leading to his large mansion, Roman's legs buckled. They were in suburbia Maryland among the rich. She never walked into anything so beautiful in all of her life and she doubted she ever would again. Every fixture in the home, including the guests, seemed to sparkle. "This is where I live," he announced as he watched the people who held champagne flutes in their hands in his honor. Although they were there for him, no one seemed to notice he was there.

"It's beautiful," Roman said, with her breath pulling in before slowly releasing it.

"As beautiful as it is, I can't wait to leave." He walked further inside and extended his hand for her but she didn't budge. "Are you okay?"

"What am I doing here?" Her body felt heavy as if she was weighed down by a ton of bricks.

"You here for me." She thought she was under-dressed and it made her feel unworthy. "Trust me, this house, and these things, don't mean anything to me." He smiled and raised is hand again. "Now come with me." He extended his hand.

Roman surrendered and with her hand nestled in the palm of his, she followed him. Her temples banged as her body experienced multiple sensations in an attempt to take in a whole new world. One she never experienced. As he spoke to different people, they all wanted to know who was the freakish girl with the wild hair he had on his arm. And most importantly, what did she want with Prince Jackson?

When he felt her disconnect he said, "Are you sure you're okay?"

She nodded yes although she was far from well.

As she observed him, she wondered why Jackson wasn't embarrassed to be with her. It appeared to be quite the contrary. He led her around that party as if she was wearing a beautiful gown and was royalty.

Once they were on the patio, Roman marveled at the scenery. It seemed as if 1 million candles outlined the backyard, giving it a soft yellow glow. For some reason Roman felt as if she were on stage with a star. "Why?" She asked again.

"Why what?"

"Why me? It doesn't make any sense."

Jackson sat down on a bench and reached for her to sit next to him. She did. The coolness of the concrete chilled her buns and she moved around until it warmed a little. He was just about to answer when a beautiful older woman in a stunning royal blue dress rushed outside. She was gripping the edge of the right side of her gown so that she wouldn't trip as she stomped forward. At first she looked around the patio as if she were on a mission until she spotted her son entertaining a stranger. Glaring at him, she charged in his direction as if she were wearing sneakers.

"Who is this person, Jackson?" She paused without saying hello to Roman. Her eyes protruded and her face reddened. "More importantly, what is she doing in our home?"

"Mom, this is Roman," his tone deepened.

"Well what is she doing here?"

"Don't be rude," he frowned as his voice shook a little. "She's a friend of mine!"

"It's not about being rude. You brought this creature into my home in front of my guests and you tell me not to be rude?"

"I thought they were here for me."

"They are!"

"Well if they are here for me it shouldn't matter who I invite." Jackson stood up and the muscles in his arm twitched as he reached for Roman. "Anyway, if she's not wanted here, neither am I."

"You can't rebel all of your life, Jackson! I know you brought her here to fuck with me. At some point, you will need me. And I want you to remember how you treated me and how badly you treated your family this night."

Without a word, Jackson and Roman walked through the party and out the front door. The moment they made it out of the house, Roman separated from him and ran away. With the exception of Billy, she couldn't bear to have anyone talk to her so disrespectfully and it had her wanting to do bodily harm to a woman she didn't know.

Also fast, Jackson caught up with her, gripped her by her arm and asked, "Why you leaving? I defended you! What more do you want?"

Roman shook her head and tried to catch her breath. "What makes you think anything about me needs defending? I am who I am, Jackson!" She pointed at the house as her pulse sped up. "And I don't belong here! I felt like a fucking joke!"

"You're with me. Of course you belong."

"Did you bring me here to embarrass your mother?" She wandered a short distance before returning to him. "To get back at her for whatever reason?" She placed her hand over her heart. "Because something about what she said makes me believe I was a weapon instead of a guest."

The look in his eyes told her she was on to something. "I know it doesn't seem this way but I swear to you...you can trust me," he said avoiding the question. "I wouldn't hurt you or allow anyone else to."

Her gaze clouded before she blinked a few times to clear her vision. "Trust me. No one will ever hurt me," she warned. "Emotionally."

"And neither will I." He paused. "My mother wants to control me like she wants to control everything in my life." He sighed and stuffed his hands in his pockets. "I was awarded a scholarship to Harvard University and I wanted to go. But she didn't want me to leave the state so she had my scholarship revoked. Suddenly, I receive a letter that Johns Hopkins here in Maryland has accepted me."

"How did she do that?"

"When you have as much money as my people do, things like that happen all the time."

"Why would she do all of that? Doesn't make any sense."

"Because in Maryland she can keep eyes on me."

"Why does she want to watch you? You're a grown man."

"She's been that way all of my life," he responded.

Her posture was rigid. It was all too much for her to comprehend and despite her attraction to Jackson, she wanted to go home. Something was right and wrong about him at the same time and she needed a moment to think. Without his influence.

"Listen, let me take you out, Roman. The proper way." He paused, stepping closer to her. Now she knew what the scent was that always seemed to follow him.

Money.

"Where are we going? Billy will kill me if I—"

Jackson grew frustrated and snapped. "Listen, I'm trying to get to know you! I realize the way we met is unconventional but it's our story! Will you allow it to play out? What's the worst that could happen? Is your world so great that you don't need me?"

For some reason, she felt he was her chance at life. And if she said no she doubted a man like him would ever come around again. Not for her anyway.

"I want to...I mean...what are you asking me? To be with you? It seems so fast."

"Why does it seem fast? Because I know what I want?"

"But you don't really know me or the things I've done. The things I've seen."

"Like I said, that's what I'm trying to do now. Will you let it happen?"

Silence.

"Yes, Jackson."

He removed the glare from his face and gripped her closely to his body. As he held her, Roman considered her life. He was right she had nothing to go home to. Even if she did go back tonight, Billy Bob wasn't there. He was with Cindy Lou getting high and she was tired of living for him. Jackson made her feel bold and that felt dangerous.

With him, everything was a dream.

Her body was pressed against the body of a man who, for whatever reason, wanted to spend time with her. A hood bitch born in Mississippi and raised in Baltimore. So she decided to give him a chance. Besides, what did she have to lose?

For the next few days Jackson and Roman were inseparable. They spent as much time as a day allowed and when Billy Bob returned home it was hard on Roman not seeing him as much. He was attending college soon and would have a life that wouldn't involve her. One with intelligent young people who upon graduation would be major contributors to society. Why did she allow herself to fall for a man out of her league?

Billy was gone again and Roman was pacing the living room floor waiting on Jackson to pick her up. His only request was that she dress presentably because he was taking her somewhere nice. But when he arrived to her house and saw her in the same jeans and t-shirt she always wore he was confused. "Babe, I asked you to wear something presentable. There's something I want to ask you and..." His words trailed off as if he was holding himself back. "You don't have anything else to wear? Anything at all?"

She shook her head no and shuffled in place. "Jackson, what you see with me is all you get. I'm sorry if it's not enough."

Jackson realized that if they were going out, it would be in what she was wearing. For the moment anyway. "I apologize, babe. I just wanted tonight to be special." He grabbed her hands and held them tightly. "Let me buy you something nice to wear."

"You don't have to, Jackson," she responded, her appetite vanishing by the second. "I don't want you for your money."

"I know and you need to know that I don't do shit I don't want to." He kissed her lips. "Let me take care of you."

Realizing she hit the lottery, she said, "I don't know why you chose me but I'm so grateful, Jackson."

"Keep that thought, babe. There's something I want to ask you after we leave the restaurant. I'll see if you still feel the same then."

The two of them went to the mall as planned and with two full bags, they were on their way back so that Roman could get dressed. Jackson took her to almost every store. Dresses, shoes, perfume—he bought it all.

Roman was overwhelmed by the smell of new clothing and new shoes. Before him, she was a t-shirt jeans type of woman but when Jackson entered the picture, she was changed. Forever. She now knew what it meant to own nice things and it altered her perspective on life. What else was she missing out on in the world?

They were walking through the mall when Roman saw Jackson's mother, Debra Tate. With wide eyes, Debra approached them and said, "Jackson"—her jaw hung— "What are you doing here?" She scanned Roman. "With this thing again?"

"Mother, I'm just—"

"What? Trying to ruin the family name?" she spat as she looked at Roman with disdain. "After I forbade you to see her again and you promised? It's getting to the point where I can't trust you anymore. We've had our problems but I have always been able to trust you!"

Roman stood in silence with a clenched fist. She didn't know how much more of Debra's insults she was going to take. But she doubted it would be a lot.

"We had an agreement, Jackson," she yelled, causing an audience to assemble. "I don't know why you must subject this child to your lifestyle when you know she can't handle it. It's madness!"

Roman eased her hand out of Jackson's and he looked down at her. "I'm so sorry about this. Let me take you home."

"Please," she said under her breath. "I don't feel well."

"Jackson, don't go anywhere with that girl," Debra demanded as they rushed away. "Jackson! Come back here now! Before I tell her everything!"

★★★★

Roman was so hurt and embarrassed by Debra that when she walked in the apartment she didn't see Billy Bob standing in front of her. He stood directly in the middle of the living room looking at her. She'd never seen him so angry in all of her life.

"Where were you?" he asked with his feet planted wide apart in a fighter's stance.

"Uh…I…was out," she responded as she stared down at her feet, trying to find another answer. One that would make more sense.

He stepped closer. "I know you were out, Roman. But with who? And where?"

Silence.

Suddenly, he laughed revealing his yellowing teeth. "Do you really think I will allow you to see him?" He moved closer. "Do you really think I will allow you to be with him?" He paused. "You will either obey me or you will be thrown out on the streets. Because I doubt very seriously those uppity Tate niggers you keep time with will save you."

"I'm sorry, Billy," she said wiping her tears upon hearing what she deemed to be the truth. "I thought I liked him…and I thought he liked me…but I know now it's not true. And it will never happen again." Remembering Debra's face forced her into that realization. "I'm so sorry for lying to you."

"Good because we're moving on Jackson's house next. And I will need you to help set him up."

"Billy, please don't," she responded in a monotone voice, disturbed by his words. "We can find someone else. Anybody else and I promise I'll do it. No questions asked."

He waved her off. "I know you ain't happy about it but it's what we got to do." His mind was obviously made up with no room for deliberation. "With the money that boy is worth, we might even be able to take him hostage and ask for enough ransom to leave this town for good."

"But what about Cindy Lou? And your shop?"

Billy frowned because he could tell she cared too much about Jackson and it ignited his rage. "The only question you should be asking yourself is this. Are you loyal to him? Or me?"

****

"Get out of that bathroom, Roman!" Billy yelled. "You been in there all fucking night!" He punched the bathroom door hard, causing Roman to leap toward the sink.

"I'm coming," she said as she struggled with the rumbling she was feeling in her stomach. She drew her mouth into a tight line and bit down on her bottom lip. She was not prepared to commit a crime, let alone against the man she was falling for. But Billy was many things; patient was not one of them. So she tossed water on her face and walked out into the hallway.

"Let's go," he said grabbing her by the forearm and ushering her to the front door. "I heard from a neighbor that the boy's going to college tomorrow. If we don't move now we won't be able to get him."

He opened the door but the moment he took a step outside, she snatched away from him and backed into the living room. "No," she said swinging her head softly from left to right.

"No?" he frowned baring his teeth. "I said come on, girl! We don't have time for this shit!"

"No," she repeated a bit louder. "I have done everything you have ever asked of me. Everything. All my life. But I won't do this."

Billy Bob slammed the door, his face reddening with each breath. As if he pressed the gas peddle on a racecar, suddenly he was in front of her breathing heavily in her face. No longer as fragile as he appeared throughout the week, he was now able bodied and strong.

"I didn't want to tell you this but Jackson was responsible for what happened to your family." His glare evaporated and changed to a compassionate smile. "He personally pulled the trigger, Roman. And if you don't go after

Goon   125

him tonight you're basically saying you're okay with it. Is that what you want?"

"How many?" she asked looking upon him with cold eyes as tears poured down her face.

"How many what?"

"How many people were responsible?" she paused. "Every time you want me to do something, you say the same fucking thing. That this person or that was responsible for killing my mother. And all I want to know is how many?"

Roman felt the rumble brewing in her chest she always did when he said she would be in the presence of someone who harmed her family. But this time she sucked it in and pushed it down.

"I know you don't believe me, Roman. And I probably have lied before but this time I'm being true. Jackson himself was responsible for their murders."

"But how is that possible?"

"How is what possible?"

"How was he responsible when he was a kid? 'Bout the same age as me when my family was murdered."

Up until that point, he thought she was mainly dumb. But upon hearing her response, he was the one who felt stupid. So he reacted as best he knew. With a raised fist; he brought it down on her face so hard her lip busted open and sprayed blood. Every fiber in her being wanted to fight him back but she loved him, despite his evil ways. Her mindset was like that of an abused dog that was being beat by its owner. Although she had the ability to tear him apart, she elected not to.

Billy Bob continued to strike her forcefully until she was bloodied, curled up in a ball and crying. "You are worthless!" he yelled down at her with a stiff finger. "As worthless as the day I found you in that house. I should've never saved your life and brought you here. And I want you out."

Fearing homelessness, she rolled over, preparing to do whatever she needed to stay there. But when she looked beyond where Billy was standing, she was staring into the angry eyes of Jackson Tate. His face was scratched up and Roman reasoned that he got into a violent altercation with someone.

She hoped not his mother.

"Get up, Roman," Jackson said with authority. "You're coming with me."

"What are you doing in my house, boy?" Billy asked walking up to him.

Jackson pressed the palm of his hand in Billy's face and shoved him back into the window. "Roman, get the fuck up," Jackson said louder. "Now! You coming with me."

The thing he wanted to ask her was to move in with him but he never got a chance to, thanks to his mother.

Upon hearing the rage in his voice, Roman leapt and hustled behind him. She clutched her lower belly as she waited for what would happen next. If she left with Jackson what would happen to Billy? He was evil but he needed her to survive.

And what would happen to her best friend Yoko? She feared the worst but reasoned even if she stayed, that was inevitable. Yoko didn't respect the code of the streets and she knew that would cause her problems.

Billy Bob picked himself up, looked at the two of them and laughed. "You are funny. Both of you." He leaned on the wall for support because the fall hurt his aging back. "You think you can save her? You think you're some hero?" he chuckled louder. "I assure you that the only thing she good for is cleaning the house."

"Don't ever come near her again," Jackson responded. He looked back at Roman. "Let's leave. Before I do something he'll regret."

"If you leave here don't ever return!" Billy threatened Roman. "Do you hear me? Never come back!"

"Don't worry," Jackson promised. "She never will. She belongs to me now."

CHAPTER ELEVEN
-YOKO-

"Thou art so full of misery."
- Edgar Allan Poe

Yoko sat on the living room sofa holding a beer with more vodka than anything inside of the can. It had been weeks since she talked to Roman and she never knew how bad it would hurt to lose her friendship until it was unavailable. Whenever she called, Roman wouldn't answer the phone and yesterday when she knocked on the door Billy Bob cursed her out and told her that bitch didn't live there anymore.

Although Roman made herself clear about the friendship being over, Yoko believed she would return to her soon enough. Who cared if she told her brothers that they murdered Damien? Now she learned that she moved. Not only out of the building, but also out of her life.

She tried to appear hard but her heart wouldn't allow her. It hurt most when she sat on the porch and watched the city alone. Roman was a real friend, the type that came around once in a lifetime if you were lucky. Yoko was able to be herself around Roman and she feared she lost her forever. She even recalled a time when they went to get something to eat at a local restaurant. They had been drinking all day and Yoko had to piss badly.

But when she walked inside and saw a huge stall she realized she couldn't get on top of the seat alone. Not only that, but how could she wipe herself when done? She left her tongs at home.

Luckily Roman was in the bathroom re-braiding one of her plaits when all of a sudden she asked, "You alright in there? Need help?"

Yoko's silence was her answer and Roman entered the stall, helped her on the toilet and wiped her pussy with tissue paper when she was done. The more Yoko thought about

Roman, the clearer it was. Being too loose with the lips may have ruined her friendship.

True blues came once in a lifetime if you were lucky and blessed.

Trying to get her mind off everything, she took another swig. Her life was fucked up but her brothers were winning. They were across from her making out with their female guests. While only men with fetishes were interested in her, her brothers always seemed to find someone to be with them. No matter how broke they were. She started to resent their longer limbs and even their manhood. She could never understand why she wasn't average height too when they shared the same mother and father.

Out of all the brothers, it was Dale who caused Yoko the most pain. He was on the right side of the sofa kissing the one person she wanted more than anything else. His mouth covered Amanda's as if he were trying to pull blood from her lips. His fingers snaked toward the entrance of her pussy and from where Yoko sat she could see her pink flesh open wide. This did nothing but send Yoko into a blind rage. At first, she thought she was reading Amanda correctly by thinking that Amanda liked her but now she felt stupid.

It was obvious she was wrong.

When Amanda cooed a littler louder, she raised her hips up higher and Yoko could see her sweetness even more. It was as if she were teasing her. Drunk and excited about the freak show, Yoko unbuttoned her pants, grabbed a remote control and used it to stroke her pussy on the spot.

Amanda was the first to see Yoko masturbating and boy did she make a scene. "What the fuck is she doing?" she asked jumping up. She pulled her collar up to cover her nose. "That's so fucking nasty!"

Upon hearing Amanda, the other girls turned their heads and saw Yoko too. When they noticed the remote in her pants, they cringed and shook their heads.

Dale looked over, saw Yoko rubbing her pussy and sighed. "What is wrong with you, Yoko? You scaring the girls!" He believed she was drunk and was willing to let it ride to continue to fool around but the girls weren't hearing it.

"I'm out of here," Amanda said as she grabbed her purse before taking one last look at Dale. "You got that for me, right?" Dale dipped into his pocket and slapped a tiny packet of coke into her palm. Before leaving, she looked at Yoko once more. First disgusted, Amanda now appeared as if she felt sorry for her. "Ya'll take care of that," she said to the boys, referring to Yoko. With a wave of her finger, she instructed the other girls to follow her too.

When they all exited the apartment Dale walked over to Yoko. "Why you do that shit, man?"

Yoko rolled on her stomach, scooted on the edge of the couch and slid down to the floor. She opened her mouth and then closed it as if she were going to say something else but changed her mind. "That bitch was flirting with me," she elected to say. "Had her dress all hiked up so I could see her shit and everything."

"So you gay now?" he asked, his head flinching back slightly.

"Not saying that." She responded as she shuffled a little in front of them. "Just telling you what happened that's all."

Dale looked at the rest of his brothers and they busted out laughing. "You gonna have to get you a nigga soon. People gonna start calling you a dyke if you keep that shit up."

"Yeah, that's the third time you ran our bitches out of here," Mills added with slight hate in his tone. "You starting to make me think you're jealous."

When Dale saw how upset Yoko really was he said, "Fuck them bitches." He slapped Yoko on the shoulder. "Pops cooking out later. So let's get some drinks and watch the city." Amanda wasn't wifey material so he had no intentions on elaborating on the matter further.

As if the women were never there, they all walked outside and sat on the porch of their building. Like she and Roman used to.

An hour passed and although only their mother remained in their apartment, since Vincent and his friends
were in back of the building grilling, the siblings stayed on
the porch. Joshua sat on the bottom step and Yoko kept a
firm hold of the leash.

They were just getting into the bottle when a woman
walked across the street and toward them. She was wearing a
soiled white t-shirt and some blue jeans that looked as if they
had never been washed. Her eyes were blackened but everyone could tell that beauty once lived on her face. At first they
thought she was getting ready to walk into their building but
she stopped in front of them.

"What you need?" Dale asked thinking she was there
to cop.

"Uh," she said looking at him before her attention fixed
on Yoko. "I'm…I'm…you don't know me but I'm—"

"Bothering us," Mills laughed. "Now if you not buying,
get the fuck up off this porch before we get you off."

"My daughter…" She paused again looking at Yoko.
"He told me to stay away but I couldn't. Your real father."
She paused. "But he died in a car accident some years back
and I wanted to meet you then. But I fell hard when he died
as you can see," she said glancing down at herself. Clearing
her throat, she said, "I should've come earlier…and I hope
you can forgive me. Maybe we can start all over."

Yoko stood up, not understanding what she was saying.
Then she focused on her eyes. It was as if she were looking at
her own face. "I think you got me mixed up with someone
else," she said as she took a swig of liquor. "I ain't got time
for this shit." When Joshua moaned, preparing to attack
Daisy, she said, "Yoko fine. It's okay."

Joshua settled down but continued to glare at the
woman.

"I know you don't believe me but you are my daughter,"
she explained. "And I'm so sorry about what I did to you. By
neglecting you. I'm sorry that I wasn't strong enough to keep
you. But ask her. Ask Maria if what I'm saying is true."
Daisy's eyes were planted on Yoko so long that she didn't see

the bottle flying toward her until it was too late. It landed on her forehead, causing blood to ooze from her pores as the glass ripped into her flesh.

"Get the fuck away from here," Mills laughed, having successfully struck the woman. "Before we fire on your dusty ass."

Having gotten the message loud and clear, Daisy held onto her face and backed away. "I'm sorry, Yoko," she sobbed. "Please forgive me."

Although the brothers continued to hold conversation about the strange woman, Yoko's mind was elsewhere. Was what she said true? Her eyes blinked rapidly as she struggled to see things clearer. Needing to know the truth, she stood up. "Dale, keep an eye on Josh." She handed him the leash.

She was almost in the building when Dale stopped her. He tugged his ear and asked, "I know you not listening to that shit, Yoko. You know that crackhead ass bitch lying, right?"

"I'm not thinking nothing about that dope fiend," she lied. "I'll be back out. Just watch Josh."

The moment she walked into the apartment, she could hear her father and his friends outside by the grill from the open window. She was relieved because she knew if nothing else, her mother would tell her the truth if he wasn't around. At least she hoped.

The moment Yoko knocked on Maria's door, she said, "Come in."

Maria rolled over and smiled, moaning a little due to the pain she was in. "Oh, hey, sweetheart. You and your brothers aren't out there——" she stopped in midsentence when she saw Yoko's stone expression. "You know...don't you?" Her chin quivered.

Without asking the question, Yoko received an answer.

She lowered her head and tears rolled down her cheeks. "Why didn't you tell me, ma? Why I had to hear it from her? Huh?" She paused. "Why, ma?"

"Because I was trying to protect you," she said taking a long, pained breath. "And I didn't want you learning about how your mother treated you." Her voice cracked. "How she tried to throw you away like trash. All I wanted was to love you. You were my little girl. You still are."

"What did she do?" Yoko huffed and puffed. "You said you didn't want me knowing how she treated me."

"Yoko, I don't think—"

"What did she do?" she yelled, her breathing noisy.

Maria had a headache before Yoko entered but now it reached astounding levels. If you looked closely, you could see her temples pulsating. When Maria looked into her eyes she knew she could no longer lie. It was time to come clean on it all. "She tossed you out of a window. And you fell on a mattress. I was there to pick you up and had you ever since. I caught you and I took you into my home. Yoko, I loved you all of your life. I still love you now."

She thought about her brothers. "So...they aren't my...my blood?"

"Yes. They are your blood but they aren't your brothers. Your real father and Vincent are brothers," she said softly. "That makes them your cousins."

"Do they know? That I'm not their sister?"

"Yes, everyone knows but you. I'm so sorry, baby."

Larger tears poured down her face, as her mind was flooded with more questions. "Is my father...is he little? Like me?"

"Yes," she said under her breath.

Yoko kicked her mother's shoe rack and paced in place. Remembering what Roman said to her the last time she saw her face, she stopped. "Is it true...about dad...I mean Vincent drugging me and making me have sex with his friends for money?"

Maria exhaled deeply and wept so hard Yoko couldn't understand her. "We needed the money. We...we...so I agreed but then he would send more of his friends into your room. Things got out of hand! A lot of people paid a lot of money to have sex with you. They thought you were different. It turned into a freak show. Before long it got to be too much and—"

Yoko was stunned. Roman said Vincent was involved but she never saw Maria being in the picture. "You knew about it? And you allowed them!"

"Yes, Yoko. I'm so sorry."

Yoko's body tensed and ached terribly. She wasn't a killer. That was Roman's job. But suddenly she fantasized about going into Dale's room, getting his gun and blowing her brains out. She set out to do just that when Vincent yelled up through the window, "Yoko!" The scent of charcoal burning oozed in the room. "Come here and dance for your pops!"

Yoko turned around, preparing to walk out until Maria said, "I'm begging you not to bring it up like this, Yoko. Wait until everyone is out of the house. Let family business remain that way. Private."

Yoko laughed and walked toward the door. She was done listening to Maria and her lies. On a mission, she grabbed her pole, opened the front door and trotted downstairs to reach the backdoor. Once there, she pushed it open and before approaching Vincent, she snatched two items off the picnic table.

"Fuck took you so long?" Vincent laughed as she approached him and his friends. "I called you five hours ago."

"I was talking to ma," she said flatly. "Just learned a lot of shit about my life."

High and selfish, he couldn't see the pain in Yoko's eyes. Nor did he care. "Well fuck all that. Do a dance for your pops." He looked at his friends. "We paying."

"No," she said. "I'm done with that shit."

"No?" He tilted his head and looked down at her. "Fuck you mean no?"

"I said no," Yoko said louder.

Feeling disrespected that his friends were looking, Vincent made a move for her but Yoko squeezed the lighter fluid she had in her hand on his shirt, struck a match and threw it at him. Yoko and Vincent's friends watched him go up in flames.

****

The streets were still wet due to the recent summer rain when Yoko was released from prison after serving six months. Although Vincent was badly burned, he lived, which was the only reason she wasn't convicted of murder.

When Vincent was released from the hospital, he didn't go back to his apartment and no one knew where he lived. There was a lot of secrecy surrounding his absence and the city talked. Some said he was killed and others said he moved with a young girl who lived down the block. But Maria believed he was out of the state. With third degree burns everywhere, he felt unattractive and couldn't face his friends.

Maria's main concern was hurting Yoko.

Although Maria and her sons tried to reach out to Yoko in jail by way of letters, she ignored them all. She blamed everyone for not telling her about who she really was. When she had Internet access, she saw the hundreds of videos that were circulating with her body and her name. She was a circus act.

It wasn't until she was released that she realized they were the only family she ever had, even if they prostituted her. She would have to deal with them or be alone.

When Yoko knocked on the door to the apartment she lived in all of her life, Maria opened the door. Maria looked frailer, as if time had not been good and this scared Yoko. "Come in, baby," she smiled. "I missed you so much." Although she wanted to hug her, she took care to maintain her space.

When Yoko walked inside she saw Joshua sitting at the dining room table. His back was faced in her direction but when he turned around and saw her he went wild. "Yoko! Yoko! Yoko's home!"

Normally his excited spirit would scare her, considering all they'd been through but today she welcomed his energy. It meant, if nothing else, that she was officially home.

After Yoko positioned herself on the sofa with Joshua next to her, she looked over at Maria and asked, "Are you okay?"

"Not really, Yoko," she smiled. "Although I'm trying to take care of myself, I can't help but think about how I treated you." She looked up at the ceiling. "I found out when you went to jail that your father...your real father...left this building to you."

"To me?" she asked with wide eyes. "But why? I didn't even know him."

"I guess he never got over how he treated you. When Vincent went to the hospital I found the papers in a chest he kept locked up. On his side of the closet." She sat down and ran her hand through her thinning grey hair. "He was planning to make you look like a drunk. Planning to get you strung out. And then he was going to submit papers to the court to have you ruled incapable of caring for this building and the tenants. Since he was the next of kin, he may have won and regained control of this building."

"But why." She swallowed. "Why would my father leave anything to me if he didn't love me?"

"Not sure if he didn't love you, Yoko. We all have different ways of showing love. Have different ways of expressing our feelings. From what I'm told, he didn't want to put the resentment he had of being a dwarf on you." She paused. "Daisy was the one who told him you were dead at first but someone told him that his brother was raising you. So he would come around in secret, never introducing himself." She sighed again. "I guess giving you this building was a way of saying sorry."

The conversation was too heavy for her. If Maria said she owned the building then so be it. She was more interested in what was happening to everyone else. "Where are my brothers?"

Pleased she still referred to them as her siblings, Maria grinned. "They were supposed to be here fifteen minutes ago, to take Joshua to the community pool." She looked at the clock on the wall. "The folks at the center are having a day for the mentally challenged." She sighed. "Joshua was so excited about going but now it doesn't seem like he'll make it. They are always so irresponsible. Without you or me, I don't know what they would do."

"I'll take him," Yoko said, eager to get back to her life.

"Are you sure?"

"Yeah, he's my little brother. It's not a problem."

Maria smiled and stood up. "Okay, and when you get back I'll make you dinner."

Although she longed for a home cooked meal, Yoko was concerned about her resting instead of slaving in a kitchen. "I'll be fine, ma. I can grab something while I'm out."

"I want to cook for my little girl." There was a deep sadness and regret in Maria's eyes. "I mean, I want to cook for you. I know you're not a child anymore." She paused. "It would be my pleasure."

"If you really want to."

"I do. And I almost forgot," she said pulling a cell phone out of the pocket of her robe. "This is Dale's phone. Take it in case I need to reach you."

****

The pool was jam-packed with teenagers and young adults with mental challenges. Yoko sat on the recliner, growing irritated at the children who either pointed at her or thought she was a child and wanted to play. But when she focused on how much fun Joshua was having she smiled brightly. No matter what, he was her brother. She would never forget what he did to her in that bathroom but she also understood that it was not his fault.

When something vibrated against her body she jumped. She forgot she had the cell phone in her pocket until that moment. Taking it out, she frowned when she didn't recognize the number. Thinking it was one of Dale's many girlfriends, she ignored it but the person wouldn't stop calling. Frustrated, she hit the button and yelled, "Who is this?"

"Dale...I need Dale."

Although the caller didn't announce her name, Yoko knew her voice very well. She thought about her most days and wondered how she was doing. If she and Dale were still good friends. "Amanda?" Yoko said sensing urgency in her voice. "What's wrong? Are you hurt?"

Although she was listening, she focused on Joshua who was playing ball with a woman in the kiddy pool. The woman's brown hair was tied in a bun on top of her head and she wore a huge smile on her face as she interacted with him.

"I'm in my apartment," her voice was shaky. "Off of Liberty Road. Somebody just tried to kill me. I need help."

****

Luckily, Amanda's apartment was around the corner from the pool because Yoko didn't have a car. Although she didn't want to leave Joshua at the community center alone, she figured she would be back quickly once she helped Amanda. Before agreeing to come over, Yoko pleaded with Amanda to call the cops but she refused, saying that she needed someone to hide her crack pipes and drug paraphernalia before they arrived.

With urgency, Yoko ascended the stairs with the assistance of her pole. When she made it to Amanda's apartment she knocked but she realized it was already open. Pushing herself inside, she called Amanda's name several times, hoping she'd answer.

"I'm back here," Amanda moaned. "Please hurry."

When Yoko reached the backroom, her stomach churned when she saw the condition Amanda was in. The back of her head was leaning against the wall while the rest of her body was pressed against the floor. Her face was beaten badly and a bloody broom handle lay on the carpet some feet away.

Yoko quickly moved toward her and asked, "What happened?"

"Some niggas broke in here," she moaned. "And tried to kill me."

"What? Why?" Yoko yelled as she continued to examine her.

"They said I owed them money for some coke. But I didn't," she cried.

Yoko knew immediately that she was lying but she didn't care.

"So he stabbed me in my pussy with that shit." Tears rolled down her face and mixed with the blood. "Yoko the inside of my body is throbbing. You got to call the ambulance."

****

Yoko was in the hospital room with Amanda. The doctor came in and told them that Amanda was assaulted so badly that the robbers ruptured her uterus and most of her reproductive organs. Essentially, he was saying that Amanda would never, under any circumstances, have children.

Yoko was still staring at Amanda, who was drugged up and asleep when the phone vibrated in her pocket again. It wasn't until that moment she realized she fucked up. The call was a reminder that not only had she forgotten about Joshua, she also left him in the pool alone.

Slowly she answered the phone. "Hello," she said breathing heavily, her hand trembling.

"Yoko, where the fuck you been?" Mills asked huffing and puffing.

"I'm so sorry, Mills! Amanda called. Some niggas almost killed her and I forgot about Joshua."

"Fuck that junkie bitch!" he yelled. "Because you left him alone, shit is fucked up over here! Joshua held some little girl under water at the pool. He raped her and tried to kill her." When he started crying Yoko's body trembled. "The little girl almost died."

"Where's Dale? And Farmer?"

"I just spoke to 'em. They coming. You got to get home."

"I'm on my way. Where's ma?"

The phone dropped and Yoko didn't receive her answer.

But later that day she would learn that Maria, out of grief, died of a heart attack.

.

PART TWO

CHAPTER TWELVE
-ROMAN-

FIVE YEARS LATER

"But we loved with a love that was more than love."
- Edgar Allan Poe

Mrs. Roman Tate climbed on top of her husband after she just sucked his dick for twenty-five minutes straight. It was like she wanted to pull the skin off. When it came to Jackson, she couldn't get enough. Wanting him inside of her, she allowed her strawberry pink flesh to engulf his chocolate stick until it could go no further in her body. His thickness felt like stiff fist bumps into her walls and she moved her waist like a mad woman, taking it all.

"Fuck me, Jackson," she begged as she worked back and forth with wide long strokes. "Give me all that good shit."

When it came to murder and fucking, Roman didn't play games. She knew she was good because of how he made her feel. She worked at it. Gone were the days of her toting guns. During sex was the only time she could act out violently and she appreciated those moments.

When Roman was too much in charge, Jackson flipped her over and tore into her like he was trying to rip her apart. The best thing about Jackson was that he didn't hold back and together they were match.

When her legs began to tremble and close for business, he smacked them apart so that he could have all of her, no restraints. From the back, he grabbed her titties, pinching them so hard she was worried he'd break her flesh. But pain was as hot as sex to hear her tell it, so she begged him not to stop.

When he felt himself about to explode, he pulled his dick out, gripped her hip and nutted all over her back. As good as she felt, they couldn't afford to have another kid. Exhausted, he fell into her warm skin before sliding off and lying to her right. "Roman," Jackson said as he stroked her yellow thigh. "Did you hear what I just said to you?"

Roman flapped her eyes a few times and looked into his brown eyes. "I'm sorry, baby. I was in my head. What did you say?"

"Damn, babe. That quick?" He paused. "I was just inside of you. I said how much I loved you. You mean to tell me that I lost you already?" He rubbed her chin. "What were you thinking about?"

When she saw his concerned expression, she rolled on her back and faced the ceiling. Tiny roaches crawled on the wall and huddled in the corners like piles of dirt. The apartment was a dump but it was all they could afford at the moment.

Roman felt guilty. Since Jackson married her, true to his mother's word, she cut him off financially. If she hadn't seen where he grew up, she would not have felt so bad. To pursue his dream, he went to Johns Hopkins anyway and paid for the apartment using the proceeds of his scholarship. His mother was serious when it came to out casting him. Either he divorce Roman or he would continue to live in squalor. Those were the only options.

The only time Debra gave him the time of day was when it came to her adorable grandson Sailor. As angry as she was, whenever she looked into the boy's light green eyes, she was in love and there was no denying it.

He was her blood.

And despite his mother, that made him perfect.

Roman closed her eyes tightly and a few tears rolled down her face as she considered their fate. "This is my fault." She paused looking at the filth. She remembered clearly the home he grew up in and it was a long way from the one they were in now. "All of this. If you didn't marry me you would have a better life. Why did you choose me?"

"I chose you because you're my bitch. So don't talk like that."

"Jackson!"

"I'm serious! I'm not a fan of weakness, Roman. You know that about me." He sat up and leaned against the unstable headboard that rocked several times before adjusting to his weight. "I wouldn't have a life if you weren't in it. I love you."

"But I wish I could help more. You're in school to be a doctor and what am I doing?"

"You're taking care of our son. I give you credit for that if nothing else. Don't be so hard on yourself. You've been trying to get a part-time job since we got married. Something will come up."

Roman appreciated his support but she knew something that he didn't. That she couldn't read to save her life. Almost completely illiterate, every time she tried to fill out an application, she would leave with embarrassment instead of a job. She had no idea, after all of these years, that she suffered from Dyslexia because she kept the fact that words seemed to move around to herself.

She rolled over and smiled at him. "I know you're right, Jackson. I'll just keep—"

"Mommy! Daddy!" their five-year-old son Sailor screamed in the other room. "Help me!"

Hearing their son's distressed voice, Roman and Jackson jumped out of bed and rushed toward his room. Jackson was quick but Roman was quicker and she reached him first, pushing the door open so hard the doorknob stabbed into the wall behind it.

When she got to him his soft brown hair was pulled on top of his head in a ponytail because it hadn't been braided yet. Sweat poured down his face. "What happened, honey?" Roman asked as she pulled him into her arms. Their pounding hearts touching each other.

"Something bit me," he cried, raising his bloody arm. "It hurts!"

When Roman examined the bruise and saw what looked like small teeth marks in his flesh she was enraged. She wanted to harm something but wasn't sure where to direct her anger. Roman loved that little boy more than a mother could and she wanted him to be safe. She needed him to feel secure. She certainly didn't want him to have the horrible life she had.

"What was it, son?" Jackson questioned as he stood next to the bed. His eyes bulging down at him. "Did you see it?"

"It was a mouse." He pointed over at the wall across the room. "I threw it over there."

When Jackson observed the area he pointed in he saw the rodent was gone. "Son, I think it got away." He shuffled a little and tried to calm down so that his son wouldn't see his anger. "I'm sorry, lil man. I'll put down some more traps."

"I'm scared, mommy and daddy," he said gripping Roman's neck. "I don't like it here. I wanna stay with grandmommy. Please."

Roman held her head down and shook it softly. To say her heart was broken would be an understatement. Her son wanted to live somewhere she was not welcome. It ripped her apart. But if she were him she'd want to stay with Debra too. But that was impossible. She couldn't see giving up her son for anybody especially to her mother-in-law.

"I know, Sailor," she said as her chin quivered. "We're going to get you out of here. I promise." She kissed him on the forehead and looked up at Jackson. "What are we going to do, Jackson?" she asked with tears rolling down her face. "We can't stay here anymore."

"I know, baby," he said. "I'll think of something. Even if I have to call my mother."

★★★★

Roman placed the groceries on the belt as she observed the total increase with each item the cashier scanned. Her cart was divided in two halves between the things she needed and the things Sailor desired. The plan was to pay for it all but if it cost more than forty-five dollars she wouldn't be able to get everything.

When she saw the total come up to $48.13, three dollars over the amount in the banking account, Roman put her hands on the counter and broke down in tears. She hated crying because although she hadn't seen or heard from Billy Bob in years, she could hear his voice telling her she was weak. But these days, she couldn't help it.

She was a mother and a wife and things were different now.

Everything she did these days made her feel like a burden. She couldn't even read the words on the items and resorted to looking at the pictures to make a decision on what she would buy. She wanted to be a good citizen but this shit was about to force her to start knocking over niggas with the barrel of a gun, which she didn't want to do.

"Ma'am," the cashier said witnessing her breakdown. "Do you want the groceries?"

Roman looked up at her and was about to take out half of the choices when a pretty woman behind her in line said, "Yes. She wants all of it."

Roman was stuck. Outside of Jackson, no one in her life ever showed her an act of kindness. As she examined the short pretty girl with the huge breasts and light brown hair, she wondered why she helped her. What was her motive? She didn't appear to be the Good Samaritan type.

"I can't afford to pay you back," Roman said.

"No need for payback," she winked at Roman. She handed the cashier a wad of cash and pushed her groceries forward. "Please bag her things separately and then do mine."

"You don't understand," Roman said wiping the remaining tears from her cheek. "I don't have any money."

"Just pay it forward."

After the groceries were bagged, Roman stood outside of the store and waited for the kind woman to come out. When she saw her she walked up and said, "I really appreciate your help. You don't know what this does for me and my family."

By T. Styles   146

"No problem, honey," she smiled brighter. "I had the money so I didn't mind spending it. For whatever reason I'm blessed and I don't mind helping out if I can." When she activated her alarm, sending a beautiful black Benz into chirp mode, Roman was even more curious.

"Do you mind if I ask what you do for a living?"

She giggled. "How about we have some coffee and I tell you my name first."

Roman smiled for the first time in a long while. "That works for me."

****
One Week Later

Roman was in the middle of the floor in Carey's basement dancing to the point of sweat dripping down her inner thighs. Carey's two cousins sat on the couch with one duty, to judge Roman's routine to see if it was worthy. Roman never imagined life as a stripper but unless she was knocking niggas over with her gun, she didn't see any other alternative.

"Make your movements smaller, Roman," Carey suggested as she sat on a couch watching her. "You have to connect with your body or you won't reach the tippers. Feel your hips, feel your legs and the men will fall."

"I think she's doing fine," Owen, Carey's older cousin, said as he sipped on his beer.

He was leaned so far back in the recliner that you could barely see his eyes. The shadows appeared to cover him and he liked it that way. His neat cornrows were tucked under his all black New York Yankees hat and he would tug it every so often so that Roman couldn't see his expression. From the moment he saw the tall cutie with the green eyes, he felt a connection, one that he couldn't deny. Although he was enamored, he told himself it would never happen when he saw the small ring on her finger but it didn't stop him from feeling her. Besides, Owen Martin was a thug who got what he wanted. And what he wanted was Roman Tate but he had no intentions on letting her know.

"You would say that," Carey said with an attitude. She knew her cousin was feeling Roman but she didn't want her to know. Married meant off limits unless you received an open invitation and as far as she knew, Roman hadn't given him the okay. "If she's going to work at Smack Back she has to be the best. Evan's not going to even give her the time of day if she's not good."

"I'm with Carey," Raymond said to his brother. "No need in sending that girl in that club unprepared. If she gonna do it she should learn from a pro."

Unlike Owen who was single, Raymond was married to Brittani, an ex-prostitute who he slept with as a gift for his birthday from Owen ten years earlier. People were surprised when after his birthday was over he was still with her. Most thought she would never change but the moment Raymond expressed how much he cared about her, she dropped the lifestyle she was accustomed to and a year later, he asked her to be his wife. Owen, who always held a grudge, warmed to his sister-in-law because despite the past, he knew she really loved him.

"Stop kissing up, bro," Owen said shaking his head. "You and me both know the nigga takes what he can get." He looked at Roman. "What I don't understand is if you're married why you got to do this shit?" Like a lovesick kid, instead of telling Roman he was feeling her, he took to bashing her instead.

"That's my business, don't you think?" she winked.

"It don't make me no never mind." He sipped his beer. "If you want to play yourself like a whore then so be it."

When he insulted Roman, Carey stabbed her fists in her tiny waist, cut the music off and looked over at Owen. Her cousin was out of line, which was unlike him, and she wanted to know what was up.

Ever since Carey met Roman, she took a liking to her and it seemed like everyone in her camp felt the same.

There was something about her quiet character that had Carey wanting to protect her like someone did for her when she first started in the game. Originally, she tried to give her enough money to help pay the bills for a month. So she wouldn't get started. Because she knew once the stripper life-style took her in, there was no turning back but Roman wouldn't accept the paper. And that made Carey like her even more. She preferred to work for her dollar these days.

"What is going on with you, Owen?" Carey asked. "I know you can be a bitch but this is even too much for you."

Owen adjusted his hat and sunk deeper into the seat. "Me and Ray fucked up Sam's package. Now they threatening to slump us."

"How you fuck it up?" Carey shrilled.

"Coming out the carryout one night," Owen explained. "I went to grab something to eat for this bitch and got caught up."

"With his work on you?" Carey stomped. "How could you be so stupid?"

"He's lying for me," Raymond interrupted. "I was the one who fucked up. Brit called and told me that the baby didn't have any diapers. So I went to get some with the work in the car. I thought it would be quick but when I stepped outside two niggas were there. Waiting. And they got me."

"But we got the money now," Owen added. "The thing is, the nigga asking for a vig. Talking about we two days late so now we owe more."

"How much more he want?"

"Five grand."

"I can give it to you," she assured them. "What I want to know is why you didn't come to me—" Carey's statement was interrupted. "Wait! I think somebody's in my fucking house," she whispered with her jaw hung. "I can't believe this shit."

"That may not be somebody. That might be the nigga we owe," Raymond responded.

Carey shook her head and looked over at her cousins. "Please say you're strapped."

Raymond and Owen looked at one another. "I don't have my heat," Raymond said. "You told us not to strap up in your crib, remember?" he whispered. "My shit in the car out front. I think the door open and everything."

Carey recalled the rule but now it seemed dumb. It happened after they all had too much to drink and Raymond accidently fired into the living room floor, missing Carey who was sitting on the basement sofa, by inches.

Carey's heartbeat quickened when she realized they were unprepared and unarmed. She didn't know what to do. And when she looked back for her friend Roman she saw she was gone. "Hold up, where your peoples go?" Raymond asked scanning the basement. "Please don't tell me you fucking with someone who set you up, Carey. Because that bitch got ghost real quick."

Owen didn't believe Roman was that foul. He knew a hood rat when he saw one and in his opinion, she was far from it. When he glanced over at the small window over the sink, he saw it was open. "Oh shit, shawty rolled out."

"You think we could get through there too?" Raymond asked surveying the window.

Owen looked at his beer belly and said, "Naw, nigga. We gonna have to wing this one out." He looked around the basement. "Find whatever you can grab as a weapon.

Although Carey appreciated that Roman was able to get away, she felt she could've alerted her. Maybe they could've followed her and everyone would be safe.

"Carey, why don't you try and leave," Owen said grabbing a pool stick and breaking it, presenting its sharp edge.

"Yeah, cousin. Ain't no need in you staying," Raymond added.

"You know I'm not leaving here without ya'll. If you down I'm down too." The moment she said that, there was some louder knocking around upstairs followed by frantic voices.

"Oh shit! Who the fuck is that?" the first intruder screamed upstairs.

"I don't know but shoot the bitch!" the second intruder yelled.

Their voices were followed by three consecutive shots and then there was total silence. Carey's heart pumped wildly in her chest and her antennas were tuned on every movement upstairs. All of a sudden, a single set of footsteps knocked against the floor leading toward the basement. The three secured what they could find to protect themselves and awaited their fate.

The door opened slowly and Roman calmly said, "You guys might wanna come upstairs now. It's all been taken care of."

Raymond ran his hand down the front of his face in relief. While Owen plopped on the sofa as he fell for Roman harder. She was pretty and handy with a gun? If she could cook, he would be gone.

Roman successfully killed two intruders by escaping the basement and catching them off guard. Using the guns Raymond said were in the car.

For Carey, it was a wrap. She knew there was something about the southern girl she liked and now she knew she was right. From that moment on, Roman, Carey, Raymond and Owen were as thick as thieves. And nothing or no one could break their bond.

Or so they thought.

****

Collections of smoke clouds ascended in the air at Smack Back as bass from the speakers appeared to make them dance. Men clutched glasses filled with their drink of choice while stacks of tens and twenties sat before the ballers with the most bread. It was time for the main event.

"Gentlemen, I hope you are ready to lose that bank. Because coming to the stage is the one and only, Romance!"

The first three beats of the song pumped way before Romance stepped to the stage sending her regulars on a frenzy. Was she coming out? Did they miss her? Sure, there were other women who commanded the stage with the right outfits and songs but no one was as luxurious as Roman's sexy tall ass.

When she was ready, and only when she was ready, she eased out from the black and gold curtains and dropped her red velvet cape on the stage. Using all of the skills Carey had given her and some of her own, she waved her hips like an American flag in the wind, causing bills to fall from the sky.

Romance's gift was not in her ability to dance better than the next. It was in her ability to be whomever she desired at the time. And at the moment she wasn't Bay from Mississippi, or Roman the killer. She was Romance, a professional dancer, a professional seducer.

After she danced, a few of her regulars tried to offer a little dick mixed in between the Benjamins but she wasn't interested. She may have showed a little pussy and popped a little ass but she would never cheat on her husband. So she said her goodbyes and walked to the dressing room only to see Carey standing in the middle of the floor. "You were great out there," she announced smiling at her. "I hardly recognize you anymore."

Roman giggled. "Stop playing games, girl," she responded as she sat down in the chair and eyed herself in the mirror. "I've been doing this for a minute now. You know I'm good. You taught me everything I know." She winked and looked her over. "But you better get dressed. You're next. Don't have Evan come back here yelling at me too."

"That's what I wanted to tell you." She sat next to her. "I'm not dancing anymore."

"What? Why?"

"Remember I was telling you I was in a weird relationship?"

"Yeah." She paused. "But I thought you broke up with him."

"I did," she giggled. "But we got back together. And they don't want me dancing anymore."

"They?" she asked with wide eyes.

"Yeah." She paused. "They're rich, Roman. I'm talking about they got enough money to take care of me for the rest of my life. I got to take this chance. They don't want me in here anymore and I understand why. I couldn't do this dance shit for the rest of my life anyway. After awhile it's a little whack. I'm too old for this shit."

Roman wanted to be happy for her but she was sad. She only worked at the club because she had her support. If she left what did that mean for her? She wouldn't feel as safe for starters and that made her nervous. "Do you really know them? I mean *really* know them?" Without saying the words, Roman wanted her to know that she would kirk out if someone was trying to get her friend wrong.

"I know them as much as anybody can know someone in a relationship."

"Who are they?" Roman asked, confused at the change of heart. One minute she was about the dollar and the next things were different.

"Race and Ramirez Kennedy. They are outside waiting on me now." She stood up, grabbed her hand and walked her to the curtain leading to the club. "You see them over there?"

Roman fixed her eyes on a cute couple. Particularly the short girl with the shoulder length brown hair and a wedding ring that sparkled when she raised her drinking glass in the air. Having seen enough, Roman shook her head and walked back into the dressing room. "I see them. They are a nice looking couple but how do you know you can trust these people?"

"How do you know you can trust anyone, Roman? Sometimes you just feel it. In your heart." Carey placed a strand of Roman's wild curly hair behind her ear. "I trusted you, didn't I? And look how it paid off."

Roman wasn't big on compliments but she took it with a grain of salt. "So basically they're swingers?"

"You can call it that if you like stereotypes. But I think it's deeper. They've invited me into their marriage and they love me as if I walked down the aisle with them, Roman. They gave me something I never had. Two people who care about me. And I love them for it."

Roman didn't like the idea of her being a swinger but Carey was too happy to bust her bubble. So instead of popping off strong, she decided to keep shit real. "Let me tell you something you need to hear. As long as they married, there will always be a divider in the relationship. If you aren't the wife, you don't have first place. And there will come a time when you will know it. And it won't feel good. Just be prepared."

"Roman!"

"I'm serious. I support you but I just want you to be smart. As long as you safe and happy, homie." She smiled. "What can I say?"

"I am. And what are you doing tonight? Wanna hang out with us?"

"I can't. Jackson coming home early from school. I'm planning a nice meal for the three of us." She paused. "Do you know after all of this time, he still doesn't know I work here?"

"Where does he think you work every night?"

"At a department store. Thank God he has school because I don't know what I would do if he walked up in here." She exhaled. "If he ever found out he'd leave me, Carey. Who am I without him?"

Carey touched her shoulder. "Now you know how I feel." She paused. "When it's love it's love. No matter who's involved." A few nosey strippers walked in and Carey lowered her voice for privacy. "I might be out of the stripper business but I told Raymond and Owen to stick around at night when you have a set. They serve dope out of here so it's not a big deal for them to stay around and keep an eye on you. I don't want you to ever think you don't have anybody in your corner."

Roman sighed because she appreciated they were looking out but she missed her already.

"Stop looking sad, friend. Be happy for me."

Roman held her head down. "I'm happy for you. I really am."

"Well it doesn't sound like it," Carey said placing her hand on her shoulder.

"I'll just miss you that's all. Am I wrong for that?"

"Don't worry about me. I'll always be here for you. I promise."

****

When Jackson Tate walked into Professor Sylvia Ortiz's office to see what was so urgent that it couldn't wait until after class, he wasn't surprised to see her sitting on the edge of the desk with her navy blue dress hiked over her hips so that he could catch the best view of her naked pussy.

She took an interest in Jackson's education in and out of the classroom from the moment she laid eyes on his chiseled physique. Unlike Martin Locks, another student who ate her pussy for breakfast, lunch and dinner, Jackson was not interested in the pretty but older teacher in the least. All he wanted was his degree in medicine and to be left alone but she didn't see it that way.

"Sylvia, what are you doing?" he asked frantically as he looked behind him to make sure nobody saw her with her legs gaped open. He slammed the door and walked further inside. "You must want to get fired."

She opened her legs wider to answer his question. "Getting fired is the last thing on earth I'm thinking about. The only thing on my mind is getting a look at that dick of yours. I know it's pretty." She ran her tongue over her lips. "So tell me, Jackson. What I got to do to get some of it?"

He slumped down in a leather chair in her office and threw his face into the palms of his hands. *Why won't this bitch leave me alone?* he thought. It was bad enough that Roman was working overtime at a department store trying to provide a home for the family, something he felt he should be doing, but now there he was the object of Sylvia's sexual harassment.

He looked up at her. "Listen, I'm going to tell you like I did the other times you made a move. I'm a married man."

She stood up and approached him before dropping to her knees. When she was situated she wiggled her warm body between his legs. "But are you happy?"

"It doesn't matter if I'm happy or not. I love my wife."

Embarrassed, Sylvia stood up, looked down at him and slapped him in the face. Angry he didn't fuck her, she said, "Let me remind you about something that I think you've forgotten. You are on a scholarship, sir. And there are a lot of things that could go wrong before you graduate. Not fucking me and losing everything you've worked for is one of them. I can be a handful when I don't get what I want, Mr. Tate. Take caution before continuing to reject me."

CHAPTER THIRTEEN
-YOKO-

"In a strange city, lying alone."
- Edgar Allan Poe

Yoko was riding Erin's little dick inside of his white Mitsubishi Outlander while trying to make him believe it was the best sex she ever had. The small SUV was parked behind a 7-Eleven while they did their thing. Normally she made the niggas she tricked off wear a condom but Erin refused and since she believed that he was her last resort in terms of money, she decided to let it ride.

Back in the day, Yoko had niggas with strange fetishes lined up around the corner. Dudes who, although weird, weren't bad to look at if you squinted a little. But since she allowed Amanda to run her into the ground, large bags rested under her eyes and the once fat ass she was possessed with flattened like a deflated basketball. She was nowhere near the bad bitch she used to be, that was certain.

Trying to speed the process up, Yoko did all she could to encourage an orgasm. From moaning loudly to gripping her breasts and squeezing them to the point of turning red, it seemed as if nothing she did worked. It was clear that Erin wasn't going to bust a nut until he got good and ready.

At the moment, the entire car smelled of fish and ass because for two days in a row Yoko couldn't find the tongs she used to wash her own pussy. She had a feeling that her drug-addicted girlfriend Amanda hid them from her like she did whenever she wanted her to get money for her fix. On more than one occasion, she blackmailed her in that cruel way, by limiting her access to life.

Amanda could be mean and nasty if she desired. From putting her books on the top shelves in their apartment so Yoko couldn't step on them and get around the house, or leaving her in the house for days without food or water by hiding the stools, for the love of drugs she did it all. In the end, Yoko would have to prostitute herself or risk losing Amanda and her sanity in the process.

Everyone said Yoko played the fool but they had no room to talk. They didn't have to meet people and wonder if they liked them for the person they were or the sexual desires they could fulfill. Amanda may have been a washed up addict, who was taking from Yoko emotionally everyday. But her presence and even her addiction made Yoko feel wanted. She could count on it.

Since Maria died, it was accurate to say Yoko fell on hard times. It didn't help that her only best friend Roman seemed to have fallen off the face of the earth years ago without the benefit of a goodbye. That fucked up her disposition and made it worse. When she asked around the neighborhood about where Roman moved, everyone said the same thing. That she got up with some rich dude named Jackson, married him and moved on with her life. And a few even went on to say that she should do the same.

This devastated Yoko because she was certain if nothing else that Roman knew she was all she had in the world. So why would she leave her alone?

Yoko was her own woman but if Roman was in her corner, dealing with her mother's death, her lazy brothers, tenants who paid late and her greedy girlfriend, life might not have seemed so bad. She received no help from her family; the Lighthouse men acted like young boys who without her couldn't do simple things like pay their own bills, buy food or get out of bed. They ran through the money that the tenants gave Yoko at the first of the month and they kept their hands out every day until the next payout. The cars they drove, the clothes they wore were all courtesies of Yoko's fuck game and the building her father left her.

Maria successfully produced lazy men all because she sheltered them too much. Now they walked around with fucked up senses of entitlement and she could not hold a productive conversation with them if she held a gun to their domes.

To make matters worse, Joshua, the one she truly cared for, was remanded to a home where he had to remain seven days a week. She visited him every weekend and was told if he continued to show improvement they would allow him to go home with her. Excitedly, Yoko brought the matter to Amanda who shut the idea down with the quickness.

"If Retard the Rapist lives here I won't. So make your decision on who you want to fuck. 'Cause it won't be both of us."

Disgusted, she knew he could never stay with her. Knowing he couldn't live on his own, she kept one of her apartments available upstairs and furnished it as nice as possible for him. She figured she'd tell the home that he was living with her when in actuality he would be living alone. She placed locks on the doors so that he could get in but not out and made certain there was nothing sharp inside that he could cut himself with. It wasn't the best but she would be sure to make it home for him.

His living arrangements would definitely be done in *sub rosa* but the biggest secret the family possessed was the death of Paige Kelly, the woman who saw Joshua hold the girl down while he sexually assaulted her in the pool many years back. Although the Baltimore police didn't know what happened, Yoko did.

When Mills found out that the woman would be testifying against Joshua, which could possibly land him in jail or a mental institution, he did the only thing he felt was possible, walked up to her in broad daylight and blasted her brains out. For months and then years, police tried to find witnesses who saw what happened at the pool but everyone remained mute. And when their only witness was killed, they felt it was over.

And now with Maria gone, it was up to Yoko and her pussy to take care of everybody. "Are you finished yet?" Yoko asked with a sexual grin on her face. She was trying to be seductive when in actuality she was annoyed. "I know you feeling good, baby, but I told you I have somewhere to be. You think you could speed it up a little?"

Erin frowned and said, "Bitch, as stank as your pussy is you ought to be glad I'm inside of you at all. Now shut the fuck up. It's bad enough I got to smell your box. Don't force me to smell your shitty breath too."

Yoko wanted to unleash on his ass but she decided to take the calmer route. While still moving her hips she asked, "You gonna give me my money, right? When we're done? Like you promised? You know I have stuff to take care of."

He frowned and turned his nose away from her face as he continued to pump into her tight pussy. "If you don't shut up I'm not paying you shit. Now quiet down so I can concentrate since you too lazy to fuck back."

Yoko remained silent but she knew one thing. If he had any intentions on not giving her the paper he owed he had better think again. She never killed a man, but she had no problem splattering his brains all in his new ride if need be. Besides, she needed the money for her girlfriend who was no doubt waiting on her.

Fifteen minutes later, after every bone in her body ached as if she ran a marathon, Erin finally busted a nut. The moment he was done, she collected her paper, hopped out of his truck and walked toward her Toyota Rav 4.

She didn't give him the benefit of a goodbye.

When she arrived at her car she stepped on the running board, opened the door and climbed on her extended seat. It sat high up so that Yoko could see over the dashboard like average height people. When she was comfortable she turned the car on, adjusted her tilt steering wheel and pressed the brake using the pedal extension.

These days Yoko was more independent and with the seventy-five bucks Erin had given her she bought a twenty-five dollar bag of crack for Amanda, some cereal, milk and bacon for the apartment her brothers lived in, and some wings, butter and milk for her crib. She was basically taking care of two households but the guilt of losing Maria wouldn't allow her to stop and tell the worthless bastards to fend for themselves. In her mind, had she not left Joshua alone at the pool, Maria would not be dead and she could've cared for them instead of having to do it on her own.

After all of these years, she still lived in the same building as her brothers, just in a different apartment. After dropping off their food, she went to her place but Amanda wasn't home. When she saw her brother Dale in the hallway she asked, "You seen wifey?"

He shook his head in disgust. Dale had no problems with his sister being gay if that was her thing. But the least she could do was find a woman he and the entire neighborhood hadn't nutted inside of. "She around the block with another nigga." He frowned. "I told you, you should've dumped that slut a long time ago."

Yoko was devastated.

It seemed as if every time she turned around, she had to deal with Amanda's disloyalty and public humiliation. The worst part was she just finished fucking a nigga to give her the dope she needed to feel better. Did Amanda have to trick off too?

Yoko cruised the streets of Baltimore and when she finally saw Amanda she was sick with pain. Amanda was standing in front of a black sedan laughing at another nigga's joke. He was 6'4" high, way taller than Yoko would ever be. Just looking at them talk to each other in the middle of the street broke her heart. Why would Amanda cheat when she would have surely given her anything if she would just ask?

"Fuck you, bitch," Yoko said as tears rolled down her cheek. "If you can cheat for entertainment I can too."

****

Felicia Horn was sitting on top of Yoko's face and Yoko was licking her pussy clean. Before they got busy, she soaked in her large tub that made Yoko comfortable because she just fucked and hadn't had a bath in two days. One of Felicia's favorite things to do, since Yoko couldn't push her off, was to smother her face with her ass cheeks. Felicia would sit on her face for long periods, forcing her to eat her pussy or die. In the midst of getting off, she would rise up a little, allow Yoko to catch a quick breath and slam on her face again. The game she played was a little rough at first but Yoko was used to it.

She met Felicia through her brothers at a cookout last year and they clicked instantly. She had a thing for little people and seemed to get off whenever Yoko would go down on her.

Although Yoko's mind was on Amanda, she couldn't help but revel in Felicia's sexiness. The girl had it all the way around in the looks department. Pretty face. Thick ass. And clean pussy. If only she could do something about her wicked personality, she wouldn't be so bad to be around.

If Felicia wasn't talking about gangs or jealous bitches, she wasn't talking about anything and Yoko found her conversation lacking. Yoko wasn't a thug anymore in that sense of the word. Sure, she did what she had to for her family but that was about it. At the end of the day, she had responsibilities and desired mental stimulation. This was one of the reasons she missed Roman. There was no one in her circle who Yoko could talk to about life.

Felicia was an entirely different story. She was a member of the Southeast Kittens, a girl gang based in D.C. whose only mission was to cause unnecessary trouble. Together with other members, she caused a lot of problems and got the wrong people mad at her.

When they were finished, they lay in bed and watched TV. Yoko flinched when her mind went back to how happily Amanda was smiling up in a man's face. "If I wanted you to do something to Amanda, would you?"

"Anything. You know I can't stand that junkie ass bitch."

"Okay, I want you to walk up to my wifey and smack the shit out of her."

"Are you serious?" she giggled.

"Dead serious. It doesn't have to be you. It can be one of your friends. I just want it done."

"Baby, I will personally smack that bitch in the face so hard she'll scrape both of her knees in the process." She kissed her on the chin. "Damn, Yoko. I hate to be on your bad side. What did she do to you?"

CHAPTER FOURTEEN
-ROMAN-

"She lived with no other though than to love and be loved by me."
- Edgar Allan Poe

Roman was dancing on stage when one of her regulars, Daw, waved her over with a fan of twenty-dollar bills clutched in his hand. Seductively, she moved toward him ready to serve, just as long as he didn't want more than a few leg waves so he could see her pussy smile or her booty pop.

He was selfish.

And known for making dancers do a little extra for a couple of dollars.

When she got in front of him she knelt on all fours, winked and turned around so that he could get a front row seat of her ass. "Damn, Romance," he said licking his lips and sitting back in his seat. "You know you get finer with time, right?"

"I'm glad you like the view, Daw." She lowered her body more so that her belly touched the stage sending her ass flying up in the air. The moment she saw him raise his hand, she figured she did what was necessary to warrant a few twenties in her boot. Instead she got a stiff finger into her pussy instead.

Seeing red, Roman spun around and gripped his neck so tightly Daw's heart stopped. She was no longer Romance. She was Goon. "If only you knew the things I could do to you right now," Roman said trembling. "How quick I could snuff out your——"

"Romance, your cell phone been ringing off the hook, girl," her partner Sparkle Skizz yelled raising Roman's cell phone in the air. She was standing in front of the dressing room, across the nightclub. Since they both had children, they would rotate phone duty if the other was on stage. To make sure they didn't miss any important calls, no matter who was dancing.

Roman released his throat and when Daw was about to talk crazy he felt Raymond and Owen standing behind him. Without turning around, Daw said, "Are those guns in your pockets or are you just happy to see me?"

"They dicks, nigga," Owen said. "The burner on that lower back too though." Owen pushed the barrel into him.

Owen was angrier than Raymond because he was feeling Roman and he saw what happened. The fucked up part was he didn't even get to feel her pussy himself.

He laughed and shook his head. He knew exactly who they were. In his idiot way of thinking, he assumed that because Carey wasn't working at the club anymore, her cousins would go with her. "I'm leaving," he responded taking one more look at Roman before walking off with his hands in the air.

While Raymond escorted Daw outside, Owen walked up to her. He helped her off the stage and stood in front of her. Standing 6'5", he was way taller. "You okay, Ro?"

"I'm fine," she said looking at the door Daw went out of. She wanted to hurt him so badly her clit vibrated but now was not the time. "I got to go see what's going on at home though. My husband probably called sounding all crazy and shit."

Hearing the word husband brought him back to reality. He took three steps back because Roman did not belong to him and she probably never would. "Well we'll be outside waiting. Do what you got to do."

★★★★

There was trouble at home. When she called Jackson he sounded frantic and her heart rapidly pumped blood. In their entire marriage, she never heard him so angry. He was always poised and acted as if he had everything under control. With trouble at home, there was nothing else to do. She had to talk to her manager and she was certain he wouldn't like it.

When she approached Evan he was sitting in his office looking at the computer screen. The same ugly navy blue hoodie he wore no matter what the season, because it was always cold in the club, was draped on the back of his chair.

He didn't bother looking up because he knew each stripper based on her scent. Roman smelled of strawberry perfume since she couldn't afford anything more expensive. "Don't tell me you have to leave, Roman," he said tapping at his computer. "Because we need you tonight. Got word that a few heavy hitters coming through VIP and they spending big."

"I know. And I'm so sorry. You know that I need this job but I have a family emergency." When he seemed unsympathetic she stepped in further. "I'll work whatever hours you need, Evan. Please. Just do me this solid."

Evan pushed the keyboard away from him and leaned back in his chair. "This is the last time, Roman. Once more and you no longer have a job here." He grabbed his keyboard again. "Now get out. I'm done with you."

****

Roman was sitting on the sofa with her elbows on her knees, trying desperately to understand what her husband was saying. "What do you mean you're about to lose your scholarship? I'm here with you every day, baby. I know how hard you work. I see the time you put into your studies."

"Some other shit is going on that I can't talk about."

"Other shit like what?" she asked with raised brows.

"I'm being sexually harassed."

"Harassed?" she repeated hoping he'd give her a name so that she could get rid of her the old fashioned way. "By who?"

"It's a long story. Just know that if I don't give her what she wants then she's threatening to go to the school board and lie on me. If she does, I'm sure it will be her word against mine. And she'll win. She's been at that school forever. It wouldn't even be a fair fight."

"What's her name?" she repeated slower. All she needed was her initial and she'd be dead before Good Morning America came on the next day.

"That's not important." He sighed pacing the living room floor. He looked over at her. "I just want you to know that I'm proud of you for stepping up. Moving into our new apartment next week will put me in a better mood. Maybe I'll be able to think straight." He sat next to her and kissed her on the forehead. "I love you, Roman. I don't know what I would do without you."

"I love you too, Jackson." She looked down. "But what are you going to do? About school?"

"I might have to do what I got to."

"What does that mean, Jackson?"

"Sleep with her."

She stood up and paced the room, her muscles quivering. The days of killing revisited her heart but she never thought she would consider murdering her own husband. "You would do that to me? After everything I've done?"

"Everything you've done?" he repeated. "Like what? Take a full time job as a cashier?" he laughed. "Ro, I know you work hard but I do too. If I get kicked out of med school, everything I went through by marrying you will be for nothing."

"But I don't want you to sleep with another woman, Jackson! What the fuck." She paced the floor some more. "You sound crazy even coming at me that way. What part of me would give you the impression that this shit is okay? That I would allow that?"

He walked over to the wall and leaned against it. "If I don't do what she wants, we have a problem. Because I need this degree to prove to everybody that they were wrong about me and they were wrong about you."

"That's all you're worried about? Your mother?" Roman shook her head and her face reddened. "You never cared about me." She walked toward the door.

"Where you going?"

"To clear my mind." She paused. "Just know that there's a part of me I never showed you before. But if it comes out again it's all your fault."

★★★★

Roman was dancing on the stage, looking for the dealer with the biggest pockets. Larceny was in her heart and robbery on her mind. She knew she would have to knock over many in order to cover Jackson's tuition, but for her husband she'd do it without blinking an eye. There was about to be major bodies lacing the streets of B-more and she would care less. Ever since she and Jackson argued last week about his scholarship, she had been an emotional wreck.

Although Jackson was still in school, she could feel his distance and every time he came home, she wondered if he slept with the professor even though he swore he hadn't.

Shit was hectic. Not only was she having problems at home but she hadn't seen or heard from Carey in months. It was unlike her not to return her calls and when she talked to Owen and Raymond she learned they hadn't heard from her either.

Where was Carey?

Her closest friend?

She just finished her set and was working the room but her heart wasn't on business. She was greeting the men who generously tipped her in the hopes that they would tip her again. But when she saw Daw, the nigga who slipped his finger in her pussy, her blood boiled over. He was on his cell phone talking to someone while looking across the club. "Hi, Romance," he said when she was walking in his direction.

"Fuck you, nigga," she responded before walking up to the man behind him who tipped her earlier when she was dancing. Turning on her charm, she said, "Thank you, cutie. I appreciate the love you showed me on stage."

He softly took her hand and said, "There's more where that came from. All you have to do is ask."

As he ran his mouth for some reason, Roman was zeroed in on the back of Daw's head. Something about how closely he held the phone against his ear captivated her attention. What was he up to? She knew the scent of larceny when she smelled it. At first she thought he was taking pictures of Honey Titties from his phone on the sly but when she looked across the room she saw Race Kennedy. He was eyeballing her like she had dollar signs on her forehead.

Race was in the VIP section and a silver bucket filled with ice and Ciroc sat in front of her. Her head nodded back and forth and it was obvious she was drunk. She was alone too. Judging by how sad she looked, Roman figured she missed Carey as much as she did. But why was she there? Was she waiting for Carey to show up?

"I'm telling you, man. This rich bitch is by herself," Daw said loud enough for Roman to hear. Although he wasn't screaming, it was obvious he was going to pull a caper. "Are you coming or not?" Daw continued. "'Cause if you don't I'ma do it myself." Apparently he didn't get the answer he wanted because he ended the call and stomped toward the bathroom.

Roman was about to alert Race that danger was near when the tipper she was talking to earlier yanked her roughly and said, "What on earth could be more important than me?" He slapped a wad of cash on the bar. "Because I'm paying if you staying."

****

Race was walking toward her car after just leaving the club. She had been sitting down so long that originally she thought she was good to drive. That she could handle the liquor she poured in her mouth, glassful after glassful. Once she got moving, she discovered she was wrong.

Race Kennedy was a wealthy woman. Powerful too. And because of it, she was wanted by a lot of jealous people, dead or alive. But at the moment she was drunk.

As a boss in the Pretty Kings organization, the largest drug ring in the DMV (DC, Maryland and Virginia), a lot of people would pay to see her returned if she were snatched. Unfortunately, Race was not thinking clearly when she chose to get inebriated. Her mind was on Carey and that she'd never see her again. How did she know?

She was responsible for killing her.

She didn't murder Carey because she was jealous of the relationship she shared with her husband. It was quite the contrary. From the moment she invited Carey into her life with her husband, she realized the three of them were the perfect combination. Race had a husband and a wife. She loved her dearly. Carey was no longer living because she violated code by getting pregnant by her husband. Which was something that Race couldn't do.

Out of guilt, Race went to the club to be next to her memory.

Race was almost to her car when Daw walked up behind her. "Don't scream," he said through clenched teeth. "You coming with me and you'll live as long as you don't make any crazy moves."

Race, considerably shorter than him, turned around and looked up into his eyes. Although drunk, she wasn't as scared of him as she should've been. She could tell he was a punk and if she had her hammer she would've brought him to his knees. But her mind was in the wrong place and she was bare. "Do you know who I am?" she asked plainly.

"Why else would I—"

Daw's sentence was severed when he felt something plunge into his lower back. When he tried to scream a hand was placed over his mouth and a silver blade slid across his throat slowly, causing the pinkness of his flesh to spill out.

All while Race watched.

When his body dropped, Race was staring up into the green eyes of Roman Tate. "Figured you could use the help," Roman said with a glistening red knife in her hand.

****

By T. Styles   170

The air conditioner seemed to be too high in the small diner that Race and Roman sat in as they attempted to get to know each other. After Roman laid Daw to rest, they tucked his body in the back of Race's car like trash. Race got on the phone and made a call to Sarge who was her right hand in the drug operation. In less than fifteen minutes, he had two carloads of loyal soldiers on the scene with one mission in mind, to make the corpse disappear.

With the realization that she was slipping, which she never did, Race's buzz vanished quickly. Now sober, she wanted to know more about the woman who killed so easily. The woman who saved her life. The way Race saw it, with skills like Roman's she could've used her on her squad. Being female would give her access to places that Sarge and the other soldiers couldn't roam.

A cup of coffee sat in front of Roman and a cup of water with lemon in front of Race. Neither was sure if they could trust the other so an intense but respectful power struggle occurred. "Where is Carey?" Roman asked flatly. "I'm looking for her." She took a sip of coffee.

Race hung her head low. "I don't know." She lied. "That's why I was in the club tonight. I talk to Carey every day and all of a sudden she's not returning my calls. It's been fucking my head up," she continued, taking a sip of water. "So tell me...were you two close?"

"Extremely. Like sisters."

"Did she tell you anything about me?"

"Not really," she said scanning Race's expression for the truth. "Just that she had a bond with you and your husband. Which I was wary about but respected."

Roman was getting mixed signals from Race so she was careful about what she said. As she looked her over, she could tell she came from money or had access to it. She was also very powerful. With one call, she made a body go away and that made Roman respectful of her but also wary.

Back in the day, Roman would've robbed her and taken everything she had on her person. But today, although she needed money, she would let her slide.

"I took care of her," Race continued. "I loved her very much. Me and my husband." She rubbed her hand down her face. "I know people might not understand our brand of love but it worked for us, you know?"

Roman shrugged. "I don't judge."

"I figured as much," she smiled. "Look, I called you here for a reason. The way you got rid of that nigga tonight was amazing. I've met killers before. Many. But your moves were calculating." She paused. "I have a place for someone of your skill set in my operation. That is, if you want it."

"Are you asking if I'm interested in murder for hire?"

"Yes."

Silence.

Roman looked toward her right, out of a window with several people walking by. She smiled at a little girl, who was certainly up past her bedtime, skipping with her family. While the young black couple held hands, the little girl was chasing the leash to the collar that was wrapped around her dog's neck.

In that moment, Roman thought of many things. She thought about her son. She thought about Jackson and losing him if he ever found out she was a stripper, let alone a murderer.

Yet there was one dominating thought above all. If she took Race's proposal, she saw herself as the animal the little girl was chasing.

She saw herself as a pet and it didn't sit well with her. Long ago, she made a decision when she left Billy Bob that she wouldn't be on anyone's leash again. "I'm sorry, Race." She paused. "I'm glad you're safe. But the life you are offering is not for me anymore."

Race reached in her purse and said, "Well let me give you something for your—"

"No," Roman shook her head when she saw she was handing her money. "Consider his death a gift from me to you. I hated that nigga." She stood up and smiled. "Good luck." She walked out, leaving Race's offer on the table.

****

Sylvia Ortiz had Jackson pressed against the blackboard in her classroom. The palm of her hand clutched his penis firmly in his slacks. She was trying to wake it up in the hopes that he would plunge it into her body. "I've waited long enough, Jackson," she said as she breathed heavily in his face. It seemed like the more he said no the more she wanted him.

Jackson's heart paced rapidly and his thoughts were fleeting. She may have thought he was resisting for the name of love but she was so wrong. There was something else he was hiding. "You don't know me, Sylvia. I'm begging you not to do this. All I want to do is take care of my—"

"Family," she said completing his sentence. "I already get it. But you're driving me crazy," she moaned. "I can't even look across the room without thinking of your dick. I bet it's so smooth. So pretty. Come on, Jackson. Let me see."

"Sylvia, stop," he yelled. "Fuck!"

"At first I was irritated but now the resisting game is turning me on. I never had to work so hard for something I wanted so badly. But let's both admit it, Jackson, this will happen between us sooner or later. Now you're going to give me what I want or I'll cause problems for you. Big ones." She leaned in for a kiss on his lips and he allowed her. "Is that what you want? Trouble?"

Although older, Sylvia wasn't an unattractive woman. She was just pushy and in his opinion that made her gross. He considered giving her some dick but when she snaked her tongue into his mouth, he pushed her away. "I'm sorry, Sylvia. I can't." He rushed out of the classroom leaving her alone.

****

The next morning, Jackson was headed for class. He was running late but he couldn't help it. He and Roman were up all night with Sailor who was running a temperature of over one hundred. As he drove to school, he replayed repeatedly in his mind how loving Roman was with their son. While he was sick, she sang to him, wiped cool water mixed with alcohol over his forehead and rocked him in her arms.

Things were different now. When he was a baby she didn't have the patience for him. His cries when he was teething or wanted to be picked up drove her crazy. She automatically assumed something was wrong with her, that she was a bad mother. And because of it, the bond between her and her son wasn't as cohesive in the earlier years.

But when he grew older and she realized the cries didn't mean she was a bad parent, things changed. Before long, they would spend hours alone in the bedroom and he always wondered what they were talking about, what she was teaching him. In the end, Sailor became her right hand man and they shared a bond that he couldn't describe.

Trying not to miss too much, Jackson ran through the hallway on the way to his classroom. He was almost there when a student instructed him to visit the Provost's office instead. His heart immediately pumped because an unexpected meeting with Matt Santos was never a good thing.

Slowly Jackson strolled toward his office and when he arrived he wasn't surprised to see him staring his way. What did shock him was Sylvia sitting on the edge of his desk with her arms folded over her breasts as she stared in his direction.

That dirty bitch, he thought as his nostrils flared.

"Jackson, have a seat," Matt said as he cleared his throat. His fingers were clenched in front of him.

"I'll remain standing, sir," Jackson said respectfully. "If you don't mind."

"Have it your way," he shrugged. "I asked you here because it has been brought to my attention that you cheated on a recent exam in Ms. Ortiz's class. I'm told you were looking at the answers on another student's paper."

By T. Styles   174

Jackson gasped. "What? I would never do anything like that! I work too hard!"

"Well Ms. Ortiz has verified it," he said firmly. "And she was brave enough to come face you directly. Even though I told her it was not necessary."

"I don't care what she says it's not true!" he yelled as his fists clenched. "She's lying on me because I won't fuck her."

"Mr. Tate!" Matt Santos yelled. "Watch your language!"

"It's the truth! That's the only reason she came to you with this shit."

"She didn't come to me with this originally. Like I said earlier, she verified the facts. It was Martin Locks who came to my office. If I'm not mistaken, he is a student in your class and this matter has been bothering him for a while." He continued, "As you know the school has a zero tolerance policy on cheating and as a result, your scholarship is under review."

Jackson stepped deeper into the office and placed a hand on his chest. "I'm begging you, Mr. Santos. Please don't do this. All of my life I have wanted to be a doctor. I have been ousted by my mother. I have been neglecting my son by working so hard on my studies. And my wife works the midnight shift as a cashier to pay the bills."

Sylvia rolled her eyes upon hearing about his wife. She was envious of a woman she didn't know.

"I have placed everything on the line," Jackson continued. "Just to be a doctor. And I can truly say that I want nothing more."

"Well you should've thought about that before violating school policy," Matt Santos said firmly. "Now leave my office. I'm done with you."

Soft tears rolled down Jackson's face. He was defeated.

As he looked at the way she felt comfortable enough to sit her funky ass on his desk, he knew what was going on. Like almost every student in school, Matt was also fucking her. It was in the way Matt held his shoulders up. In the way he allowed her to run the meeting even though she was silent. Like so many other men, he fell victim to her charms. Still he had to try to stay.

"Please, Sylvia," Jackson pleaded. "You know this isn't true. Don't do this to me. Don't do this to my family."

"You should've done what was necessary to complete your studies," she said hinting to Jackson's constant rejection of her pussy. "Now you heard Mr. Santos. Please leave."

****

Roman tried to console Jackson but he pushed her away, forcing her into the flimsy television, which sat on the stand in their living room. Most of their things were in boxes because they just moved into a new apartment in Baltimore County. Courtesy of Roman's job as a stripper.

It wasn't the mansion Jackson was accustomed to but it was far better than where they had been living for years.

"Give me space, Roman," he barked as if she were the enemy. "I don't need this shit right now. All I wanted was to be a doctor! That's it! And they took that from me! My life is fucking ruined."

"Don't say that, Jackson," she said calmly. She was trying to be a supportive wife but he was treating her as if she was the one who did him wrong.

"How the fuck you sound? Huh?" he looked over at her. "I possibly lost my scholarship, Roman! Why isn't my life ruined?"

"Because you have me! And your son! If you can't get a scholarship from there maybe you can go to school somewhere else. I'm not as smart as you but I do know we can work through this," she said trying to fill his mind with hopes of the future. "As a family."

"And tell me how that will be possible? On your cashier salary?" he frowned. "You can't even read, Roman!"

Upon hearing the truth, she threw her hands over her lips and her face trembled. Immediately, she was brought to tears. She assumed he didn't know and when she learned he was aware it was during a moment of anger. When he tried to use her problem against her, she felt devastated. "You knew?"

"Of course I did!" he yelled.

"But you never said anything?"

"No!" he yelled as he continued to pace the room. "I figured you'd tell me when you were ready. Plus, it didn't matter. You were supposed to be a housewife." He paused for a breath. "I don't even know how you got that job." He paced more. "I hate to be mean but you need to stop being naive. I have sheltered you all of our marriage, Roman, and I'm tired of it. You don't know nothing about the dark side of life. I tried to keep that from you."

She shook her head and remained silent. If only he knew how many funerals her crimes caused.

"A medical education is not cheap and at the end of the day I can't afford it without the scholarship. Neither can you working as a cashier. Like I said, it's over for me. I might as well go back to being the nigga I used to be."

As he continued to verbally bash her, Roman felt worthless. He was right. She couldn't afford an education, even with her stripper salary. There was one thing she could think of to save his career. "Maybe you should call your mother again, Jackson." She exhaled. "It's time."

Jackson paced the floor before stopping in front of the phone. Before picking up the handset, he took a moment to look down at it. As if he were trying to predict what Debra would say ahead of time. When he was ready he took a deep breath as if he were about to jump in a pool and called. The phone rang once before she answered. "Jackson," she said flatly in lieu of hello.

"Mother."

"Is my grandchild okay?"

"Yes," he cleared his throat. "He had a fever the other day but now he's fine."

"I'm not surprised that he was sick. He has an ignoramus for a mother."

Jackson looked at Roman and made a decision not to tell her about what she said. "Mother, I need help."

"Tell me what's new. You always need something."

"Mother, this is serious."

"Everything in your life is serious. But things were serious when you married that girl. Things were serious when you had a son with her, whom I love dearly. So tell me, my son. What do you deem serious now?"

"I lost my scholarship, mother. It's gone."

"Jackson, how?" she gasped. The concern was written all in her voice.

"It's a long story. Just know that it's not because of anything I did. I worked hard. Poured all of my heart into my education and it was for nothing."

She sighed. "Well…as you know, education has always been important to me." She paused. "Okay, Jackson." She exhaled. "I will help you."

Jackson smiled and looked at Roman with a large grin. "Really, mother?"

"Of course. All you have to do is bring yourself and my grandson to my house by the end of this week. You do that and you can have anything you need to carry out your degree. If you don't I don't know what to tell you."

"And Roman?" he said in a low voice. "What of my wife?"

"She is not welcome in my home. And you know that."

Jackson rubbed his throbbing temples. "Mother…she's my wife. And I'm her husband! I can't leave her!"

"Another bad decision that was made without me."

"Are you trying to push me back over the edge?" He paused. "When you know what can happen?" he huffed and puffed. "Mother, I can't leave her. I just can't."

"I don't want you over the edge, son. It took many years of therapy to get you to the point where you are now. This is why I didn't want you to leave the house so soon. You weren't ready." She paused. "Now I have delivered my terms. If you disagree, remain where you are." She sighed. "Call me when you've made your decision. Either way, you must live with it."

Click.

Jackson sat the phone on the hook softly.

"What did she say?" Roman said in a hushed tone.

"She said she'd help me if I moved back in with her. She wants me to bring Sailor."

Her shoulders dropped. "Without me?"

He nodded his head. "I can't concentrate right now. I got to get out of here. I need some air." He grabbed his wallet and car keys and walked out of the door.

****

Jackson sat in his car looking at a group of white women walk on campus. They were carefree. Totally unaware that a troubled man was about to resort to his old ways of resolving issues. The moment they split into three different ways, he followed who appeared to be the meeker.

As she texted on her phone, while walking into her building, her guard was totally down. But the moment she stuck her key into her apartment door, she felt an evil presence behind her. Horrified, her voice was trapped in her throat when she turned around and looked up into the eyes of a serial rapist. One who tried to deny his past by focusing on his lifelong dream of being a doctor.

"Please—"

She tried to scream but he stole her in the face with his leather glove covered fist. She dropped to the hallway floor and he pulled her inside of her apartment by her red hair. He had two things on his mind.

Extreme torture.

Extreme rape.

****

Roman sat in the middle of the floor on a leather recliner. Before her were the most beautiful women she'd ever met in her life, and this group included Race. The leader, a brown-skinned woman about 5'7, smiled at her, although Roman could feel her danger. Dressed in green fatigue pants and a black t-shirt, Roman wondered what pattern life designed to cause her to be a drug lord. Behind her was a gorgeous white woman with red flowing hair and to her left was another woman with blue dreads and tats on every visible part of her body.

Roman never saw women drug bosses before and she respected them immediately.

"My name is Bambi Kennedy," the leader announced. "And you are here because Race has told me great things about you." She walked closer and stopped, allowing Roman the proper amount of personal space. "I don't know what we would have done if she would've died. I do know the city would have been red with blood." She paused. "I appreciate your diligence." She paused. "We need people like you on our team."

Roman remained quiet. She thought it best to listen instead of speaking. It was a goon's way of life.

"We have an issue with a recent enemy who has moved into our territory," Bambi continued. "Worthy soldiers are not an issue for my organization. I command a huge team of killers who are able bodied and ready."

"So what is the concern?"

"We need someone who can act as a chameleon. A person who can move around easily without being spotted. One with experience." She paused. "Before I go any further I must know something. And I would appreciate your candor."

"What is it?" Roman swallowed in suspense.

"Are you the one they call Goon? From Baltimore? The one who seemed to disappear without ever getting caught, leaving a trail of bodies behind?"

Roman wondered how she knew. "If I told you then you'd know more than is necessary."

Bambi laughed having her question answered in a satisfactory way. "Before I saw you, and your height, I knew Goon was a woman. Only a woman could keep a secret this long and get away with it. Men often require the credit for such acts. So they boast. But you don't."

Roman smiled at the compliment but remained poised. "Who do you need done?" She asked plainly.

"It's not necessarily who but how many."

"I'm listening."

"Before we get into that let's talk about what you desire."

"What makes you think I desire anything?"

"We all want something, Roman. And I'm told that you have needs that we may be able to meet."

Roman sighed as she considered her home situation. When Jackson left the house last night, her heart was torn when he didn't come home. He may have thought she couldn't help. He may have thought that she didn't have any valuable skill sets but he was wrong. There was one skill that she was good at. One that she could always fall back on if need be.

Murder.

"I need money. For my husband."

"And we have plenty," Bambi assured her.

"But he can't know what I'm doing. This has to remain anonymous."

"I respect anonymity," Bambi nodded. "And we never get involved in personal affairs even if we become enemies." She paused. "I'm about money. And since we're on that issue. What is your fee?"

"Twenty-five thousand dollars." Roman had no idea how much money she needed for his education but she was hoping that would be a start. But when the women giggled Roman moved uneasily in her seat. She was tired of people laughing at her intelligence level. "What's funny?"

"Roman, for the people we need you to murder, we are willing to pay you one million dollars."

Roman swallowed hard and her eyes widened upon hearing their proposal. When she was in route to the meeting, she never dreamed they'd offer her that much cash. The most paper she held at once was a few thousand from the hustlers she knocked over who carried more than necessary on them at one time. But a million? Would her lifestyle change? Would she be able to hide her newfound wealth?

She adjusted uneasily in her seat. It was the first time she lost her cool manner. "Excuse me...did you say a million?"

"You heard me correctly," Bambi confirmed. "I don't want you to knock over a few dope boys. We have a squad for that. The people I'm seeking your assistance for have caused major problems for my organization. So they require care and confidentiality. You've demonstrated that when you killed back in the day and maintained your silence...even now. Mellvue, the girlfriend of our biggest enemy, has family in the area but she won't be as easy to get as the others. Her movements are sporadic and he takes care to protect her."

"I understand. But I will need help."

"You can use some of our men."

"I'm sorry, Bambi. But in order for me to do this properly, I need to work with men I trust. I hope that's okay."

"We will have Sarge run a background check on the men you've chosen. If they come back clean I'm okay with that."

"A million dollars is a lot of money," Roman continued. "Just for a few people."

Bambi walked closer and looked down at her. "I know, Roman. A million dollars is hefty." She paused. "That's why I must tell you. For the money, you will owe me a hundred lives."

CHAPTER FIFTEEN
-YOKO-

"That the play is the tragedy, man."
- Edgar Allan Poe

Yoko's relationship was in trouble.

Ever since Felicia slapped Amanda in the face, Amanda was afraid that someone was out to get her. Yoko tried to play up that insecurity by telling her to stay home to be safe and it worked for a few days. But as time went on, she was back ripping and running the streets. Nothing Yoko did could save her relationship because Amanda appeared to be encased in the streets.

Yoko's answer to help her broken heart was Felicia.

She needed someone who wanted her around. Although they couldn't maintain a conversation with each other without fighting, the sexual chemistry was explosive.

They were just finishing up their sex session and were lying on their backs looking up at the ceiling. "You've been here a lot lately, Yoko."

"You don't like me here?"

"I love it."

"So what's the problem?" Yoko sat up and looked over at her.

"I want to know if you're trying to make this into something else." She paused. Being with Yoko surpassed the fetish thing when it came to Felicia. She actually liked her. "I haven't seen you this much since never."

Yoko grew weary of the questions. The only reason she was around so much was because she wanted her to help with the pain. It hurt Yoko to come home only for Amanda not to be there so she wanted to give her a taste of her own medicine by not being available. Not being home didn't stop Amanda from seeing her new man but it made her feel better.

"I'm here because I want to be," Yoko said honestly. "Now you trying to go to your spot?" She sat up on the bed before hopping down.

"Whaaaaat?" she said tilting her head. "I must've laid it on you good this time. Since when do you treat for dinner?"

"You trying to eat or what?" Yoko asked with an attitude. She had a little money on her because she saw Erin earlier in the day and he laid two hundred on her even though he complained the entire time. She gave one hundred bucks to her brothers and without Amanda begging for cash, she was left holding something. "I'm hungry and I want you to order some food."

"So you really treating me to Ships? The one in B-more?"

"Whatever you want," she responded. "I'll call Erin and he'll bring it to us. He talks shit but he always does what I want him—"

When there was a knock at the door Yoko dipped and hid in the supply closet in the kitchen. Even though Amanda was doing her thing, she didn't want anybody to see her at Felicia's house. The last thing she needed was the hood to be talking.

"I can't believe you hiding," she giggled. "In the closet at that."

"Bitch, just go see who it is," she whispered. "I have to hide. There's not a lot of red midgets in Baltimore."

Felicia shook her head, got up and answered the door. She thought she was being ridiculous since Amanda was being a whore around town. "Who is it?" Felicia asked trying to conceal her laughter at Yoko hiding.

"UPS," a woman said.

The moment Yoko heard the voice, chills ran down her spine. Although she was trying to conceal her speech, and did a good job, Yoko was with her when she killed many. She knew the voice belonged to Roman.

What was she doing at Felicia's?

Clueless that her life was in danger, Felicia did a little dance thinking that the new shoes she ordered finally arrived. But the moment she opened the front door, a knife was plunged into her stomach, piercing both her small and large intestines. Roman preferred knives as her weapon of choice because it was minus the gunpowder and evidence.

From inside of the closet, through the slats, Yoko saw it all. Roman was dressed as a white woman delivering packages and the costume was so good that at first Yoko thought she was wrong. Maybe she wasn't seeing Roman. Until she said, "Goon."

There was the proof!

Yoko's heart beat rapidly upon hearing her moniker. Part of her wanted to come out and ask her where she'd been and why she broke her heart by leaving her life. But the other part of her was angry and wondered if she was still in the city why she never reached out. It wasn't like Yoko's residence changed.

But now was not the time to approach Roman about the past. She wanted to know where she was going. When Roman left the apartment Yoko quickly ran out of the closet. When she saw Felicia lying in her doorway with her eyes open, she felt slight remorse but the feeling exited quickly because she had to know where her friend was going. What she had been up to.

Carefully Yoko peeked her head out of the door and when she saw Roman hop into a white van with a UPS decal she shook her head. Everyone knew the UPS vehicles were brown and Yoko felt Roman could have done a better job faking it.

Everything about Roman was illegal at the moment. She just committed murder. And was driving with a fake license since she couldn't pass the driver's test due to not being able to read. Although Billy Bob taught her how to operate a car years ago, she needed GPS just to tell her where to go and when to turn.

Yoko hopped in her Rav 4 and trailed Roman until she was in front of a warehouse. Once Roman parked, she whistled loudly and the dock's door rolled upward. Two men stepped out, dressed in all black with hoodies. They signaled for Roman to back in the vehicle slowly. When she stopped the back of the van was blocking the dock's entrance.

Roman didn't come out of the driver's side door. Instead, she entered the warehouse through the back of the van. Once she parked, there was no activity for about fifteen minutes. Then suddenly an elderly man, who was really Roman, came out of the warehouse's office entrance holding onto a cherry wood cane. The two hooded men followed.

One of them, Raymond, yelled back at the other and said, "You got the batteries for this joint?" He raised a tiny speaker in the air. It was small enough to be concealed on his body and the curiosity was killing Yoko.

"Oh shit! Give me a sec!" Owen yelled.

A minute later, Owen returned and placed batteries into the device. "Let me put 'em in."

"Can ya'll hurry up," Roman yelled from the driver's seat. "We gonna miss him."

Raymond and Owen busied themselves with the speaker and after a while, gunshots rang out. They were so loud that Yoko ducked lower in her truck, thinking someone was shooting. When she realized the sounds came from the speaker she frowned. "What could you be doing with a speaker that makes gunshot noises?"

Owen stuffed the speaker in his jean pocket and Raymond tore the UPS decal off the van and changed the license plate. When they were done they got into the van and pulled off. There was no way Yoko was getting left. She stuck with them close enough not to lose them but far enough not to be spotted. The scene was getting more interesting by the second.

When the van finally stopped they were in front of Mondawmin Mall. Roman hopped out of the van holding the cane and suddenly her gait changed. She was no longer Roman. She had successfully transformed to an older man who could barely walk.

"This bitch is good," Yoko thought to herself. "Outstanding even!"

She remained seated in her truck for a moment when all of a sudden a crowd of people rushed outside of the mall yelling and screaming. They were clearly terrified.

"What the fuck are you up to, Roman?" Yoko asked to herself as she watched the frantic crowd spill into the parking lot and street. To prevent from being seen, she slipped further down in her seat. But she was still spotted.

"Somebody shooting," a woman yelled as she banged on Yoko's window, startling her to death. "Save yourself!"

But Yoko didn't move. She wasn't certain about what was going on in the mall but she was sure Roman had everything to do with it. Twenty minutes passed before Raymond and Owen returned, with Roman coming some moments later. Yoko was so amused by her ex-best friend that she felt as if she were watching a movie.

"I don't know what's going on, Roman. But I have all intentions on finding out."

CHAPTER SIXTEEN
-ROMAN-

"Is conquered at last."
- Edgar Allan Poe

Roman killed two people in one day. And the only thing she could think about was that she was certain that someone followed her.

But who?

Killing Felicia was cut and dry. She had her name and picture so she buried the knife into her intestines the moment she saw her face, before slicing her throat. But trying to get a hold of Larry, leader of the Reapers, was challenging so she didn't cover her tracks like she normally did. She was too excited. Which may have been why someone was able to trail her.

Larry didn't have a set routine. His moves were erratic and because of it, he wasn't home every night. As a hired killer, it took Roman a moment to figure out a creative way to catch him. And then it dawned on her after watching him in places she couldn't reach him. He had a shoe passion. And passions could be used as weaknesses. So she decided to use his against him.

Roman spent months trying to figure out a plan of action and ironically it came to her when she was taking Sailor to the park. It rained the day before and he ruined his shoes. He loved them so much he slept with them due to not being used to new clothes. He was so sad and even though she promised she'd buy him more he was still unnerved thinking that they couldn't afford them. And that's when she got an idea.

She would place mud traps along the place where he parked his car. Knowing that whenever he did show up, he would walk into it and be forced to replace his footwear. It wasn't an easy job to keep the traps moist. She would have either Raymond or Owen go to his house every other day to water the traps that lined his streets. It didn't matter that Larry had over fifty pairs. They were all unique and one ruined pair would destroy his entire wardrobe. It was a weak idea but at the time, it was all she had.

Since Larry didn't come home often, the matter was time sensitive. Roman received the call from Owen that he was home after he saw him in the camera they placed near his house.

When his shoes were ruined Larry didn't even go into the house; instead, he turned around and headed to the mall. Part A worked but Part B would not be simple. Larry watched his back a lot and would never allow someone to get close enough to kill him. Roman could've sprayed everybody near him in a drive by shooting but she didn't believe in killing innocents. So she thought of another plan instead.

Cause a diversion in the mall.

Using the small speaker, Raymond turned it on and the moment he stepped inside of the building he yelled, "Someone's shooting!" Without anybody seeing the killer, they ran for safety based on the sound of gunfire. This allowed Roman to follow Larry and then pass him and find the closet.

In the end, Larry was dead.

She slit his throat and the job was done.

Putting the matter out of her mind, when she got to her apartment she slid out of the car and approached the door. Jackson hadn't been home in two days so she didn't expect him to be there now. He wasn't even aware that she had a plan. That she was now a wealthy woman.

The possibility of his scholarship being revoked brought him down and he disconnected from his family. Realizing she only had a little time to pick up Sailor, she wanted to shower, get dressed and make herself presentable before going to his school. But when she opened the door Jackson was there.

"Baby, I'm sorry," he said standing in the middle of the living room. "For not being here for the last couple of days. I know that was weak on my part." Instead of feeling rage, she rushed toward him and wrapped her arms around his waist, squeezing him tightly. He kissed the top of her head and looked down at her. "I didn't think you would forgive me so easily. I'm so grateful."

"Where have you been, baby?" Roman asked gazing into his brown eyes. She hugged him again.

"I just needed some time away. But I was out of line for not coming home and not calling."

"It doesn't matter. I'm so happy you're home. There's some rapist roaming around the city and I was concerned for me and Sailor's safety," she said trying to appear meek so that he would stay home more. To protect them both.

"Well I'm here now," he said. "And no one will harm you or my son." He would know since he was the one committing the rapes.

She gripped him tighter, afraid to let him go. "You were right, Jackson. You were so right about everything you said. With your scholarship and stuff."

The smile wiped off his face and he walked away. "It's over now, baby." He sat on the sofa. "I'm just going to have to see if I can find another way to go to school. They officially revoked my scholarship today."

"That's what I'm trying to tell you. It's okay," Roman said as she sat on the floor between his legs. "I have a plan. I know how to make it work."

He sighed, thinking she was being naive again. "Let me worry about my education. You just take care of our son. He's going to need you because I might be in my head over the next few days. I might need some time away from the house to get my shit together but I won't stay out anymore."

"Jackson, I'm serious this time. I have a new job now. That's why I'm looking all crazy. I found a job at a call center that will help pay for my education and the education of my spouse." She rubbed his leg. "I'm going back to school too. To learn how to read," she lied.

"I'm confused."

"I know," she kissed his knee. "You might not be able to go to Johns Hopkins because of the trouble you're having but there are other medical schools in the area. Your grades are great and I don't think it will be a problem."

Jackson looked down into her green eyes and saw that she was serious. "Are you really saying that you can afford my tuition, Roman?" His eyes were wide and hopeful. "Is that what you mean?"

"Yes," she giggled before kissing his lips again. "And with the extra money I'm making, we could get a better spot. I know we just moved here but I want you to have a comfortable place so you can focus on your studies. And I want Sailor to have a backyard so he can be a kid."

He stood up and wiped his hands down his face. He was suddenly sick with jealousy. "Roman, are you selling your body? Are you giving my pussy away for profit?"

She rose up quickly, hoping to get that notion out of his mind. "No! Why would you ask me something like that?" She paused. "Think, Jackson. If I was a whore, I doubt very seriously I'd make enough money for a new home and your education too. You're not going to school to be an electrician! You're getting a medical degree! Being a whore or even a stripper is not in me," she lied. "I'd be too scared. You know that about me." She giggled. "Aren't you always the one calling me naive?"

He looked deeper into her eyes. "You do know if I find out you're lying to me it's over, right? I would take Sailor from you and you'd never see him again."

"I'm not lying, Jackson."

He shook his head and wiped his hand down his face. "If only I knew earlier," he whispered to himself, thinking of the ten women he raped so far, which reignited his fire.

Roman stood up and followed. "What do you mean?"

"Nothing, baby," he said as he pulled her in and rubbed her shoulders. "Roman, I'm so sorry for asking you if you would sell your body. I know you aren't that type of girl and I'm grateful for you. And for staying loyal to me and our family."

"I'd do anything for you, Jackson. Anything."

****

Roman and Jackson lay on their bed that was dampened with their sweat. Roman just finished giving him the blowjob of a lifetime but for some reason he couldn't cum. In all of the years they'd been married, he always responded to her sexually, except now. "Baby, are you okay? Am I doing it right?"

"Get on all fours and turn over!" he yelled.

When she moved too slowly, he flipped her over roughly and tore into her pussy like a dog in heat. At first he was gentle but the more he thought about his latest rape conquests the wilder he got. His last victim was about twenty-five and fought him so hard that when he finally raped her he felt as if he came inside of her body for hours. It was the best feeling he'd ever experienced.

As Jackson spread her legs wider, she closed her eyes and visions of her latest murders visited her mind. But he successfully pushed her out of those thoughts when he pounded her harder. "You dirty, bitch," he said. "Look at you lying down there looking like a slut. You like this rough dick, don't you? Tell me, slutty bitch! Talk to me!"

"Jackson, are you okay?" she asked as she looked back at him. He never talked to her in that manner and it surprised her more than anything else.

His face contorted in an evil glare but softened when her green eyes lay upon him. "I'm sorry, honey," he said pulling out of her. "I went too far. Please forgive me."

She was just about to ask him what was wrong when her flip phone vibrated on the dresser. It was for Goon business only. She scooted toward it and saw it was her new boss. Race. Roman exhaled because she knew Jackson would not like the late night calls. Since she took the money, her time was no longer her own. Whenever Race called, she was on the clock. "I got to answer this real quick," she said raising the phone. "It's my new job."

"Your new job calls you this late? It's 10:22 at night, Roman. You're a married woman."

"I know, baby. But what can I do?"

He jumped out of bed and snatched his jeans and shirt off the floor. "You do what you got to. I'll be home later."

Roman knew he was angry but she had to give up a part of her life to fulfill his dreams. She only hoped he'd appreciate her for it later. When he left she focused back on the cell phone. "I'm here."

"It's time for the next one. Her name is Lisa Sport."

CHAPTER SEVENTEEN
-YOKO-

"Hell rising from a thousand thrones shall do it reverence."
- Edgar Allan Poe

I t finally happened.

The thing Yoko had been trying to avoid. Mills Lighthouse was arrested for Paige's murder.

Yoko sat across from Mills, a partition separating them. The words snitch bitch, although faint, were etched into the hard plastic divider. Yoko focused on the harsh words as her brother said something she never wanted to hear. "Somebody talking, Yoko. About Paige Kelly."

"How do you know?" Yoko asked although she knew they couldn't speak much. Everything they did was recorded and watched.

"The police know too much. About what I was wearing and shit like that."

Yoko hung her head down. It seemed like she was having bad day after bad day with no end in sight. "Okay, Mills. I'll ask around."

"I don't think you'll have to go far. Whoever talking is close to home." He hung up the phone and walked toward the guard. "I'm ready."

****

Yoko was on the road, about a mile from her house when she reached a red light. Since trouble was brewing with her family, she needed to speak to her other brothers at once. Everything was urgent and there could be no delay. "What's taking so long?" she asked as she pushed back into her seat.

When she glanced to the right, she noticed someone had a car just like Amanda's. A beat up silver Honda. But when Yoko leaned closer to peer into the car she saw it wasn't a car like Amanda's.

By T. Styles   194

It *was* Amanda's.

Amanda was alone so Yoko pulled some feet ahead to prevent from being seen. Who was she waiting on? From where she parked, she was able to look at Amanda through the rearview mirror. She appeared jittery and kept looking out of her window. As if she was afraid of something or somebody.

Five minutes later, the same man Amanda was with some weeks earlier approached the car and eased into the passenger's seat. Yoko trembled and tears rolled down her face although she swatted them away.

She's in love, Yoko thought. *She fucking loves him!*

It was one thing to have sex with someone but if Amanda fell in love, who would care about Yoko? She didn't even have Felicia anymore thanks to Roman. No one cared if she lived or died. She needed her attention no matter how wretched.

Amanda and the stranger spoke for an hour, Yoko watching it all, before he got out and slid into his own car, a blue sedan, about six spaces back. When he left Yoko hopped out of the car and knocked on Amanda's window, catching her before she pulled off. At first Amanda's eyes widened upon realizing her secret was now revealed. Then she lowered her head, unlocked the door and allowed her inside.

Before saying a word, Yoko looked ahead for a moment to gather her thoughts. It was hard to express herself. Since she was a little girl, she was taught that emotions were weak and left you vulnerable. But Maria was dead, Roman moved on with her life and her brothers were too self-centered to care about her. She needed Amanda if for nothing else because she was there. "Do you love him?" Yoko finally asked.

"What are you talking about?" she said anxiously. "No, Yoko! Of course not. It's not like that."

"Then are you pregnant with his baby?"

"No! Don't you remember? I can't have kids!"

"Then what the fuck is going on? I'm confused! You're never home! You got me running around Baltimore whoring myself for your drug habit. Tell me what's up now!"

"I never asked you to—"

"No you didn't but you made me feel like I didn't have a choice," she replied, cutting her off. "Blackmailing me for your love! I would've done anything for you, Amanda! When my best friend left me you were all I had and you said you would never leave." She paused. "I need to know right now what's going on!"

Amanda opened her mouth and instead of words pouring out, she sobbed. She lowered her face on her steering wheel and wept for what felt like an eternity. Yoko allowed her that time, just as long as when she was done she would make everything clear. When she was finished howling she eased up, wiped her face and looked at Yoko. "He's a detective."

"A detective?" she frowned. "What kind?" she roared.

"A homicide detective. He's asking about Paige Kelly."

Now it all made sense. Amanda betrayed her just like Mills said. She betrayed her family. So she pulled the gun from her waist that she recently stole from Erin's house. Angry, she pointed it in her direction. "I need you to give me one reason why I shouldn't kill you right now." The gun trembled in her hand as she awaited an answer.

"Because I haven't told him anything, Yoko." She covered her mouth with her fingers. She knew Yoko could be violent but never towards her. "He doesn't know shit. Think about it, you only told me a little bit!"

"But I saw you with that nigga. Twice. Today and some weeks back. You were laughing and shit with him. Like ya'll were together or something."

She sighed. "I admit. I was extra friendly. But you must believe me; he hasn't gotten any information from me. The only reason he hasn't pushed more and locked me up is because he likes me and he flirts with me a little."

"You fucked him, didn't you?"

"No. I mean, not really."

Yoko looked into her eyes and lowered the gun. When it came to Amanda, she never knew if she was being honest or not. Yoko was too weak in love with Amanda to know if she was telling the truth. She leaned back into the seat, taking a moment to look at the roof. "Then who is talking about the case? Because I saw Mills in jail today and he said they know something. About everything."

Amanda glanced over at Yoko and then leaned back into her seat. With a shaky voice, she said, "They found five witnesses, Yoko. One person who saw Mills shoot Paige and the other four who were at the pool the day Joshua almost killed that little girl. They are building a case."

Yoko's hand suddenly felt clammy and she wiped them on her jeans. "How do I know you ain't one of the five?"

"Because I know their names." She swallowed. "He told them to me one of the times we met."

Yoko's eyes bulged. "And you didn't fuck him for the information? Because if you didn't it doesn't make any sense. It don't add up."

"I sucked his dick," she said, her lip quivering. "That's it, Yoko. I didn't want to tell on you. And I didn't want to get locked up so I did what I had to."

Yoko's entire disposition changed. Through clenched teeth she said, "Give me every one of their names. And don't leave out an initial."

CHAPTER EIGHTEEN
-ROMAN-

TWO WEEKS LATER

"Men die nightly in their beds."
- Edgar Allan Poe

Roman was leaned to the side in the driver's seat of a rented black E Class Benz. When she glanced in the rearview mirror she was surprised because even she couldn't recognize her reflection. A baseball cap concealed her green eyes, giving her a smooth, masculine flow. The gold chain that hung from her neck rocked against her fresh black Polo shirt as she went deeper into character. She succeeded in looking like a fine ass nigga and she knew it too.

Now it was time to meet, seduce and kill her next victim.

Lisa Sport was outside with her friends in front of Rich Mane Hair Salon in Washington D.C. On her VIP shit, she called an hour before she was coming and told Donna to get her chair ready. Lisa was a member of the Southeast Kittens and had been trying to throw salt into the Pretty Kings organization by arranging for a few of their dealers to get robbed of their packages.

She was good too because men could not deny her sexuality and for their lust they paid with their lives.

But unlike a few members of her crew, including Felicia, she was not easy to predict. But her weakness, just like Larry's, would be her undoing. For Lisa it was her hair. And she didn't let anybody touch it but Donna so all Roman had to do was wait for her to make an appointment. After paying one of the new hairdressers five hundred, she told Raymond when she would be coming in.

Even though Lisa had a hit on her head, she took a few moments to kick shit out in front of the shop. The girls were in all talk mode until Roman pulled up on them and rolled the window down. In a deep voice she said, "'Scuse me, ladies. Is Joy still inside?"

Lisa proved to be the car freak Race told Roman she was because the moment she saw the luxury car, she was ready to slide a condom on it and fuck it on the spot. "Why you looking for Joy when you could be hanging with me?"

"Work, bitch!" her chubby but cute hairdresser cheered. "Good gawd, that nigga fine."

Roman fake blushed and leaned back in the seat. "Come on, ma. I 'preciate the compliment but Joy's my cousin. It ain't even like that." Roman looked at her expensive watch, hoping Lisa would spot the luxury timepiece. Lisa did and she licked her lips. "She was supposed to be here earlier. I guess she got tired of waiting and bounced."

"I don't know where you going but the trip up here doesn't have to be in vain," Lisa said walking closer to the ride. The vanilla air freshener brushed her inner nostrils, getting her more aroused. "Ain't nobody in the shop but the stylists and they getting ready to close. But I have all night." She licked her lips. "If you do."

Roman appeared frustrated upon hearing the news that Joy left. "Damn, I had to give her this paper too." She patted the large wad in her jean pocket. Lisa's eyes roamed toward the baggy True Religion jeans Roman wore and her mouth watered as she calculated the fund. "Well thanks anyway, ma." She threw the car in drive as if she had intentions on leaving without her next victim.

"Wait a minute," Lisa said walking closer to the car and leaning in the window. "The least you can do is ask for my number. I mean I'm doing everything but throwing myself on top of your windshield. Got me looking pressed in front of my friends and shit."

Roman chuckled heartedly like a dude. "I got one better, ma. How 'bout you slide in and we grab something to drink right quick." She looked at her watch again. "I got a few minutes to spare."

Before Roman could change her mind, Lisa went into morph mode and before long was in the passenger seat with the seatbelt pressing against her breasts. "See ya'll later," she said as she waved at all of the jealous bitches who were angry that she didn't give anybody else a chance to book Roman. "So where we going?" Lisa asked.

"Somewhere nice," Roman said a little colder than earlier. She caught her fish and didn't feel like playing the games anymore.

This was business.

With her victim on her hook, she pulled off and eased into traffic.

Not trying to anger him and get thrown out like she had before, Lisa decided to chill out until ten minutes passed and they still hadn't reached a restaurant despite passing five. "I don't mind riding in this sexy bitch all night," she said looking around the ride, "but can you tell me where we going now?"

Roman heard remnants of what she was saying but she didn't care. She was already within the caves of her mind preparing herself to do what was necessary.

Kill.

This bitch killed my mother. When my mother begged her not to she did it anyway. It's 'cause of her I don't have no family. Roman looked over at her and frowned before focusing back on the road. She was trying to hype herself up to murder as usual. *She ain't nothing but a funky dirty whore. I hate whores.*

"Excuse me can you—"

Lisa's sentence was cut short when Roman removed the gun from the driver's door. The gun sat in Roman's lap and she tugged the trigger, sending a bullet flying into Lisa's gut. In extreme pain, Lisa doubled over, looked over at Roman and said, "Who are you?"

It was the last thing she ever said and she would not receive an answer. Had she known she would not survive, she would've said something worth remembering. Instead, her head slumped forward and she closed her eyes as Roman whispered, "Goon".

****

By T. Styles   200

Roman just left Raymond and Owen to get Lisa's body dumped. Aware of her surroundings again, she glanced in her rearview mirror and saw the same car following her. But when she saw the face of the person in the driver's seat her heart thumped.

Roman always wondered how things would be if she saw Yoko again. She wondered if she would miss her or if she would cry. When she left to be with Jackson without saying goodbye to Yoko, she felt warranted. Yoko was a hothead and she couldn't afford the liability. Although she would ask people how she was doing, she demanded that no one tell her she asked about her. For Roman, it wasn't about the friendship. She just wanted to make sure she was safe.

Realizing it was time to finally face her, Roman pulled over to the side of the road, in the parking lot of McDonald's and got out. Not knowing Yoko's mood, she placed a gun in her waist, got out and walked to Yoko's car. "Hey."

Yoko shook her head. "After all this time all you gonna say is hey?" She paused. "You treated me like a punk, Roman. Why didn't you tell me I'd never see you again?"

"Because I was angry." She exhaled. "And I guess I can hold a grudge."

Yoko didn't like the response. "Anyway, I'd figure you'd have more to talk about after everything I've seen." She looked at her dress. "Today you are a dude, you were a white UPS driver the other day and even an old man." She paused. "You're a jack of all trades these days, aren't you? Looks like your operation is expensive. Who's funding you?"

"Since it doesn't sound like this is a friendly visit, what do you want?" Roman asked firmly.

"Get in." When she didn't she said, "I know you know that I've been following you. The way you were slipping by not checking your surroundings, if I wanted to kill you you'd be dead already. Now get in the car, Roman. No matter what happens, we were once best friends." She paused. "Let's not act like enemies before it's time."

Roman got in and placed her hand on her waist. At one point, she loved Yoko but she could tell by the way Yoko looked at her that she held a lot of resentment for the way she bounced out of her life. "So what's up?" Roman questioned. "So how have you been?"

Yoko shook her head and laughed. "Not good. Not good at all." She paused and looked ahead. "Let me ask you something I always wanted to know." She swallowed. "How come you didn't tell me my father was spiking liquor and letting his friends rape me? Before I made you mad?"

Roman shook her head. "You're fucking kidding me, right? I told you when we were drinking one night. It was the night I had to help you on the toilet. We were at the restaurant. You got mad and went off on me. Said if I ever said something again, you would tell people about the murders. You don't remember that shit?"

Yoko shook her head no.

"It don't even matter. What do you want with me, Yoko? I know you aren't following me without a reason."

"I really just want to kick it, Ro. Loosen up a bit."

Roman was about to get out of the car so she could see her son when Yoko stopped her.

"Hold up," Yoko yelled. "Just give me five minutes and you can go. There's something in the glove compartment I want you to see. Can you get it out?"

Roman opened the glove compartment carefully while keeping eyes on Yoko. She pulled out a manila envelope. "What's this?"

"Open it."

When Roman pulled out a sheet of paper she saw a long list of names and addresses. "Fuck is this?"

"A problem for me."

For two weeks, Yoko tried to kill the witnesses on the list to end the issue for her family to no avail. After all of that time, she finally came to the realization that she always knew, she didn't have murder in her heart. Plus, she was a dwarf. Even if she built up the heart to commit the crime, she would stand out like a dick with herpes. In order to get the job done, she needed someone who could blend in with the world.

She needed a professional.

She needed Roman.

Roman dropped the list on the seat. "After all this time, you still in over your head." Roman exhaled. "Why can't you just be regular like the bitch you are, Yoko? Why can't you let shit be? You not a gangster and you'll never be."

"You mean like you are?" she asked. "A gangster, that is."

"That's right. I'm the mothafuckin' killer," she said pointing to herself. "You're a wannabe." She paused. "Always have been. I'm not asking nobody to do my dirty work by following them around B-more. I put my own work in and you should too."

"Roman, I need you to take care of the people on that list for me. They causing issues for me and my brothers and I need that to stop."

Roman laughed. "Is this related to what Joshua did to that little girl at the pool? And how Mills killed that woman all those years back?"

"Yeah. How you know?"

"Everybody knows, Yoko. The shit was sloppy at best. I told you your brothers weren't shit. I even found out they not even your brothers but your cousins instead," she laughed. "The funny thing is, even if I cared enough to put myself on the line, I can't trust you. You talk too much. That's the problem we've always had. Give me one reason why I should do this?"

"Because I need your help, Ro," she pleaded. "I don't want my brothers going to jail."

"You mean your cousins."

"I mean my family."

"They ain't your fucking family. This shit don't involve you. If it did, the job would've been done already. And you would not have known I was even associated with it because that's how I move. And I cared about you that much."

With a lowered brow, Yoko said, "You know murder doesn't have a statute of limitations, Roman. I know about all of the niggas you killed back in the city. Remember? When we were coming up? I was there! Even if the cops didn't get you, I know a few hood niggas that would want you dead."

"You threatening me?"

"I'm asking for your help."

Roman was overcome with rage. She couldn't believe she allowed Yoko in her life to begin with. She was a fucking snake. But she decided not to let her know how much she hurt her feelings. Besides, little doo-wop wasn't worth it. "Yoko, you on your own. And you and I know that threatening me is dangerous for your health." She hopped out of the vehicle. "Don't ever contact me again. That's a warning."

Yoko was so mad she was trembling. "You know for some reason, I have a feeling you'll come around." She grabbed the list and handed it to her and Roman accepted. "Keep it. And hit me when you change your mind."

****

Roman pulled up in front of the new house she bought for her family. It wasn't anything big or fancy but it was theirs and Sailor had a backyard he could run around in. Ever since Roman decided to murder for hire, she told herself that she would not take the problems from the street into her home. It was hard. But she didn't want Jackson feeling her negative energy or Sailor for that matter.

As she sat in the car, she thought about Yoko. It was amazing how a good friend could turn enemy with the flick of a switch.

Then there was the matter that Roman was slipping. Yoko trailing her that easily made her realize that everything had to change and that included the location of her warehouse and her way of doing things. The only people who would know her whereabouts would be Raymond and

Owen. She wouldn't even allow Race the honor because she figured the less she knew, the better.

Roman got out of the car and walked into the house. When she saw Jackson frantically pacing she slammed the door and rushed up to him. "What's wrong, baby?"

"Where the fuck were you today, Roman? Huh? I've been calling you nonstop!" He looked at her clothes. "And why you dressed like a nigga?"

She took the cap off her head and tossed it to the recliner. "I'm sorry, baby." She forgot to change clothes because Yoko tossed up her mind. "It was dress down day at work." She swallowed. "But what you talking about you couldn't reach me? I told you I have to work and I'm not allowed to take calls."

She didn't carry her personal cell phone on her when she was out doing work. The last thing she needed was one of her capers being tracked on the cellular towers. Even the GPS system she used was connected to a fake person at a fake location.

"I called you about our son, Roman. Where's Sailor?"

Her skin felt like it was crawling. "What? I don't know! You were supposed to pick him up!" she screamed hoping it was a grave mistake. "Didn't you get him?"

"Fuck no! That's why I'm asking you! He's not at school!! They said he was last seen with some little girl outside! Our son has been kidnapped!"

CHAPTER NINETEEN
-YOKO-

"He had come like a thief in the night."
- Edgar Allan Poe

Just thinking about how crazy Yoko knew Roman was going with her son being stolen brought Yoko extreme pleasure. Getting Sailor away from his school was easier than she thought. Taking a note out of Roman's playbook, she dressed up like a little girl and requested to be friends with Sailor. He accepted the invite and the next thing he knew, he was in Yoko's trunk with the assistance of Erin.

Duct taped and gagged.

She was riding on cloud nine when she walked through the front door of her new apartment and saw Amanda tied to a chair in the middle of the floor. Now she had a taste of her own medicine. Her face was bludgeoned and only three teeth remained in her mouth. One was hanging by a flesh thread connected to her gum and was bound to drop at any moment.

When Vincent, the man she thought for most of her life was her father, stepped from the kitchen, her heart pounded. His face was scarred from the last time she saw him and set him on fire. She hadn't seen him since. "Hello, Princess." He looked from her toes to her head. "You look beautiful," he lied.

Yoko slammed the door closed and approached Amanda. "What is going on, daddy? Why would you do this?"

"I know it looks bad, Yoko," he said stepping closer to her. "I went too far." He glared down at Amanda. "But I know that she has been speaking to the cops."

Outside of the fact that they were his sons, Yoko was confused on why he cared so much. He never took an interest in his sons so she wondered what was different now. "Dad, please listen to me," she said looking at Amanda and then back at him. "She hasn't said a thing. Trust me. I asked her several times and I believe her."

"Shut the fuck up, midget! You don't know what you're talking about!" he yelled. "A friend of mine works for the police department. He told me she has been talking to him. And since she wasn't there the day at the pool or the day Mills shot Paige, she had to have heard it from you."

"I know it looks bad, daddy. But she hasn't said anything. I promise. Five other people you don't know about, that were around that day at the pool and when Mills shot Paige said something to the cops." She wiped the tears rolling down her face. "But I promise I have everything under control."

"I do too," he said before he raised the gun and held it to Amanda's head. "If you wasn't fucking with this bitch, none of this would've happened."

Amanda closed her eyes. "I'm sorry, Yoko. For everything."

Vincent was about to pull the trigger when Yoko yelled, "I'm begging you not to do it! Let me show you what I have. Let me show you how I have things under control. And then you can do whatever you want and I won't try to stop you."

****

Yoko was standing next to Sailor Tate who was sitting on the floor in the corner of the basement. They were in a row home that Erin was renovating for his real estate business. She looked up at Vincent and said, "You see? This is our answer."

Vincent looked at the little boy with the tearstained red scarf tied around his eyes. His eyes roamed toward the dried snot oozing from his nostrils and back to Yoko. "Who is this?" he asked.

"He's Roman's son," she said with a grin.

"What you doing with her fucking kid? And how will it help us?"

The smirk melted from her face. "I kidnapped him. I asked her to get rid of the witnesses and she refused." She paused. "The thing is she's good at murder, dad. And since I have him, she has a little motivation to do what I'm asking. Trust me."

"This had better work, Yoko," Vincent warned. "Because all of this is your fault. Had you not left Joshua to go see about that bitch, the boys wouldn't be in the situation now." He paused. "Make the shit go away or I'll make that bitch of yours disappear." He stomped up the stairs and out of the house.

When Vincent left, Yoko looked at the child. She wanted to feel some remorse but there was none in her heart. She blamed everybody but herself for the mess she was in but she especially blamed Roman. Who was Roman to have a son and a life when hers was fucked up? Jealousy was ripping her apart. With anger in her heart, she walked up to the child and slapped him before kicking him in the shin.

Upon feeling the blows, Sailor cried out in pain. "Leave me alone!" he yelled. "I'm gonna tell my mommy and daddy!"

"Tell them then, nigga," she yelled. "If you keep screaming I'm gonna give you something to cry about too!"

When Yoko's cell phone rang she took a few steps away from Sailor and answered. "Hello." The person on the other end of the phone was so hysterical that she almost didn't recognize her voice. "Who the fuck is this?" she said drawing things out, knowing full well it was Roman.

"Yoko, do you have my son?" Roman cried. "Do you have my baby?"

Yoko grinned and licked her lips. "What do you think?" she said flatly. "You took from me and now I'm taking from you."

"I'm begging you," Roman pleaded. "I'm begging you to please not hurt my baby. Bring him back to me. To his family. He's innocent. You don't know what I went through to have him, Yoko. I'm begging you."

Yoko thought her attitude was hilarious considering how big and bad she was earlier in the day. "If you do what I'm asking he will be okay. If not…well…I hope your ovaries still work because this one might be dead."

Roman sniffled a few times before taking a few deep breaths. "If you hurt my son I will kill everybody you love. Do you hear me, Yoko? I will kill everything you love!"

Yoko looked over at her whimpering child. "Then I guess this is war."

Silence.

"No, Yoko. This is far worse."

CHAPTER TWENTY
-ROMAN-

"They who dream by day are cognizant of many things which escape those who dream only by night."
- Edgar Allan Poe

Although Roman begged Jackson to let her handle things, he called the cops anyway. He didn't trust that she knew enough to bring his child back and why should he? As far as he knew, she was a customer service rep with zero experience in the streets. How would she get their son? She knew nothing about the ways of killers and kidnappers. This mess was epic.

And now she was standing in the middle of her living room, looking down at two officers sitting on her sofa. Equipped with pens and pads in their hands, they diligently took notes.

Although they wanted to be helpful, Roman was beyond irritated. She wanted them out of her house so that she could go about the business of getting her son back. For a quick moment, she thought about telling them everything she knew but she decided against it. Besides, telling them too much would expose Jackson to what she did for a living and the murders she committed in her lifetime. She was willing to sacrifice herself until she realized that no one would be invested as much as she was to get her son back. If she wanted him home, she had to remain out of jail.

She had to remain free.

"Ma'am, is there anything else you can tell us about the call you received later in the day when your son went missing?" Detective Mickens asked. He was a tall white man with frizzy brown eyebrows and an uncomfortable glare.

"No. Just that we weren't supposed to alert the police or they'd kill him. Which is why I asked you to come in unmarked cars." She paused. "That's all I was told. The fact that you're here is jeopardizing his life."

By T. Styles   210

"I know it feels that way but we are going to find your son," Det. Mickens said.

"It just doesn't make any sense," Jackson said as he circled in place. "We aren't wealthy. We don't have money."

"We aren't wealthy but your mother is," Roman reminded him.

"So you're saying this is my fault?" he asked stopping in place.

"No. I just wanted to remind you that your mother is paid. That's all." Sweat poured down her face and she wiped it away with the back of her hand. "We don't know why they took him."

"It sure does sound like you are coming at me!" he yelled. "You aren't the only one who lost a child! I did too!"

"I know this is rough," Detective Speller added. She was an African American woman with kind eyes and an amazing detective brain. When she was on a case, it got solved. "But you shouldn't be fighting one another. Everyone needs to keep a level head and stick together."

"I have to get some air," Roman said as she grabbed her purse and car keys. "I'm sorry but I'll be back." She quickly moved toward the door.

"Do you really think it is smart to be leaving right now?" Det. Mickens questioned. "I think we all need to stay here and wait for another call."

Roman shuffled a little as she fought to find out how to get out so that she could find Sailor.

"Let her go...I'm here," Jackson said looking over at Roman. "My wife has led a sheltered life. Give her some time alone."

Roman looked at him and rolled out before someone else could combat. She needed to get to work to find her baby and she didn't care what anyone thought of it. She was almost to her car when Det. Mickens walked outside and called her name. "Mrs. Tate," he said raising his finger. "Give me one second of your time."

She turned around and sighed. "I have to go now. If I don't leave I'm going to scream." She deactivated the lock on her car. "I'll be back soon. I'm so sorry for leaving like this."

As he watched her pull off, Det. Speller walked outside and over to her partner. "Is everything okay?"

"I think she's involved," he said watching her drive away.

She smiled and shook her head. "She isn't responsible."

He looked over at her, secretly resenting that most of the times that she had a hunch she was right. "Why do you say that?"

"I know a loving mother when I see one." She sighed. "Someone took that boy but it certainly wasn't her."

****

Roman was standing in the middle of her warehouse and the whites of her eyes were red from crying all day. She, Raymond and Owen spent hours visiting the people on Yoko's list, preparing to do whatever she had to return her son, including kill. But when she saw one of the women was pregnant, and that the rest were what she considered innocents, people uninvolved in the crime world, her good conscience wouldn't allow her to murder them.

Looking at Raymond and Owen, she pulled out her cell phone. "It's time." Taking a deep breath, she dialed Yoko's number. "Yoko, I want to give you one last chance to bring back my son. Please." She was calmer but still devastated.

"Did you do what I asked?"

"You know I can't hurt innocent people, Yoko."

She laughed. "After all these years, you still hold onto that belief. That code of yours. Sadly enough, that shit is going to cost you."

Roman's nostrils flared wildly. "I'm trying to save you unnecessary pain," she pleaded. "I don't want a war with you. Just bring him back and I won't bother you, Yoko. Please."

Click.

When she saw she hung up she shoved the phone in her pocket and looked at Raymond and Owen. "So she not giving up?" Raymond asked.

"No. And the bitch moved from that apartment building too. Everybody she loves is gone."

"They're hiding somewhere but I'll find them." Angrily, she stomped over to the desk and handed Owen a list. Because she couldn't read well, Raymond wrote the list as she dictated. "I need everything on here."

Owen looked down at it. "A bus?" he asked.

"I need everything on that list. I'll explain why later." She walked over to a red plastic container in the corner of her office. It was filled with gas and she poured it over everything in the warehouse. When she was done they got out of the warehouse via the open dock door and she tossed a match inside, causing the entire place to go up in flames.

They all jumped in their cars and went their separate ways to handle the assigned tasks. As she drove down the street, Roman could hear the fire alarm sounding in the background. She wasn't concerned about the burning warehouse being connected with her in any way. If they wanted to arrest the person whose name it was in, they would need to find a Gerry Shumaker who didn't exist.

When she was far enough away, she made another call. "Race, I need a favor."

"You due for one," she responded. "Especially after saving my life. What's up?"

"Actually I need a favor from that white girl you roll with."

Race chuckled. "You mean Scarlett?"

"Yeah."

"Depends on what it is but I'm sure I could get her for you. But you have to give me more detail."

Roman explained everything she could minus the part about her son being missing. She told her that she needed Scarlett to throw her husband off. She didn't involve her in the kidnapping because she wanted her to think that she had everything under control. The less people knew about the situation the better. Besides, she needed the money to continue to roll in because they paid her in installments. It would be difficult to find Sailor if she was broke. "It's just a diversion for my husband that's all."

Race sighed. "Yeah, I got it." She paused. "What's up with Mellvue? Is that done yet?"

In all of the action, with losing her son, she forgot that she had an important job to do. "Not yet, but I'll handle it. I just need a little more time. I promise."

****

The view from the roof of the building at night was spectacular as Roman, along with her partners Owen and Raymond, stood on top of it. It was as if the city was showing off and wanted this moment to remain etched in Roman's mind forever, no matter how deadly the event was.

In front of her, close to the ledge, was her latest victim. His ankles were connected with rope, duct tape and chains and his hands were bound behind his back. His mouth was stuffed with a soiled sweat sock and a rope was tied so tight it cut off the blood flow to the top part of his face, causing an extreme headache.

Roman untied the gag and the victim ran his tongue over his lips. "Please don't do this," he pleaded. "I'm begging you!"

Roman looked away from him and out at the sparkling city. "I was hoping that this would give me satisfaction." She looked at him. "You know, when I pushed you off the building and all." She looked at the city again and exhaled. "But now I think I'm doing you a favor. I mean look at this shit. What a beautiful way to die." She paused. "Don't you agree?"

"Why you doing this to me, Roman? I never did anything to you."

"You were right that day. When you said I was the one."

"Who?"

"Where is my son?" she asked calmly with a lowered brow, skipping the subject. "Where is he?"

"I swear to God I don't know what the fuck you talking 'bout! If I did—"

Tiring of his speech already, with one firm push, she sent him plummeting thirty feet to his death. His loud screaming grew fainter and fainter the closer he got to the ground. And then there was silence.

With the mission completed, Roman looked at Raymond and Owen and they nodded at her. This part of the plan was over but her job was far from done. Although she came a long way from dancing at Smack Back, she certainly proved each day she was built for this life.

"Ray, did you do what I asked?" Roman said calmly, getting right back to business.

"It's done, baby girl."

With that acknowledgement, Roman removed the phone from her pocket and dialed a number. It rang once before Yoko answered. "Hello, Roman. Did you take care of the people on the list?"

"I got a better question for you, Yoko. You know where your brother Dale is?"

CHAPTER TWENTY-ONE
-YOKO-

"Death has reared himself a throne."
- Edgar Allan Poe

Yoko crashed into the trashcan in Dale's driveway as she parked sideways, hopped out and rushed to the house Dale was hiding in to avoid Roman finding him. When she made it to the door, she banged heavily trying to reach him. "Dale, open up! It's Yoko!"

Her heartbeat went into overdrive as she peered through the windows, hoping to catch a glimpse of him or one of the cuties he bedded on a regular. Because it would mean they were alive. But after a minute there was nothing. Yoko banged on the door again and when he didn't answer she tossed a stone through the window, pushed a lawn chair in front of it and crawled into the house. She went through the entire place and still did not find him.

When her phone vibrated she removed it and held it up to her ear. It shook a little due to her nerves being all over the place. Trying to get herself together, Yoko walked over to the couch, sat down and reluctantly answered. "Hello."

"Where the fuck is Dale?" Vincent yelled at her. "Huh? We can't find him, Yoko! I thought you told me this shit would work!"

"Daddy, you know how he is. He's probably with some bitch," she lied knowing he was possibly dead. The idea alone caused her physical pain.

"For your sake, he'd better be, Yoko. For you and Amanda's sake."

****

The television blasted in the background as Yoko and Amanda argued about the obvious, that Dale was missing. They were in one of Erin's rental properties hiding out. Although Vincent released Amanda, they both knew he would have no problem finding them if need be so there was no use in running too far. Plus, Yoko needed to be there for her brothers.

"Where were you earlier, Amanda?" Yoko asked sternly. "Because Vincent not fucking around with you. You can't see that detective anymore. He don't believe me when I say you ain't snitching."

"Why is he back in the picture?" she asked off subject. "It doesn't seem odd to you that suddenly he cares about his sons so much?"

Yoko took a deep breath and held it in. She felt despite the beat down, Amanda didn't understand what was going on. "I don't know why he's back. All I know is that I don't want him thinking you talking to police because he may kill you." She paused. "Now where were you?"

"I told you I went to get a bag and came back," Amanda yelled as she sat on the edge of the bed. "Look at my face, Yoko! After everything I've been through, I wanted to get high." She pointed at herself. "Is that so wrong? Vincent almost killed me." She paused. "So what do you think happened?"

Yoko paced the floor. "I think she got to him. Even after I told him to be careful."

"Don't think the worst. You know Dale. He's probably with—"

"I know what you about to say. That he's with some female, holed up somewhere. That's the shit that I told my father but I don't believe it any more than you do."

"So where do you think he is?"

She exhaled and sat on a chair built for her height across the room. "Dead." She chewed on her fingernails. "And Roman actually did it." Her hands dropped to her side when she realized what she said. That he may actually be gone.

In a shaky voice, Amanda asked, "So how do you know you're not next? Or me?"

"Because I know where her son is." She exhaled. "And as long as I have the boy, I'm safe."

"Yoko, if you don't end this now I fear things will get worse. I remember the stories you told me about Roman. I mean...aren't you scared of what she's capable of?"

Yoko drew back into the chair as if she were trying to melt away. Part of her was jealous that everyone feared her so much. What about her? Wasn't she just as threatening? "You really think it's that easy?" she said softly. "For me to walk away? I started something that I have to finish. Her child is being held in a basement."

"Yoko, please. Let the police do their work. Don't worry about the witnesses. They can't convict Mills unless they have a good case and it's obvious that they don't. If they did they wouldn't need us so badly. Return her son. Please."

Yoko considered what she was saying. She saw the look in Roman's eyes when she killed. She knew she was great at her job, which was why she wanted her so badly. "Maybe you're right," she sighed. "I'll make the call in a—"

When Yoko saw Amanda covering her mouth as she looked at the television, she hopped off the chair and walked toward it. As the blue hue from the tube glowed in Yoko's face, a vision of a body covered under a sheet flashed on the screen. But it was the name at the bottom of the screen that stopped her heart.

Dale Lighthouse was officially found murdered.

CHAPTER TWENTY-TWO
-ROMAN-

"Die with despair of heart and convulsion of throat."
- Edgar Allan Poe

Roman sat across from Race as Race sipped a glass of whiskey. The restaurant was small and quaint but it didn't ease Roman's stiff demeanor. She didn't want to be there. She wanted to be out in the streets finding her son.

Race leaned back in her seat with one question for Roman. "Why is Mellvue still alive?"

Roman's head fell back as she tried to think of a reasonable lie. Although she successfully killed five people out of the first batch of names given, Mellvue was harder to locate. For starters, her schedule was difficult to follow and she could never get her alone. To make matters worse, the only thing on Roman's mind was finding her son, which she dedicated most of her mental energy to. "I'm working on her," she admitted. "That's all I can say right now. I mean I've gotten everybody else you—"

"I vouched for you, Roman," she said cutting her off.

"I know and I appreciate it."

"If you appreciate it, talk to me. What's going on for real? I can tell in your eyes that something's up. Let me help you like you helped me. I owe you my life."

"It's not that simple."

"Why not? I'm a very powerful woman. And that makes you powerful too."

Roman wanted to seek her help but she feared the more people involved the worse it would be for her son. It was bad enough she invited Yoko to a game of war, believing that when she saw what happened to her brother she would bring Sailor back.

Well Dale was dead and Sailor had not been returned. Things didn't look good at all.

"I appreciate the offer but I really am okay, Race."

Race nodded. "I'm a good judge of character, Roman. I always have been. And since you refuse to accept my friendship by being honest, I'll treat our relationship in kind."

"Meaning?"

"Meaning this is business." Race clasped her hands together on the table. "With that said, I feel the need to remind you that you are being paid very handsomely for a service." She paused. "I want that job done. If it's not done you'll have problems you won't be able to slice yourself out of."

****

With no new information on Sailor, the moment Roman opened the door to her house and saw Det. Mickens and Det. Speller sitting on her couch again, she was irritated. She had been in contact with everyone she could to find out where Yoko and her brothers were staying and she still came up short. Through her travels, she still had not learned a thing. Why was Yoko able to elude her unlike the other people she hunted and killed?

The moment she closed the door, Det. Mickens chose rudeness instead of pleasantry as a way to greet her. "Where the fuck were you, Mrs. Tate?"

"Where is my husband?"

"He's at his mother's house," Det. Mickens advised. "Picking her up I believe." He paused. "Now answer the question. Where were you?"

Roman tried to conceal her anger about Jackson picking up Debra but she was certain she was doing a bad job of hiding her feelings. The last thing she needed was that hateful bitch hanging around her home, asking her a million questions. "But he wasn't supposed to tell anybody," Roman said as she wiped her hands down her face. "Not even his mother! Why doesn't he get it?"

"That may be true but when are you going to answer me? Where...were....you?"

"I was at work."

By T. Styles   220

He stood up and tapped Det. Speller on the arm. "If this is true take us there now."

"Where?"

"To your job."

Roman's eyes bulged. "But...I..."

"No more excuses, Mrs. Tate," he said with a raise of the hand. "Let's go now."

Against her will, she was whisked outside to go to a job she didn't have. As she sat in the back of the police car and directed them where to go she sent a text message to Race indicating that she needed the favor from Scarlett she requested.

"Handled," Race responded five minutes later. "She said she will meet you there. But make this the last favor you ever ask of me. This is a business relationship. Remember?"

When she tossed her cell phone in her bag she looked up at the detectives with irritation. Det. Mickens' eyes met hers as they scanned one another in the rearview mirror. "Is that the same cell phone you registered with the department?"

"Yes," she lied looking out of the window. "Don't worry. I didn't take my son and you already have my phone records, which I'm sure you've combed through." A tear fell down her face and she wiped it off. "Besides, I would never hurt Sailor. Ever." When she remembered an important fact she said, "I have to remind you that you can't let my job know about my son being missing. This is very important or he may be hurt."

"Let me ask you something," Det. Mickens asked suspiciously. "Why hasn't your suspected kidnapper tried to reach out to your husband? At the house? He has the money, not you." He paused. "We have your home phones wired and ready. Where is the request for the ransom?"

Det. Speller shook her head at her partner's tactics. She was as disgusted as Roman about his line of questioning.

"I don't know why the person hasn't called. Maybe we'll find out soon enough." When she saw the new building she rented she prayed that Race came through as promised. "Park over there."

They placed the car where she directed and walked into the location. The moment they opened the door to the building they saw two women answering phones that appeared to be ringing off the hook. The Pretty Kings organization went all out to protect their murder star.

Wasting no time, Det. Speller walked up to the counter dividing the back of the office and spoke to a pretty girl with long brown hair. "Excuse me, young lady. But is your manager here?" she asked.

"Sure. One moment please." Before leaving she said, "Oh, hi, Roman."

Shocked she knew her name, Roman waved. The young woman who Roman didn't recognize walked into the back and reappeared with Scarlett. The moment Roman saw her face, she exhaled.

"May I help you?" Scarlett asked the detectives, sliding thick strands of her red hair behind her ear. She was wearing a serious navy blue suit and was dressed for business.

"Uh yes, uh," Det. Mickens said. Stunned by her beauty, he forgot the reason he was there. She looked more like a movie star than a manager. "Do you...can you..."

"What my partner is trying to say is we are here to verify Roman's employment," Det. Speller said saving her partner from further embarrassment.

"Sure, but is something wrong?"

"Of course not," she responded. "Roman has applied for a program to purchase a new home. It's for first time buyers. And we wanted to make sure everything she provided on her application was correct. We are her real estate agents and wanted to rush the project along."

Scarlett smiled. "Wow, I never had this happen before. Most agents request the information be faxed."

"I realize this is unconventional but as we said, we are hoping to push her through this program. Can you help us?"

"Normally I would request that Roman send over documentation giving authorization the proper way. Using the appropriate channels. But since you are here and with

Roman, I will say she is an exemplary employee. One of our best, if I'm being honest, so of course she works here."

"When was the last time you saw her?" Det. Mickens asked as he suddenly regained his composure.

"She was here earlier today actually," she responded. "Why, is everything okay? Because I'm really worried now."

The detectives took a few moments to assure her that things were fine. And although she didn't have to, Scarlett spent five more minutes answering their other questions with fake responses that sounded realistic. When they were done, they walked out of the business and Det. Mickens said, "Go sit in the car, Roman."

Roman did as she was told but her eyes remained on them as they spoke in front of the building. "I still think something is up," Det. Mickens said to his partner.

"What I think we need to do is focus our attention on other sources," she replied. "Like I said before, this young lady is not involved in the kidnapping of her child. It's just time for us to do good old fashion police work and discover who is," she continued, slapping him on the back. "Let's get to it."

****

Farmer and his family buried his brother Dale in secrecy last week and his mind was all over the place. Everything the Lighthouse family did these days had to be thought out to prevent Roman from finding them. Although he wasn't as worried, Yoko acted as if Roman was a ghost, able to move in places they didn't have access too. In his mind, she was still a bitch and he was sick of it all.

The only thing Farmer wanted was to go out, get some drinks and clear his mind. Yoko pleaded with him earlier to stay in but he wasn't feeling the restriction. Even at the moment, she was calling his cell phone, which he ignored repeatedly.

After the liquor and the music got to be too much for his buzz, Farmer gave Keisha, a chick with a fat ass that he just met in the club, the keys to his older model Escalade. "Have the valet bring my truck 'round front. I'm gonna go piss right quick." He was so inebriated that he didn't even know who Keisha was. All he knew was that since the first drink he bought her four hours ago, she was stuck closer to him than his rotator cuff.

While she got the truck, he stumbled to the bathroom and drained his stick. And when he was done, he shook his dick and hobbled out without washing his hands. Once outside, he saw the chick he had been nursing all night smiling up in another nigga's face. Worried she was about to get him for his ride, he grabbed her by the arm and yanked her back. "Fuck my car at?"

She snatched her arm away and said, "Get the fuck off of me, drunk! Anyway your shit is over there." She pointed at the curb. "It ain't even new."

He turned around, saw his truck and sighed in relief. "My bad, shawty." He leaned up on her neck, even though she was posted on another man. "Still coming with me?"

"Damn, nigga. Don't you see me with my dude?" She rolled her eyes. "You and I had a little fun in the club and now it's over. Fuck off before you get your feelings hurt."

The dude she was referring to looked at her as if she lost her mind. As if he didn't know her for real. All he said was hello and she ran with it like they were newlyweds. Farmer was about to walk away until he noticed she was trembling. Like she was scared of something. His theory was proven when urine ran down her inner thigh and painted the concrete beneath her. Something or somebody had her shook.

"Damn, ma, thanks for doing me a favor. I didn't know you were a pissy type bitch."

She ignored him as he bounced toward his truck without a care in the world. A dark-skinned, tall young guy with a Jamaican accent opened the door and said, "Your keys are in the ignition."

Farmer slid inside. "Thanks, man."

"You sure you fit to drive?" the valet said, leaning on the window. "If you look up the block you'll see they're pulling cars over left and right. Maybe you should call somebody to come get you since this is a one way street and you can't go the other way."

Farmer felt like he wanted to shit on himself. Up ahead, he could see red and blue lights inside of an unmarked car. The last thing he needed was to get locked up. Outside of wanting some pussy, that was the main reason he wanted Keisha to drive. "Listen, how much you make an hour?" Farmer asked the valet.

"About ten bucks plus tips."

Farmer reached in his pocket and slapped a fifty-dollar bill in his palm. "That should cover you for an hour. All I need you to do is drive me up the block, past the cops. And make sure I get there safe. You with it?"

CHAPTER TWENTY-THREE
-YOKO-

"And Darkness and Decay and the Red Death held illimitable dominion over all."
- Edgar Allan Poe

Yoko was already having a bad day when all of a sudden she experienced a bout of nausea. Thinking something was off, she went to the doctor's to find out what was up. Something didn't feel the same. She thought it had to do with losing her older brother Dale and the fear that there was more to come.

"May I come in?" the doctor asked as he knocked on the door before entering.

Yoko was in the bed with a white nightgown hiding the framework of her body. "Yes, doctor," she said scooting up. "Is everything okay?"

"Of course. You're pregnant, Yoko," he smiled. "I don't know if it's good news but I certainly hope that it is."

Yoko grew unusually silent. Her vision blurred and she batted her eyes several times to clear her sight.

"Ms. Lighthouse, are you okay?" he asked in a concerned tone.

She moved uneasily in the bed and cleared her throat. "What...I mean...how?"

"How?" he repeated, leaning in. "Are you asking me how babies are conceived?"

"No, I mean, how can I have a child? I thought...'cause I'm...a dwarf that it wasn't possible." She pulled on her nightgown, trying to get some air.

"Oh, no, Yoko," he said compassionately. "You can certainly have children. And there is a good possibility, that he or she could be average height too." He paused. "Not assuming it's a problem for you."

Yoko felt the breath releasing from her body. To know that she was capable of having a normal baby perplexed her. Even though she was sure Erin was the father, she wouldn't worry about him being in the child's life if he didn't want to. She wasn't even sure if she'd tell him. But she had all intentions on having her child, with or without his help.

Now she had to tell Amanda, which she was sure wouldn't go over well.

Before she could think about it some more, she received a text from her father. "Come to your house! I'm waiting!"

****

When Yoko arrived to the house she lived in, her father was chain smoking. Pillows of smoke bounced around his head and his eyes were bloody red. "Bout time you got here."

"What happened?" Yoko asked in a surprised tone.

Vincent got up and walked over to the remote control on the table. He calmly hit the on button and scrolled through the channels. He stopped on a news broadcast and blasted the volume. Yoko was stunned as they recounted the breaking news story of the day.

Authorities are saying that last night, Farmer Lighthouse was murdered and placed in front of a police station. Since he is related to another recent murder victim, an investigation is being launched as the events may be connected. Police say that based on camera footage from the station, at about 1:00 am the victim was driven up to the precinct in his own vehicle. Then another male, about 6 feet tall, dressed in a black hoodie and black sweatpants exited the vehicle before getting away on foot.

If you have any information about this case or the other, please contact authorities.

When the program was over, Vincent threw the remote down, stomped over to Yoko and slapped her in the face, causing her to fall on the hardwood floor. She immediately backed into a corner and covered her belly. "That bitch Maria may have considered you a daughter but I never have!

Now two of my fucking sons are gone! Two of them! To top it all off, police keep coming around my house like I know something about who killed them. Even with my brother dead, he's still haunting me! Through you!"

"I'm so sorry," she sobbed as the realization hit her that she lost two men she cared about.

"I thought you had it under control, Yoko. I thought you handled it!"

She stood up and hid her face, fearing he'd strike her again. "I'm gonna make it right."

"Make it right? How the fuck you gonna make it right? My kids are dead, bitch! Return the little nigga you kidnapped before I lose it."

Still devastated that she lost both Dale and Farmer, Yoko was unforgiving and unrelenting. "She killed my brothers. Your sons! There's no way I'm gonna let her get away with this shit." Yoko was about to walk back out of the house when her phone rang.

It was Roman. "Yoko, please bring my son back."

"It's mighty funny how you won't kill a few people on a list but you'll kill everybody I love," she cried. "You never gave a fuck about me! Ever!"

"I warned you, Yoko. I didn't want to go this far but you pushed me. All I want is Sailor. Please."

Her lips flattened and her nostrils flared. "I'll bring him to you in a body bag before I give him back alive!"

CHAPTER TWENTY-FOUR
-ROMAN-

"In many of my productions terror has been the thesis."
- Edgar Allan Poe

Roman was in the shower, on her knees allowing the hot water to soothe her body. She was an emotional wreck and she had a feeling things would get worse. Losing her son was beyond overwhelming and she felt as if the air was being ripped out of her lungs. Not only did she miss him terribly, everywhere she went in her own home she had someone judging her and asking questions. *Did you kidnap your son? Is he alive?* It felt as if there was never an end in sight.

"Baby, are you okay?" Jackson asked as he opened the bathroom door slightly. "I heard you crying."

She stood up and wiped the tears from her face. "I'm fine," she lied.

He removed his clothes and slid in the shower with her. Taking her face into his hands, he looked deeply into her eyes. Her body trembled as he held onto her. "We will find our son, Ro. Don't worry about it. I know things look bad right now but I'm confident we will find him." He paused. "I just want to ask you one thing." He wiped the wet hair from her face and pulled her head toward him. "Are you telling me everything you know? Is there anything you're leaving out?"

"What do you mean?" she frowned.

"My mother says she feels that you know more than you're letting on."

"Jackson, your mother doesn't like me. Of course she feels that way!" she yelled. "She's been making me uncomfortable ever since she's been here. Now I don't mean to be rude but your mother has her son! And she can lay eyes on him anytime she wants. Mine is gone!" She was so angry she slammed her fist into the wall, almost fracturing it.

"Okay, Roman," he said kissing her softly. "Okay, baby. I didn't mean to make you upset. I'll ask her to leave tomorrow."

"Thank you," she said softly. "I really need a calm environment right now." Roman placed her head on his chest and noticed some scratches. "Baby, what happened?" she ran her hand over the wounds. "Are you okay?"

He pushed her hand away. "Nothing you should be worried about. I was doing some work outside of the house and scratched myself. Being careless that's all." He kissed her on the side of her neck and lifted her up with the mission of easing inside of her.

"Jackson, not now," she said softly. "It doesn't feel right. With Sailor being missing."

He looked into her eyes, rage all over him, and stepped back. "I hate when you deny me. I fucking hate it!" He paused. "I'm used to getting what I want, Roman. Remember that." He exited the shower, grabbed a towel and stormed out, slamming the door behind him.

Although he was upset, she was relieved he was gone. She wanted to be alone with her thoughts. Since she had more work to do, Roman cut the water off and got out of the shower too. The moment she stepped out her phone rang. It was Yoko. "Where are my witnesses?" Yoko yelled breathing heavily.

"Where are the witnesses?" Roman repeated.

"Yes, bitch! Where are they?"

"I have them. What did you think; I would let you take my son and your witnesses too? I had them pulled up a long time ago, Yoko. Shipped away on a bus. All I want is my child and I'll release them to you. Where is he?"

"You don't realize what you've done," she said angrily. "Do you even care about your boy? If you did you would've given me what I asked a long time ago."

"Why? So every time you have a problem you can snatch him? Or my husband?" she asked. "I'm not stupid, Yoko! I love my baby more than you know," she whispered. Outside of Jackson, he's all I have in this world. And you don't know the limits I will go to, to bring him back. I'm different these days. Haven't I shown you already?"

"Do what I want or I will fucking kill him!" she screamed.

"Yoko," Roman said in a calm tone.

"What, bitch?" she replied, hating how poised she was.

"Where's Joshua?" She ended the call.

CHAPTER TWENTY-FIVE
-YOKO-

"Coveted her and me."
- Edgar Allan Poe

Yoko was standing in front of Erin, her eyes swollen red from days upon days of crying. Things had gotten way out of control and several times she told herself if she could take it all back, with kidnapping Sailor, she would. But now it was too late.

A large blue bin that was big enough to fit her body sat in front of her. She needed to get out of the house to see if what Roman said was true.

Was Joshua murdered?

"I don't know if this is going to work," Erin said. "The cops are outside watching and shit. I can't believe I let you rope me into this mess! It's obvious they think you did it. Why else would they be here?" He paused. "First you ask to use a few of my houses and then this."

"I'm not being watched because they think I killed my brothers. I'm being watched for protection, Erin. They saw you come in and out of here recently. They know you are a friend so they have no reason to check this bin."

"Like I said, I don't know about this," Erin said ignoring everything she said as if he wasn't going to do it anyway. "I already got a strike against me for that assault charge some years back. This is just begging for another."

"I'm asking for your help, Erin."

"Where is Amanda? Why can't she help you?"

"She's not here," she said under her breath. "And even if she was she couldn't pull this bin with me in it." She paused. "Come on, Erin. I'm asking for your help because I'm pregnant."

"By who?" he asked with wide eyes. "Because I'm not having no midget baby with your red ass. Fuck that shit!"

Yoko felt gut punched. "I never said it was by you," she responded while trying to conceal her feelings and save face. "I was just telling you that I am, that's all. Now will you help me or not?"

He sighed and said, "Get in before I change my fucking mind. I'm sick of this shit! I don't know what's up with you and these cops hanging around but I don't want you asking me for nothing else after this. You hear me? I'm done after this shit!"

Yoko hopped in the bin and using the dolly he pushed in the house earlier, Erin opened the door and walked out of the house with the bin on top of it. When he got to his work van, he opened the backdoor and pushed the container inside. The officers were parked out front of Yoko's house but they didn't seem interested in Erin in the least. They were more concerned with the house.

When Erin got five blocks away from the house, he parked and opened the back door. He took the lid off and asked, "Were you serious? About me not being the baby's father?"

"Why? It's obvious you don't care, Erin. So just drop it."

"You're right, I don't give a fuck," he lied. "I was just saying that if you do have it...I mean...if you need help, I'm here," he said grumpily. "That's all I wanted to say."

Although she faked hard, she was relieved by his answer. She needed all of the help she could get. "Can you take me to the mental home? I need to see if my brother is okay."

****

Yoko just returned from the mental home and at first she thought they would commit her too. She had lost what was left of her mind. She had gotten the news that she didn't want, that her brother choked on a quarter and died in his sleep. He begged her to visit him the weekend prior but she was busy dipping in Roman's life and now she was consumed with guilt.

Her stomach ached as she walked through the door of her house only to see Vincent sitting on her sofa. He smelled of liquor and it seemed as if it permeated through his pores. Although afraid he would attack her, Yoko slowly approached him. "Daddy, what's wrong?" she asked trying to hide her emotions. "What are you doing here?"

"She killed him!" he yelled wiping his hand down his face. "She fucking killed my son. Who is this bitch? The grim reaper?"

"I don't think it was her, daddy," she lied. "They said he choked. That he——"

"Stop fucking lying to me! She took everything from me! Everything! I would've wrapped my hands around her neck a long time ago had I not trusted you! You said you had it under control!"

Yoko swallowed when she saw the blood on his t-shirt. "Where is Amanda?"

"Fuck Amanda!"

"Daddy, where is she?" she asked as she ran through the house as fast as her legs would take her.

"Take me to that boy first. The one you're keeping hostage. And then I'll show you your little bitch."

****

Vincent held the camera phone, which was recording video as Yoko beat the boy until he was bloodied. It was Vincent's demand. Despite being pregnant herself, she no longer saw a child when looking at him. Sailor was the son of a woman who successfully took everything from her and she didn't care if he died. When she was done slapping the boy around enough, she said, "Cut the video off, daddy."

When he did she used the phone to call Roman. "Are you ready for this to end?" Roman asked Yoko. "I told you what would happen if you didn't return my son but you didn't believe me. All I want is Sailor back," she said firmly. "And then it will all stop."

"You overplayed your hand, bitch. You killed everybody! I don't have nobody else left." she yelled.

"What about Mills? You don't care about him?"

When Vincent heard his son's name he snatched the phone from Yoko and said, "Listen here, you stupid bitch, if you do anything to Mills I will find you and kill you myself. Do you hear me?"

"Is this Vincent?" Roman asked calmly. "I didn't know you were still in the picture. Seeing as how you were raping your own sons and all. I would think you'd want to move far away."

Vincent stepped away from Yoko a little. "Fuck are you talking about?"

"I heard about you, Vincent. I needed to know what I was working with. Who Yoko may have on her side. And imagine my surprise when I found out the reason why your children were so fucked up in the head." She paused. "Every night, you were raping each one of them. You raped Dale until he was eighteen. You raped Joshua for all of his life and he took it out on Yoko, and that little girl at the pool. And you raped Mills and Farmer too. It's not your fault though, is it? Since your father raped you also. I heard he's in the walls of that apartment building. Where you spent all of your life after finding out what he was doing to other boys who lived there. Talk, Vincent. Tell me I'm not right."

Vincent's hand trembled. "If you tell anyone that, I will—"

"You will what?" she screamed. "I don't know what Yoko told you about me but I'm not a fucking joke. All of my life I have been around death and I won't stop until my son is back or the world is dead!"

Vincent was seething. "Since you got so much mouth, bitch. Check out your phone in a minute. You have a video coming your way."

****

Roman's fingertips trembled against her lips as she watched the video of her son being treated so violently. Up until that point, she thought Yoko didn't have the heart to harm him in that way. She thought she was a punk who had limits and would never hurt a child.

She was wrong.

Roman tossed the phone on the sofa and paced the floor in her office. How could she be so stupid? How could she be so reckless? She knew the situation was dire but seeing it in that way fucked up her mind. She should've killed the witnesses long ago. Maybe her son would be home by now.

It was settled. After seeing her child on that video, she didn't care who was on that list. She would murder every one of them and their children if it meant bringing back her boy. Picking up the phone she sobbed, "Okay, Yoko. You won."

"Okay what?" Yoko responded sternly.

"I'll do it. Just don't hurt my son anymore."

"I knew you'd come around," Yoko responded, hoping to at least get Miles out of jail and save Amanda. "It's high time you got rid of that code." She giggled. "And don't be slick. I want video showing me that you killed them."

CHAPTER TWENTY-SIX
-ROMAN-

"And tempted her out of her gloom."
- Edgar Allan Poe

Roman's big toe felt as if it were being bent backward as she pressed the gas pedal on the way to Billy Bob's House of Horrors in Essex, Maryland. Although Billy Bob's business failed, the property still stood and she took the hostages there to keep them safe.

However, the hostages didn't feel protected at all. Being forced to be somewhere you didn't want to be felt like anything but solitude. But she needed them to be away from the city, away from Yoko, in case she tried to get to them. The witnesses were her last play.

It took an hour for her to make it to the property. The moment she pulled up, it gave her bad memories. Not only of missing her family but also of Billy Bob and the murderous lifestyle he forced her into. She hadn't spoken to him since she left and part of her felt like she should make amends so that she could move on. But first, she had to get back her son.

Roman opened the door of the property and stomped down the dark hallway leading to the basement. Once inside, she rushed downstairs and saw the witnesses. Five of them, huddled on a sofa and chained to one another. They had the relative comforts. Blankets and a television. And during the week, either Raymond or Owen would stop by to make sure they had food and water and could go to the bathroom. Now everything seemed like it was for nothing because she would be forced to kill them all.

Realizing she had to do what she must to get her son, she approached them hurriedly, with the gun pointed in their direction. Everyone screamed but it was the pregnant woman who pleaded with Roman.

"Oh, my God! Please don't," she yelled louder while clutching her belly with one hand. "I'm…I'm begging you. I don't know what's going on but you don't have to do this." She paused. "We won't say anything." She looked down at them. "Will we?"

"You don't understand," Roman wept as the gun swung around. "If I don't do this she will take everything from me. She'll kill my son!"

"Why can't you make her believe that the work is done already?" a man asked calmly with his hands outstretched, as if he could stop a bullet. "It's not like we aren't already gone away from our families."

"It won't work," she yelled with spit flying out of her mouth. "She'll never believe it. And she asked for video."

"Then let's think of something together," he continued. "But please, don't make her change you into something you're not." He paused. "A killer."

"You don't know anything about me," Roman said angrily as her heart softened by his kind words. "You don't know the things I've done in my life to become the person I am. The last thing I deserve is respect or kindness from anyone."

"Does the soldier who killed for his country deserve any less respect?" He paused. "You're right. I don't know why you do what you do. I don't even know what keeps you up at night. But I can tell that you are a reasonable young lady. Please don't kill us. You kept us alive this long for a reason. Let us help you."

CHAPTER TWENTY-SEVEN
-YOKO-

"Horror, the soul of the plot."
- Edgar Allan Poe

Yoko sat on a red plastic chair across from the police officers while telling them the same thing she did from the start. That she knew nothing about who was killing her brothers. "I don't know how else you want me to explain myself. I've said the same thing over and over since you asked me to come to the station. All I want to do is go home."

"Yes, you sound quite rehearsed."

"You don't need rehearsal when you're speaking the truth."

"Then why did you sneak out of the house in a bin? If you had nothing to hide?" a detective questioned as he looked down on her. It was obvious that he was trying to intimidate her using his height. If only he knew the things she'd gone through recently, he would never have used that method. No one could intimidate her anymore.

"I left because I didn't need you following me. I can protect myself, you know. Now if you don't mind, I would appreciate if you either charge me with a crime or let me go." She moved as if she were about to walk out of the door.

"Actually, hold your horses," one of the officers said. "Do you know anything about Nora Coffee? She had some information about an open case concerning your brothers."

"A case on what?"

"We can't get into all of that."

"Then I don't know what to tell you," she responded.

He sighed and said, "Mrs. Coffee's family received a picture of her lying on an unidentified sofa with her throat slit. She appeared to be dead but we can't find her body to verify."

Yoko did all she could to try and conceal her excitement. Roman finally did what she wanted after all of that time. The saddest part was that even though Roman fulfilled her end of the deal, Yoko had no intentions on returning Sailor.

He knew too much.

He saw her face.

He had to die.

In fact, she was having Sailor transported to another location where she would have him killed once it was safe. "Like I said, I have no idea what you're talking about."

"So you have no information about Nora? Even though the case involves your brother Mills? Who's in prison as we speak?"

"Sir, I am going through a devastating loss right now," she said honestly. "And I'm pregnant," she continued, rubbing her belly. "My brothers have been murdered and all I want to do is spend time with what's left of my family. And I can't do that if you have me pinned up in a precinct like I'm already convicted of the crime. So unless you are charging me, am I free to go?"

"Yes," he responded. "But don't go too far. We will be watching you."

****

The moment Yoko stepped outside, she received a call from Roman. "It's done," she sobbed. "I made each situation look unrelated like we talked about. The pregnant bitch I set up to look like she was robbed and raped. And the older man I set up to make it look like he was involved in a car accident and—"

"Why are you so hype?" Yoko said rubbing her belly and cutting her off. "No need to scream, Roman. I can hear you."

"I'm hyper because I need my fucking baby back, Yoko. Now I did what you asked. Can you tell me where my son is? Please!"

"Roman, do you remember when we first met?"

Roman tried to respect her need for reflection but truthfully, she didn't give a fuck. "Yoko, where's Sailor?"

"I'm asking you a question! Do your remember when we first met?"

"Vaguely."

That hurt Yoko's feelings because she had a lot going on in her world but she would never, ever forget the day they became friends. "Well I do. I had just checked a crackhead who tried to cheat me out of my money. I thought my life would be the same each day, plain awful, but then I met you. I knew we would forever be connected."

Roman wept louder. "Yoko, please. Tell me where my child is! I'm begging you."

"Your kid is dead, Roman. I warned you what would happen if you ever turned your back on me. Now you're learning what it means to feel real pain."

Roman screamed in agony and Yoko hung up the phone.

****

When Yoko stepped back into her house she could feel something was off. She saw her father's car out front and when she walked into the living room, Vincent was smoking a cigarette and he was intoxicated. "Mills may be released from prison soon," he said calmly. "No witnesses...no case." He paused. "Good job, Yoko." He clapped his hands. "Good fucking job! Did I ever tell you about your father? Your real father?"

"No," she said eager to hear something about him.

"He was a drug dealer. A big one too. Although I never understood why so many people feared him. He was as tall as you. No bigger." He stood up and leaned against the wall. "Anyway, when we were kids he and my father used to do so much together. They went fishing, to the movies." He shook his head. "They basically did everything a father and son would...all without me."

"But why?"

"Because I reminded my father that he wasn't average. Wasn't normal. My height made him feel inadequate and he made me suffer for it. Including the nights he made me give him oral sex, and piss and shit on me like I was some fucking toilet!" he screamed. "He didn't do Andrew like that. Just me! I hated my fucking father and I hate him even more now!"

Yoko's breaths burst in and out of her body.

"And then you know what this bastard does in his will? He gives the place he tortured me in, Magnolia Gardens, to my brother. And when my brother died he left it to you." He broke out in laughter. "But let me tell you what else my no good ass brother did. He put a clause in his will that if something were to happen to you, the building goes to my sons."

Yoko swallowed, finally understanding what was going on. Why he wanted his children to remain alive and out of prison.

"But why? Why do you want a building that you were tortured in?"

"Because I killed my father and buried him in that building! I couldn't fucking take the rape anymore! Couldn't taste him in my mouth anymore! So I waited until he was sleep and stabbed him in the throat with a spatula. When he was dead, although I was a kid, I was big enough to pull his body to the basement, where fresh cement had been poured. He's buried in the fucking floors of that building! It's a tomb! And I want to make sure it isn't pulled up. I want to make sure he rots there for the rest of my life!"

"You mean you don't want to get caught," she said under her breath.

"That too!"

Yoko could feel the anger pouring out of him. She swallowed and said, "But, daddy—"

"I'm not your fucking father!" he yelled pointing at her.

She trembled and said, "Vincent, where is Amanda? You promised to bring her back to me if I made sure Mills was okay. I did that."

"Amanda." He laughed hysterically. "You so stupid, Yoko. Just like your father. I killed that black bitch days ago." He paused. "For revenge on what you did to my face."

CHAPTER TWENTY-EIGHT
-SAILOR-

"With a love that winged seraphs of Heaven."
- Edgar Allan Poe

Sailor lay horizontally on the backseat in Erin's van as he drove him to the next destination. His eyes were covered and his arms and legs were bound so he wouldn't get away. As the vehicle drove down the highway, his lips trembled due to being so frightened. All he wanted was his mommy and daddy but they never came.

Maybe they don't love me anymore, he thought.

For some reason, in that moment, Sailor remembered the long conversations he would have with his mother in his room. When they were at home. At first he thought it was weird that his mother would talk to him about what to do if someone kidnapped him but now he realized he was wrong.

Sailor, although young, knew he had to think if he wanted to stay alive. It was time to revert to the nights Roman taught him basic survival techniques. "I have to go to the bathroom," Sailor announced as he turned his head in the direction of the driver. Although Sailor couldn't see Erin, he could feel his evil presence.

"You gonna have to hold it," he said groggily. "You gonna be where you going in a minute so relax."

"But I can't hold it," he whined. "Please. I got to go pee-pee. You want me to do it here?"

"If you piss in my ride, little nigga, I'll break your fucking neck," he growled looking at him in the rearview mirror. It was already annoying that Yoko asked him to take the kid to his cabin in a rural part of Maryland. He didn't feel like doing that. But he'd long since learned that for Yoko there wasn't much that he wouldn't do, no matter how much shit he talked. At the end of the day, he cared for her, always had and always would.

"But I got to go now," Sailor persisted. "It's coming out."

"Fuck," he yelled as he hit the steering wheel. "Don't piss in my van. I'm pulling over now."

The last thing he wanted or needed was his van smelling like urine. So with an attitude, he steered to the gas station even though Yoko told him not to make any stops. Since he was the man and she wasn't, he figured one pause wouldn't stop the show.

Once parked, he crawled in the backseat and removed the boy's ties. Before getting out, and with a long finger pointed in Sailor's face, he said, "If you try to escape, or if you tell anybody anything, I will kill you." He pulled Sailor's ear. "Do you understand me?"

"Yes," he nodded wiping the tears off of his face with the back of his hand.

"Then come on. We got to hurry up."

Erin grabbed him by his arm and hustled him toward the bathroom at the gas station as if he were a bag of garbage. A few tenants thought he was handling the child a bit roughly but Erin's mind was too unfocused to recognize that he was gaining unwanted attention.

When they finally made it to the men's bathroom, Erin pushed the kid in a stall and slid inside with him. Erin dropped to his knees and unzipped the boy's pants. From the outside, it looked bad but again Erin didn't care.

"I can do it myself," Sailor said, not feeling how close he was to him.

"Listen, you little fucker," he said gripping his arm. "I'm not letting you out of my sight. So either you piss while I'm in here or you don't go at all! What you wannna do?"

"What are you doing in there with that little boy?" A woman asked Erin from outside of the stall.

Erin's heart pumped wildly and he looked at Sailor in a threatening manner again. "Stay quiet," he whispered through clenched teeth. He directed his attention to the woman. "Ma'am, this is my son. I'm simply taking him to the bathroom." He paused. "Furthermore, this is the men's bathroom. Not sure why it's any concern of yours."

"I know what it is. I'm in the right place. And if you're helping the same kid I saw you walk in with, he seems old enough to go to the bathroom himself if you ask me."

"Well thankfully, no one's asking you."

Ignoring Erin, the woman said, "Son, are you okay in there? If you're not you can tell me."

Erin pulled his fingers into a fist and pumped it several times in Sailor's face.

"Son, are you okay in there?" she persisted, taking one step closer to the stall.

Sailor swallowed and said, "Yes, ma'am. I'm fine."

"Okay then. Just checking."

"Are you satisfied?" Erin said taunting her. "If you want to see a man's dick so bad why don't you get one!"

"Fuck you, pervert!" she said before storming out slamming the bathroom door behind her.

When they were alone Erin continued to help Sailor with his pants. But when Erin turned his head, Sailor grabbed the small knife his mother gave him that was strapped to the inside of his pants leg, next to his sock. It had been there the entire time but when they checked his pockets for a cell phone, they didn't bother to think that he'd have anything at the lower part of his pants leg. He almost forgot about it himself.

With the weapon in his hand, Sailor stabbed him in the neck just like Roman taught him. Firmly in the carotid artery.

Erin's eyes widened and he held onto his neck, giving Sailor the time he needed to rush out of the stall.

CHAPTER TWENTY-NINE
-ROMAN-

"And my soul from out that shadow that lies floating on the floor."
- Edgar Allan Poe

Roman didn't care about anything anymore.
Not her life.
Not her responsibilities.
And without her son, not even her marriage.

Roman was sitting over at Owen's apartment on the couch crying her eyes out. "I fucked up, O. I let this bitch kill my son. I should've did what she asked." She wiped the tears away from her face.

Owen got up from the recliner and moved toward her. He wanted to console her. He wanted her to know that he was in her corner and was willing to do whatever he could to help. All she had to do was say the word. "Can I touch you?" he asked.

Without saying yes, she fell into his arms and wept hard. "I'm going to kill her," she continued, her tears dampening his shirt. "When I get my hands on her I'm going to kill her slowly, Owen. Won't nobody be able to tell who she is when I'm through. I'm gonna take my time. I promise!"

"I don't know what to say to you right now," he said as he ran his hand up and down her back while she sobbed. "But I want you to know that whatever you want to do, I'm with you."

****

Roman was driving in her car on her way home to deal with her life. She could no longer hide. It was time to admit everything to Jackson.

Her mind was on five hundred when Race called. She had been calling religiously but Roman had been treating her like a non-essential type bitch. Someone she couldn't

Goon   247 waste her time on. To make shit worse, Mellvue was still alive. Roman would've killed her a long time ago if their rules weren't so specific.

"No one can see you kill this woman," Race said. "She is not like the others. She's the side bitch to a very important man. It has to look like an accident or he'll suspect us," she repeated.

The restraint Race put her under made it harder to do her job. Slowly she placed the phone to her ear and said, "Yes, Race."

"Why is she still alive?" she asked getting straight to the point.

"Because I—"

"I think you've allowed my kindness to give you the wrong impression about me," she said cutting her off. "About who I really am. So let me be clear. I am the most dangerous woman you know."

Roman's nostrils flared as Race continued to talk to her as if she were a peon. With losing her son, she didn't care anymore what she or anyone else thought. "You want that bitch dead?" she yelled.

"I want you to do your fucking job!"

"Is that what you *really* want?" she said pressing her foot harshly on the gas as thoughts of not having her son drove her insane. "Then I'll give you what you asking for!"

She tossed the phone in the passenger's seat and drove 90 mph to where Mellvue lived. Roman was certain she wasn't home. Unlike Lisa who was aware she had a hit on her head, Mellvue didn't know people wanted her dead.

But surprisingly enough, when Roman pulled up in front of her house she was shocked to see a barbeque in session. And in the middle of it all, in front of a grill, was Mellvue swinging her long blonde hair. It wasn't Christmas day, yet there was Roman's present. A smile was etched on her pale face, as she was unaware of what was coming.

Roman grabbed the pistol, stomped out of the car and walked up on Mellvue just as she flipped over a burger. The people around her hustled out of the way to save themselves, without alerting her that Roman was moving in her direction.

The moment Mellvue raised her head, Roman pulled the trigger and shot her in the middle of the face. Her body slumped forward and fell on top of the grill and Roman squeezed the trigger three more times.

Now the bitch was dead.

With her work done, she rushed back to the car and sped away from the scene. She was a block away when she picked up the phone, knowing Race was still on the line. "Satisfied?"

Roman could hear Race breathing angrily on the line. "Meet me. Now."

"I got shit to do. I can't do it today."

"That's not an invitation. Look in your rearview mirror." When Roman did as requested she saw a trail of green Hummers following her. One of them, which held Sarge, pulled up next to her car. He frowned.

"Follow him, Roman," Race said to her. "He'll bring you to me."

****

Race stood in front of Roman as she sat in a chair inside of one of the Pretty Kings organization's buildings. Sarge and five other men stood behind Race as they waited for her word. "Before I kill you, I need you to tell me what the fuck were you thinking today?" Race asked calmly. "I'm a good judge of character but I must admit, I didn't see your unprofessionalism coming. First time for everything."

Instead of answering the question, Roman focused on the army of men behind her. "Let me ask you something. If you have all of them, why did you want my services? It's obvious anybody could've done the job."

"I don't answer your fucking questions!" Race yelled stepping toward her. She looked back at Sarge. "Kill this bitch. I'm done with her."

They were about to put her out of her misery until Roman yelled, "My son was kidnapped. And now he's...now he's dead!"

Upon hearing Roman's words, Race raised her hand, stopping the bullets seconds before they zipped through the air and toward her body. Turning around, she strolled back up to her and said, "Who kidnapped your son?"

"Her name is Yoko Lighthouse."

"You mean that little bitch?" she said raising her hand like she was measuring an invisible child's height. "Who lives in Magnolia Gardens apartments?"

"Yes." She paused. "She wanted me to kill some people. Some witnesses involved in a case against her brother. When I refused, she took my son and then...and then killed him."

For the first time, she broke down in front of them, releasing all of her pain. And every thug in the building felt for her.

Sarge and the other soldiers exhaled, realizing everything now made sense. He liked the hotheaded killer but didn't understand her recent moves.

"You should've come to me earlier, Roman," Race said. Killing a child was already bad but killing a child on purpose drove Race up a wall. "I could've helped you!"

"I wanted to do it on my own," she said as tears rolled down her face. "I was afraid the more people involved, the harder it would be to get him back. And I rejected your friendship in the process. I'm sorry." She shook her head. "I just wanted my baby."

"Are you sure he's dead?" Race asked calmly.

"Yes...I mean no. Yoko said he was dead but I haven't seen his body yet."

Race exhaled. "Carey trusted you. So I will too." She paused. "What do you need?"

"I want my son back, so that I can bury him." She looked at Race's men. "But if I can't...if I can't...I want Yoko's life. And then I want out of this contract."

CHAPTER THIRTY
-YOKO-

"Death looks gigantically down."
- Edgar Allan Poe

Yoko sat in her car clutching a bottle of vodka. She wanted to drink all of it but the baby she was told was growing inside of her would not give her the honor. For some reason, she cared more about the growing child in her gut than she did herself. Angry for feeling real love, she rolled the window down, tossing it across the street and the bottle crashed against the ground. Fracturing into many pieces.

An outcast since birth, it seemed as if nothing she set out to do worked in her favor. From her mother dying, to her brothers dying, to Vincent killing her girlfriend. All she touched failed. All her loved died. There was one bright side. She committed her first murder, against Vincent and she felt liberated. He killed Amanda and he paid with his life.

Through it all, there was one person she blamed for everything she was going through. Roman Tate. To hear Yoko tell it, it seemed as if some crazy force protected everything she did, no matter if it was right or wrong. Roman murdered many…when was she going to get her karma?

To make matters worse, she learned that Erin, who was in a coma, was fighting for his life in a hospital due to a knife wound he sustained to his neck. Apparently, Roman taught her son to kill too and that sent Yoko up a wall.

When Erin awoke, he would have to explain to detectives about why he had the boy who escaped from his custody.

When the person Yoko was waiting for pulled up in his driveway, she got out of her car. Using her height as concealment, she dodged between five vehicles until she was directly behind Raymond as he was removing his infant child from the car seat.

With a heart as cold as the arctic, she pulled the trigger, killing both Raymond and his child.

CHAPTER THIRTY-ONE
-ROMAN-

"In her tomb by the sounding sea."
- Edgar Allan Poe

Roman was a goon.

She was born to kill.

Yet there was something about the woman standing before her that made her feel as if she'd seen far more blood than Roman ever had. The weirdest part of it all was that her beauty acted as a disguise for the monster she really was. "I'm disappointed in you, Roman," Bambi said softly. "And it isn't for the reason you think."

"Then what is it for?" Roman asked through clenched teeth.

"I'm disappointed that you didn't come to us from the onset. When you first needed help. We could've ended this along time ago."

"I didn't want to get you involved. But now I need to be there for my family. My husband doesn't know that our son has been murdered and I have to go home and explain everything to him. All I want is to get out of the contract after I find Yoko."

"I'm sorry, Roman. I really am. But I can't let you out of the agreement. Over the past couple of weeks, you have proven to be invaluable to my organization. And even after your mishap today with Mellvue, for some reason you were able to complete the job without people recognizing you. You're an enigma. And I'm at war with the Russians." She paused. "I need the best on my team. I need you."

Roman held her head down. It was not the answer she was looking for. "But it's not in my heart anymore. To kill, I mean."

Bambi laughed hysterically. "Of course it's in your heart, my dear. Once a killer always a killer. Use the anger and continue to be the best. In the end, for people like you and me, anger and murder is all we have." With a lowered brow, she said, "Live with it or die."

****

After the meeting with the Pretty Kings, Roman felt it was time to face Jackson and tell him about everything. Her murder career. Yoko kidnapping Sailor and any other secret she hid. But when she arrived there were so many police cars in front of her home she thought she was dreaming.

What the fuck is going on now? she thought to herself.

When she rushed inside her front door, she saw a huddle of people on the couch. With their backs faced in her direction she could not tell what was going on. But when she saw Jackson emerge with a smile on his face she felt like she was in the Twilight Zone.

Why was he happy?

Their child was gone.

"Oh, my God, you're home! Baby, come over here," Jackson smiled brightly.

When the huddle of police officers opened wider Roman saw what captivated everyone. She was looking into Sailor's big brown eyes. He was sitting on the sofa, beaten but alive.

Believing she lost him forever, she passed out cold.

****

"He says he doesn't know anything," Roman said to the officers as Sailor sat next to her, clutching her hand. "He's had a long day and we've allowed you several hours to interrogate him. Now I don't mean to be rude, but I really need for you all to leave." She paused. "I need to spend time with my family to sort all of this out."

"My wife is right," Jackson said. "I need everybody who doesn't live here to get out. We need privacy."

Det. Mickens, with his pen and pad clasped in his hand, looked at Sailor once more. Although the child was home, it

By T. Styles   254

irritated him that he didn't solve the case in the fashion he wanted. It was almost as if the case solved itself.

Basically the kid was found wandering the street when an elderly lady asked him was he lost and took him home. It was uneventful, cut and dry and he hated it. "Son, are you sure there isn't anything you can tell us?" he asked the little boy, offering a fake smile. He wanted to catch the kidnapper so he could become the hero. "A face? A name? A van? Anything at all."

Sailor looked up at his mother. Although she didn't speak or shake her head telling him to be quiet, he knew family code. *Do not tell anyone anything you haven't told your parents first.* So he remained silent. "No, sir," he said focusing on him. "I don't remember anything."

Det. Mickens wiped off his fake smile and stood up. "Well, I guess we'll be in contact."

He may have been mad but Det. Speller was grateful that the child wasn't speaking. She saw too many children murdered in their lifetime for giving up valuable information on criminals. The fact of the matter was that the police couldn't always protect them so when best, she preferred them to protect themselves. "Well, you heard the young man," she said. "He doesn't know anything." She looked at the young couple. "Take care," she continued, touching Roman softly on the arm. "I'm happy for both of you."

****

Sailor was in bed and Jackson and Roman were having a heated argument that they were trying to keep quiet. "Roman, why do you keep taking Sailor to the side without me? Huh?" He paused. "Having private conversations? I want to know what happened to our son too!"

"I took him to the side so that he didn't have to be around so many people, Jackson. I'm his mother. Don't take it personally!"

"Why do I feel like you took him to the side to prevent me from finding out something?" he asked huffing and puffing. "Do you know what happened to him? Do you know who took my boy?"

"Baby, I don't know anything outside of what I already told you," she lied. "All I wanted was for him to have a little privacy. That's all. I figured since I'm his mother, I would find out some stuff that he was too afraid to tell everyone else." She walked up to him and kissed him on the lips. "You got to believe me. Please."

****

The Tate family finally drifted off to sleep at about three o'clock in the morning when suddenly glass broke in the front room. Roman thought she was losing her mind and she sprang up, in a sitting position and listened to the darkness. When she heard another noise, she knew someone was in her home.

Looking to her right, she exhaled a sigh of relief when she saw that Jackson was still asleep. So she snatched her phone off the nightstand and texted Raymond and Owen. She needed their help.

When she finished she grabbed her gun from underneath the mattress and tiptoed toward the door. Once she reached it, she turned the knob slowly, looked back at Jackson again and slipped into the hallway, closing the bedroom door behind her. Carefully she crept toward the sound, stopping at the entrance of the hall.

Any other time, she would've come out blazing but the creeps, whoever they were, were on her territory. She couldn't risk Sailor or her husband getting hurt. So she stepped out into the living room, eager to kill the intruders when Jackson walked up behind her and said, "Baby, what's going—"

"Jackson, get down!" Roman yelled when the intruder stepped into view.

Fighting for their lives, she squeezed the trigger multiple times but the killer fought back with more fire. In that instant, Roman was taken back to the day her name was Bay and the last day she saw her mother's face. When someone who wasn't supposed to be in her house entered her home in Mississippi.

She was a long way from that little frightened girl in the oven. So much changed mentally and physically in her world. She decided in that moment that she would fight, no matter what she had to do. And unlike with her mother, she knew that in the end she would remain standing.

She knew she would return to her child.

A fierce gun battle ensued and Roman handled her gun like a soldier. Although afraid for his wife, Jackson hung in the background, peeping how comfortable Roman was with the weapon. She manipulated the gun like it was an extension of her body. She was far from the naive girl he thought he married. She was powerful and in the end, the intruder was slumped over the recliner with his chest muscles hanging out of his upper body.

Carefully she walked toward him and fired again, causing his body to jerk before mouthing, "Goon."

When she looked past him, into her doorway, she saw Owen aiming also. "It's me, Ro. Don't shoot," he said. With the barrel still hot, he placed his gun in the back of his pants and walked over to her.

"Who the fuck are you?" Jackson frowned when he saw Roman wasn't shooting him. Wasn't he also an intruder? "And what are you doing here?"

Roman slowly turned around and looked at her husband. "Jackson, he's my friend." She focused back on Owen, the dead body and then Owen again. "Where's Ray?"

"Aw fuck," he sighed wiping his hand down his face. "You don't know?"

"Know what?"

"Raymond," he responded. "He was murdered. I'm so sorry, Ro."

Roman's legs buckled under her body and she almost hit the floor but Owen caught her.

The moment Owen laid his hands on her in front of her husband she was brought back to reality. She was a mother and a wife and Jackson didn't know anything about this lifestyle. Shaking her head she separated from Owen, placed the gun on the table and considered everything that went wrong in her life.

Ironically, the dead man on her floor entered her home to rob them, and was unrelated to anything she had going on. It was as if she was being paid back for all of the days she robbed and stole from others.

Karma was home.

Her mind was moving fast.

Raymond was dead.

And she had some explaining to do to Jackson.

"Mommy, Daddy," Sailor yelled rushing up to them. "Are the evil people coming back?"

Jackson hoisted him in his arms before he could reach Roman and her male friend. "Everything is fine, son." He eyed the strange man. "You're safe." He paused. "And I'm never going to let anything happen to you again."

He walked over to the phone to call the police but Roman stopped him. "Wait," she said placing her hand over his.

"For what?" he frowned. "I got to call the cops! Somebody came into our house and tried to hurt Sailor again."

"You can't call the police, Jackson. I have to tell you everything."

****

Roman was standing in the room watching Jackson remove the last suitcase from their home. The door was wide open and his mother was sitting in a minivan in front of the house, eager to take him back to where he belonged.

She finally won.

After learning everything about what Roman was involved in, the murder for hire, Yoko, all of it, he decided to move back with his mother. And he was taking Sailor with him. He felt validated when the Pretty Kings organization had men dressed in fatigues come by to get rid of the dead burglar in her house. Like it was just another day at the office. He certainly didn't want his son around mafia type behavior.

Although things were heated in the household, Owen was still there. He tried to leave but the look in Roman's eyes let him know that if he walked out she wouldn't have the strength to deal with her husband alone. "I'm begging you, Jackson," she said getting on her knees. "Don't leave me. You don't leave people you say you love."

"Everything about you has been a lie," he explained as if he didn't hold secrets. In fact, one of the main reasons he was returning to his mother was because she knew he was involved in the string of rapes in the neighborhood. Using blackmail as a weapon, she told him to either come with her or she'd go to the police.

So he relented.

"Please don't leave, Jackson," she said running after him. "Everything I've done is for you. Even the murders. All of it! I need you. Please!"

"You should've thought about that before you put our son in danger." He grabbed Sailor's hand.

"Before you leave, I got to know something," she said huffing. "When you left with me, and asked me to be your wife, it was to anger your mother." She paused, wiping her tears. "Wasn't it?"

With a sly grin on his face, he said, "Yes. I knew it would kill her for me to be with someone like you. And then I fell in love." He paused. "I guess that was my karma."

CHAPTER THIRTY-TWO
-YOKO-

"Nameless here for evermore."
- Edgar Allan Poe

Yoko felt as if she had the entire world against her. She lost three of her brothers, Amanda, her mother and now her freedom was in question. Even the witnesses she thought Roman killed came forward and lied. They claimed that Yoko had them kidnapped, in an effort to free Mills. Because of it, he still remained in jail facing the murder charge. It was as if Roman never existed.

She knew that in any minute, the police would be at Erin's house, since he told them about all of his properties and where she might be hiding. Erin didn't have a choice. When he came out of his coma, he had to tell the police why Sailor was in his possession. He didn't know the details about the beef between Yoko and Roman. As a matter of fact, he knew nothing about it at all. The only thing he could tell the police was that Yoko wanted the boy taken to another house and he was fulfilling that request.

Although she was angry, she was grateful that he felt enough of her to have someone contact her from jail to warn her that the police were on the way.

So she packed the cash Erin had hidden in the house, and a few pieces of clothes she could carry and rushed toward the door. But when she got outside her heart stopped.

It appeared she wouldn't be going anywhere, anytime soon.

It was eerily silent and the right side of the street was lined with eight Hummer trucks with green matte paint jobs. Three men stood in front of each with the exception of the Hummer directly across from where she stood.

In front of that vehicle was a group of women Yoko never saw before. One of them, Bambi, stood out among the others. She wore green fatigues and her long flowing brown hair blew in the wind. Behind her stood Scarlett, Race and Denim. But it was the person who was leaning on the truck, shrouded in a black hoodie with white paint over her face and black over her eyes that caused her to weep.

Yoko remembered that same face paint job from when they completed their first crime together, a robbery in which their victim fell down the steps and hit his head on a railing, resulting in him being paralyzed for life.

"So this is how I die?" Yoko yelled to Roman who remained in the background. "Your son is safe, Roman," she yelled. "I didn't kill him even though I told you I did. I would've never hurt him." She rubbed her growing belly. "I'm pregnant too, you know."

Silence.

"When we were younger you had a code," Yoko continued. "To never kill the innocents." She swallowed. "Will you keep my baby alive? Do you still honor that code?"

Roman spotted her bulge before Yoko spoke on the pregnancy but she didn't care. Because of her, she lost everything important. Her husband. Her life. And more than anything, her son.

Roman chuckled. "You right, Yoko. When we were younger, I did operate by a code. But you taught me that having a code was dumb. Do you remember what you said?"

"N...no," she stuttered.

"Well I do. You told me to leave the code shit to computer programmers. And I told you that one day you'll want someone to have a code." She paused. "Well I guess that day has arrived."

"Roman, please, I'm begging you."

"I know you're hurting, Yoko. I cried too. I lost the only people I cared about because of you. So tell me something. What the fuck I look like caring about that demon growing in your belly now?"

Silence.

"You ready?" Bambi asked Roman.

"Yes."

"Give the word and the men will act."

The soldiers cocked their weapons and aimed at Yoko.

"Wait a minute," Roman said raising her hand. Instead of letting them shoot her, she ambled slowly across the street. It was so silent you could hear the leaves rustle on the trees. Roman's hands were stuffed in her pockets and her eyes were dark with despair. When she was finally upon Yoko, she looked down at her. She wanted Yoko to know how she felt about her, wiping away any love she had in her heart for her old friend in the process.

Without a word, Roman removed two switchblades from each pocket and plunged them into the sides of her neck. Blood spurted out of Yoko's flesh and Roman mouthed, "Goon."

The Cartel Publications Order Form
www.thecartelpublications.com
Inmates **ONLY** receive novels for $10.00 per book.

Shyt List 1	_____	$15.00
Shyt List 2	_____	$15.00
Shyt List 3	_____	$15.00
Shyt List 4	_____	$15.00
Shyt List 5	_____	$15.00
Pitbulls In A Skirt	_____	$15.00
Pitbulls In A Skirt 2	_____	$15.00
Pitbulls In A Skirt 3	_____	$15.00
Pitbulls In A Skirt 4	_____	$15.00
Victoria's Secret	_____	$15.00
Poison 1	_____	$15.00
Poison 2	_____	$15.00
Hell Razor Honeys	_____	$15.00
Hell Razor Honeys 2	_____	$15.00
A Hustler's Son 2	_____	$15.00
Black and Ugly As Ever_____		$15.00
Year Of The Crackmom_____		$15.00
Deadheads	_____	$15.00
The Face That Launched A _____		$15.00
Thousand Bullets		
The Unusual Suspects_____		$15.00
Miss Wayne & The Queens of DC_____		$15.00
Paid In Blood (ebook)	_____	$15.00
Raunchy	_____	$15.00
Raunchy 2	_____	$15.00
Raunchy 3	_____	$15.00
Mad Maxxx	_____	$15.00
Jealous Hearted (ebook)	_____	$15.00
Quita's Dayscare Center_____		$15.00
Quita's Dayscare Center 2 _____		$15.00
Pretty Kings	_____	$15.00
Pretty Kings 2	_____	$15.00
Pretty Kings 3	_____	$15.00
Silence Of The Nine	_____	$15.00
Prison Throne	_____	$15.00
Drunk & Hot Girls	_____	$15.00
Hersband Material	_____	$15.00
The End: How To Write A _____		$15.00
Bestselling Novel In 30 Days (Non-Fiction Guide)		
Upscale Kittens	_____	$15.00
Wake & Bake Boys	_____	$15.00
Young & Dumb	_____	$15.00

Goon

Young & Dumb 2:	_____	$15.00
Tranny 911	_____	$15.00
Tranny 911: Dixie's Rise	_____	$15.00
First Comes Love, Then Comes Murder	_____	$15.00
Luxury Tax	_____	$15.00
The Lying King	_____	$15.00
Crazy Kind Of Love	_____	$15.00
Goon	_____	$15.00

Please add $4.00 **per book** for shipping and handling.

The Cartel Publications * P.O. BOX 486 OWINGS MILLS MD 21117 *

Name: _____

Address: _____

City/State: _____

Contact# & Email: _____

Please allow 5-7 business days for processing then shipping.

The Cartel is not responsible for prison orders rejected.

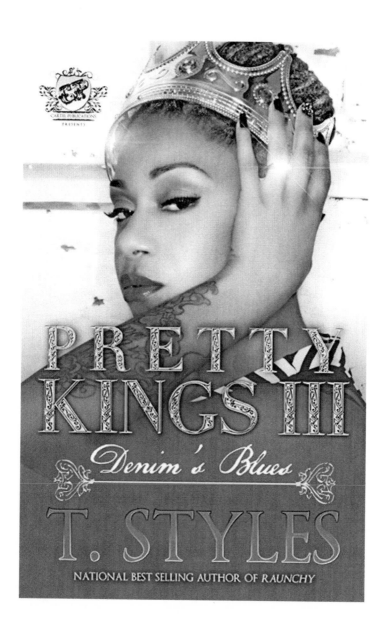

PRETTY KINGS III

Denim's Blues

T. STYLES

NATIONAL BEST SELLING AUTHOR OF *RAUNCHY*

CPSIA information can be obtained at www.ICGtesting.com
Printed in the USA
LVOW06s1952071014

407667LV00002B/314/P